NOW THAT SHE'S L[...]
CAN SHE KEEP U[...]

$\mathcal{G}$od help her, she wanted him, and she hadn't told him. Maybe that's what she should do.

"For you," he said, his words feathering against her neck.

She turned and ended face-to-bloom with an exquisite pink rose.

"You didn't seriously think an afternoon coffee would be enough, did you, Lettie? You do want more. A date. With me," Bill said.

It wasn't really a question, but she nodded. "Good," he said, brushing the petals down her cheek, "because I want to get to know you, Lettie. Even better than before. And I plan to start tonight."

"A sexy read and pure, fabulous fun!"
—JULIE LETO, **author of** *Dirty Little Secrets*

"Kelley St. John's sexy debut, GOOD GIRLS DON'T, delivers both heat and heart, making St. John an author to watch!"
—JULIE KENNER, **author of** *The Givenchy Code* **and** *Carpe Demon*

"Wow! This is over the top, and all the fun of a sweet *Sex and the City*! Debut author Kelley St. John spins a tale of Colette, who can't get over the gorgeous guy she loved and lost, and her sister Amy, a designer of award-winning sex toys! Fans of sizzling romance will have a ride on cloud nine with this one."
—MAGGIE DAVIS, **author of** *Hustle Sweet Love*

Don't forget to turn to the back of this book
for a preview of Kelly St. John's sexy new novel,
Real Women Don't Wear Size 2.

Good Girls Don't

KELLEY ST. JOHN

NEW YORK   BOSTON

Copyright © 2005 by Kelley St. John
Excerpt from *Real Women Don't Wear Size 2* copyright © 2005 by Kelley St. John.

Cover design by Diane Luger
Cover photograph by Daly & Newton/Getty Images
Book design by Giorgetta Bell McRee

Warner Books

Time Warner Book Group
1271 Avenue of the Americas
New York, NY 10020
Visit our Web site at www.twbookmark.com

Printed in the United States of America

First Paperback Printing: December 2005

10 9 8 7 6 5 4 3 2 1

To my boys. Who'd have thought having teenagers could be so *fun*?

And to my husband, my hero. With you by my side, I can do anything. Your support means more to me than words can say. I love you.

Acknowledgments

Monumental thanks to my agent, Caren Johnson, who found the perfect home at Warner for *Good Girls Don't*.

Extreme thanks to Beth de Guzman for noticing my work, and to my editor, Devi Pillai, for saying the words that make any writer's heart stand still: "I love this book!"

A sincere thanks to Diane Luger for a cover that absolutely rocks.

And last, but not least, my unending gratitude to Susan Goggins. You urged me to share my writing with the world and never doubted I would achieve my goal. I owe this dream's fruition to you.

CHAPTER 1

Digging through her briefcase, Colette Campbell snagged her cellular phone in one hand and her contact's information sheet in the other, while her sister rummaged through her green glitter-embellished duffel bag to grab a bright pink, misshaped vibrator. Both girls were notorious for bringing their work home; tonight was no exception.

"Amy, what the heck is that for?" Colette eyed the odd curve at the end of the oversized contraption. In her opinion, Amy's current employer had taken its passion line to the extreme, with the most popular products designed by her imaginative sister. But they were shooting for the next must-have sex toy. And Colette had to admit several of Amy's creations were already must-haves for her own bedroom.

Too bad they were the ones meant for singles.

"This baby will put Adventurous Accessories over the top," Amy said, grinning with unabashed pride. She made the same claim with each of her toys, though Colette chose not to point that out.

At merely twenty-two, Amy Campbell already had a mind for business. Coupled with an affinity for the intricacies of sex, which she'd obviously acquired from their mother, Amy had a hot combination for today's boudoir market. Consequently, she fully intended for one of her personally designed products to become the next Jack Rabbit.

Like practically every other female in America, Colette had watched Kim Cattrall's Samantha lose her senses over the unique vibrator on *Sex and the City*. And, like practically every other female in America, she'd wasted no time purchasing a set of talented rabbit ears of her own.

Thank God. Lord knows that battery-operated bunny helped her numerous times when Jeff hadn't got the job done. At least she had one "energize-her" in the apartment during her six months dating Mr. Perfect.

"So what does it do?" Colette asked, accustomed to Amy's tendency of bringing her sex trinkets home to show off her latest idea.

While Amy played Vanna, running a finger down the smooth length of the toy, Colette scanned her client's data sheet. My Alibi's customers were extremely specific regarding when she should make calls. In this case, the woman wanted a message left while the contact was gone. A typical request. For some reason, the lie seemed more believable when heard on an answering machine.

Colette's eyes ventured to the referral line on the bottom of the front page. "Amy?"

"Yeah?" Amy said, still grinning at the toy.

"What's up with this?" She pointed to the name scribbled across the page. "Referred by Amy Campbell?" Colette read the annotation made by the My Alibi sales associate.

Client specifically requested Colette Campbell as her sales representative.

"Oh, I can't believe I forgot to tell you," Amy said, scooting closer to Colette on the couch. She pointed to the data sheet. "That's a friend of mine. She needed a way to spend a week with her boyfriend, and I told her about My Alibi."

"You're helping your friend cheat on her husband?" Colette didn't like lying for a living, and she didn't plan to do it much longer, only until she had enough money to start her boutique. "I thought you agreed that what these people do isn't right."

"I know it isn't, but Erika isn't lying to a husband."

Colette's attention moved back to the information sheet, specifically the "Relationship to Client" line. "Her uncle?"

"She's found the love of her life, but she doesn't think her uncle will approve," Amy explained, shrugging as though this were no big deal. "She needs an alibi for a week to spend some alone time with Butch and see if he really is the one."

"Why does she have to lie to her uncle to spend a week with her boyfriend?" Colette didn't like the sound of this. What was Amy getting her into?

"He's her guardian, and he's a bit overprotective," Amy explained; then, at Colette's raised brows, she continued, "Listen. I knew you wouldn't help on your own, so I had her go through My Alibi. That way it's merely another client, right? And besides, she's my friend and needs help. You won't let me down here, will you?"

Letting Amy down was something Colette was determined not to do. And Amy knew it. Occasionally, like right now, she used it to her advantage. However, there was no way Colette would help if Erika wasn't an adult.

"You can't hire My Alibi unless you're eighteen. And if she isn't eighteen, I can't help her."

"She is eighteen. Her birthday was last month."

Sure enough, the client's date of birth on the application matched Amy's statement.

"Come on, she's an adult looking for an alibi, and she isn't lying to a husband. She simply wants to spend some time with her boyfriend. You'll help her, right? Give her a chance at true love?" Amy asked. "For me?"

Colette sighed. "All right," she conceded. "I'll help her."

Amy leaned forward and hugged her sister, while her long ponytail smothered Colette's face and made her smile.

"You're rotten, you know that, don't you?" Colette asked.

"Yep," Amy agreed, moving back to her bag and holding up the new toy. Her mission had been accomplished, so naturally, she turned her focus back to her newest product.

"Tell your friend I'll help her this one time, but I don't plan to do it again. She really shouldn't be lying to her uncle."

"Got it," Amy said, punching a finger in the air for emphasis, but her eyes never ventured from the vibrator. "Isn't it amazing?" She switched her voice to produce infomercial appeal, flicked the switch and started the thing buzzing. "This exclusive curve allows the smooth, pulsing tip to hit the G-spot precisely. Every time. And if that doesn't pique your interest, feast your eyes on this." Sounding like a late-night home-shopping host, she pushed a small button on the handle with her index finger. "Ahhh, see? The end lights up like a rainbow."

Holding the glowing contraption against her forearm, Amy let the pulsating head play against her skin while she giggled. "Cool, huh?"

Okay. Colette failed to see why illuminating like a multicolored strobe light would be of importance, particularly if you considered where those colors would be located *if* and *when* they hit the proverbial bull's-eye. But she humored Amy, nonetheless. "Yeah, sis. Real cool. If you have a spot to find."

Amy punched the switch and dropped Pinky to the couch, where it rolled like a deformed banana until lodging between the back of the sofa and the cushion. "No way. You haven't found it? *Jeff* hasn't found it? Geez, you don't know what you're missing."

Colette merely smirked. From what she could tell, Jeff did good to find his own part, much less hers. But rather than elaborate on how extremely dull those six months had been, she dialed the number listed on the My Alibi fact sheet.

"Seriously? Did he, you know, even look for it?" Amy asked, obviously bewildered at this revelation.

Did he look for it?

Hmmm. Let's think about it. Well, that'd be a definite no. Matter of fact, all he looked for, as far as Colette could tell, was his own satisfaction. Which he obtained. Every time.

And pretty dang quick, at that.

Funny thing was, Jeff looked and acted every part the ladies' man. Strutted around with his much-too-muscled chest puffed out, his politician's smile plastered on tight and every wavy hair in place. Oh, and not a single tan line on his body, thank you very much. Or thank his home-tanning bed, coupled with his ritual to make certain he stayed on each side the same number of minutes.

Colette had mistakenly believed the attention he paid to his looks stemmed from his business, rather than his mega-ego. He'd used his primary asset, his body, to promote a growing chain of health-food stores; therefore, he had to look healthy, right?

Of course, the result was quite phenomenal. Folks saw him as their goal and bought his stuff aplenty. The fact he'd tacked on a couple of Atlanta's Best Body titles didn't hurt either. Yep, he was pretty to look at, all right.

But a dud in the sack.

Heck, Colette would've bet plenty of money on his ability to please.

She'd have lost that bet.

Shoot, she'd have put money on him staying true too. Ditto for losing the wager.

"In case you've forgotten, Jeff and I have been over for two months. Matter of fact, I heard he put a ring on Emily Smith's finger last weekend. Just as well, since he was banging her the whole time we were together. Hey, who knows? Maybe he found *her* G-spot. He sure never found mine."

That sounded bitter. And she was *not* bitter. Relieved was more like it. She'd tried to make the whole commitment thing work, in spite of Jeff leaving much to be desired in the bedroom. In her bedroom, anyway. As she learned two months ago, he'd made his way through plenty of other beds during their time together.

"Maybe you should try this out. It'll find the spot." Amy picked up the translucent pink vibrator and held it to her cheek. "It's waterproof too. And you don't even need a man. Really, you should give it a trial run."

Don't need a man. Yep, that'll fit the bill.

"Maybe I should." Colette laughed. Heck, maybe a pink, rainbow, light-up G-spot finder was what she needed to get her out of this funk. Twenty-nine-and-knocking-on-thirty, she was still searching for a guy who could carry on an intelligent conversation, had at least some semblance of a career plan and—wonder of wonders—could make her toes curl as much as one of Amy's toys. She was beginning to think she might have to let go of one of the three qualities. But if anything had to fly out the window, it would *not* be curling toes.

Amy lowered the vibrator and focused on the phone perched against her sister's ear. "Hey, Colette, you dialed the number, didn't you?"

Colette's laughter lodged in her throat. She hadn't heard the answering machine pick up. But there'd definitely been a ring on the other end.

Hadn't there?

Yeah, she'd heard a ring. When had it stopped? More importantly, how much of their sisterly conversation had been recorded?

Dang.

A path of heat blazed from her throat to her face. She'd have to do major damage control at the office tomorrow for this faux pas. How do you explain leaving a message about sex toys on a customer's voice mail?

But she couldn't hang up. She'd used the cellular provided by My Alibi, and the fictitious name Amy's friend had chosen for her company would be displayed on the caller ID.

She gathered her wits. So this wouldn't be her best performance as a My Alibi representative; it'd be okay. She'd simply apologize and begin her regular spiel.

Taking a deep breath, she prepared to start the process of prevarication via the uncle's answering machine.

Then she heard a responding exhalation on the other end.

No. Way. There was *not* a living, breathing person listening to her now. Hearing her discuss G-spots, no less, when she supposedly represented a computer-graphics training company. Certainly Erika's uncle hadn't answered the phone, heard her talking and eavesdropped on that steamy little conversation with Amy. Had he?

Only one way to find out. Tossing a wary glance to her sister, she mustered up her courage. "Hello?"

"Well, hello."

*C*HAPTER 2

Colette's eyes bugged at Amy, while Amy mouthed a shocked, "Oh. No."

Erika had placed a big checkmark beside the best time to call, when her uncle wouldn't be home. She'd even handwritten that My Alibi could simply leave a message letting him know she'd arrived safely at her destination and be done with it. Simple as pie.

Not. Because the sexy hello sending a shiver down Colette's spine definitely didn't come from a machine. Flustered, she couldn't remember the name of the fake company.

Time to stall . . .

Scanning the data sheet, Colette fumbled over the conversation. "Please accept my apologies. This is Colette Campbell with"—her eyes struggled to find the name—"Integrated Solutions in Tampa. I was talking to a coworker, and I'm afraid I didn't hear you pick up."

"Obviously not." Muffled laughter echoed through the phone.

"Right. Well, I was calling to inform you that"—she

pulled her finger across the page and read the full name—"Erika Collins arrived safely and has already started her training seminars. She asked that I call and inform you everything is going according to schedule. Also, if you need to get in touch with her at any point throughout the week, you can contact her at this number." Colette recited the toll-free number established by My Alibi, the one that would ring directly to her cellular. If he did call, she would field the message and notify his niece.

"I appreciate your help, but I'll call her cell phone when I need her."

A usual response. And one Colette was prepared for. "I'm afraid the conference center rarely picks up cellular signals, but I will be happy to relay your messages, Mr."—another glance at the form, "Brannon."

Her brain clicked madly as she read the name again. *Uh-uh. It couldn't be.*

"Bill Brannon?" she questioned.

"Yes."

"From Sheldon?"

A slight pause echoed from the other end. This wasn't Bill. Surely not. There were bound to be several Bill Brannons, right? Probably plenty of them in Georgia, in fact. This wouldn't be—couldn't be—the Bill Brannon she remembered.

But she did remember *that* Bill Brannon. She could see him so clearly, black hair cropped close on the sides, longer on top. Thick, dark brows. Eyes the color of mocha. Full lips. Strong jaw. He had the looks of a guy she'd date in a heartbeat back in Sheldon High. But she didn't. That wasn't the type of relationship they shared.

Because Bill Brannon also listened to many of her worries throughout middle school and high school. The nervous ramblings of a girl not nearly as confident as she let the remainder of the world believe. A girl who wanted more than what Sheldon offered, who wanted to be a successful businesswoman and have a real family one day, the kind of family she and Amy dreamed of.

Bill Brannon had been the best male friend she'd ever known, and the one she'd left on graduation night, when he confessed his true feelings—and she left Sheldon without looking back.

"I'm afraid you have me at a disadvantage," he said.

Oh. My. God. The Bill Brannon she knew—remembered—*was* on the other end of this line. With a deeper, richer voice than she recalled.

Her hand clenched the receiver.

"What did you say your name was again?" he asked. "Colette?"

Oh boy, she'd dug herself right into a hole. A big wide black one. With, sure enough, no end in sight.

"Colette," she said, then swallowed. Maybe he wouldn't remember. And maybe her mother would become a nun. "Colette Campbell."

"Lettie?" Recognition slammed through both syllables. "Is that you?"

She hadn't heard that name in twelve years, since the night she graduated from Sheldon High. The same night she'd told him the truth, then witnessed the pain in her friend's eyes.

Her stomach knotted. "It's been a long time," she said, while her sister leaned forward, steadying her palms on the mound of sex toy paraphernalia she'd dumped on the sofa.

"Whoops," Amy mouthed, her green eyes wide. "You know him?"

Fighting the way her throat closed in, Colette nodded.

"It *has* been a long time," he said. "At the ten-year re-union, your last-known address was your house in Shel-don, and we all knew you'd kissed that place good-bye. So you're in Tampa now?"

How was she supposed to answer his question? No, she wasn't in Tampa; she was in Atlanta, the same as he was. In fact, she hadn't moved that far from their small town in the North Georgia Mountains—merely far enough to reach a big city where she could make her mark and achieve her goals.

However, he thought she was in Tampa. Well, of course he did. Because *that's* where the fictitious Inte-grated Solutions was located and *that's* where she told him she worked. Heck, not only was Colette not in Tampa, neither was his niece.

Oh God, how could she lie to Bill?

As if on cue, Amy edged closer. "Don't tell him," she mouthed. "Please."

Damnation.

According to the information sheet, Erika was cur-rently on Tybee Island. Undoubtedly having a hot and heated time with her boyfriend while Uncle Bill thought she was working at a training conference. Lettie shook her head in disbelief. This was *so* not happening. Of all the people she'd never *ever* want to lie to, the name at the top of that list would be Bill.

Well, close to the top. The very tip-top name, of course, would be Amy. And therein was the problem.

"Yeah, Tampa is nice," Colette said, while a wave of nausea covered her like a thick black cloud. She'd never even been to the place. Man, why did Erika's uncle have to be Bill?

Colette had sworn she wouldn't keep this job long. It was wrong, and she knew it. But it paid a heck of a lot more than a waitress, or a checkout clerk, or a salesperson, or a dog walker—or any of the other bizarre jobs she'd had in the past. And it helped her save the money she needed to get her business started.

She'd been convinced that was a good enough reason for helping cheaters. And she'd promised herself she'd only do it a few months. Half a year, tops.

Unfortunately, lying to Bill Brannon, the one guy who'd treated her better than any other—and the one guy she'd hurt more than any other—hadn't figured into her equation.

"And you're working for the company holding the conference?" he continued, aiding her eternal free fall into the black abyss.

"Yeah." God, she needed to get off the phone. Guilt washed over her like a mudslide down the Appalachians. Any minute now, she'd need to hurl. Violently. With gusto. No, she hadn't relished lying for cheaters, but all in all, lying to strangers hadn't seemed so bad. Lying to someone who'd been her best friend as a teenager, on the other hand, was a different story entirely.

"I'm glad to hear it's a reputable business. When Erika told me she had to spend a week in Tampa to train for her new job, I admit I had my doubts about whether the company was on the up-and-up. She has a tendency to act first and think later."

I'll say. She's definitely not thinking now, or she'd be truthful with you.

"Glad to help," Colette said, her insides churning miserably. Lying to Bill Brannon hadn't been on her list of things to do today. Hadn't been on the list of things to do this lifetime, truth be told, and she was ready for it to be over. And was he going to bring up the last time they saw each other?

Amy touched her hand. "It's just one week," she whispered. "And she's really in love."

As if *that* would make Colette feel better.

She decided to keep the charade moving and get off the phone before they traipsed down memory lane. "If you need to contact her, you can call the number I gave you."

It's completely bogus, you'll be talking to me and I'll be lying through my teeth. But, yeah, call it. And pray for me, by the way. I need all the help I can get.

"Wait. Lettie?"

Why the devil wasn't he hanging up the phone? Probably because they'd been so close before and hadn't talked in, oh, twelve years. Surely he'd want to play catch-up, even if their last conversation had been less than pleasant.

"I'm leaving Sheldon, Bill. I have to." She took his hand and held it tightly. *"And I—I don't think of you that way. You're my friend."*

And his response . . .

"It's not enough." Then he slid his hand from her grasp . . . and walked away.

"Lettie?" the deep voice on the phone repeated.

She swallowed. "Yeah?"

"How are you?"

How was she? She was making a living lying for frauds, one of which was his niece. In other words, she was pretty dang crummy, thank you very much.

"I'm fine," she said. Another lie. What was one more now?

"That's good. I always hoped you'd end up happy, with everything you ever wanted."

Guilt, a mighty heavy emotion. Right now, she'd estimate its weight at two tons and climbing. She knew the truth. Her years at Sheldon could've been sheer hell if Bill hadn't been there, the shoulder for her to cry on when her mother's reckless antics had caused those telltale whispers whenever Colette neared. In response, she'd smiled, flirted, acted as though it didn't matter. But it did. And she had dreamed of the day she could leave. Start a new life and pave the way for her sister.

The day after she graduated, she did. But in following her plan, she left behind the two people she cared about most. Amy . . . and Bill.

"I guess I'll let you go now," she said, while Amy sat beside her with her hand over her mouth.

"Lettie?"

Colette closed her eyes. Why did that name sound so sweet when coming from his mouth? She'd always thought "Lettie" held a hint of sordidness. But with Bill, it sounded almost angelic.

"Yeah?"

"Do you ever get to Atlanta? Does your work at Integrated Solutions put you traveling at all?"

Her eyes slowly opened. "Atlanta?"

Well, sure she got to Atlanta. Every day. When she drove down Interstate 85 toward the My Alibi office in Marietta. Or when she bought her groceries. Or when she slept in her apartment. Yep, she sure enough got to Atlanta.

"Right. You ever travel here?" he repeated.

"Sometimes." Shoot, she was already heading to hell in a handbasket. What was another fabrication filling the lining?

"Next time you're coming to town, give me a call. We could get together for old times' sake. You know, go out to dinner or take in a show. The Fox Theatre puts on quite a few Broadway productions throughout the year." He paused, while her heart started a slow, steady thump; then he exhaled thickly. "We shouldn't have let things end like that."

Colette smiled, recognizing the tone of her teenage friend in the husky male voice. He was right, after all. They shouldn't have ended things like that. And for her part, she shouldn't have left town before they worked things out.

"That sounds nice," she said. It sounded very nice, in fact. She'd cut ties with Sheldon, hadn't wanted reminders of the people who never saw beneath the facade of the perky cheerleader. They didn't *know* her.

But Bill did.

"So . . . what do you say? Next time you're coming to Atlanta, look me up."

She blinked. Could she look him up? Bill Brannon, the one guy who probably knew her better than any other, to this day. And yet she hadn't tried to find him after high school. Why not?

Simple. Because she'd hurt him, and she hadn't wanted to look back. But the truth was, she missed that relationship. Wouldn't it be wonderful to have a boy— correction, a man now—whom she could connect with, the way she and Bill connected back then? Could they still sit and talk for hours?

Colette glanced at the paper in front of her, the one stating all pertinent information about Bill's niece. Why did they have to reconnect this way? With a lie? But even so, she relished the idea that she could have a male friend once again. It'd been a long time, and she really hated that they'd lost touch after being so close.

"Okay," she said, deciding to venture across the point of no return. "I'd love to get together when I come to Atlanta."

Amy fell over on the couch and smothered her sucking gasps with a pillow.

"Any idea when you might be coming to town?"

He sounded almost . . . anxious. And—sexy?

Colette blinked. Where did that come from? She'd never looked at Bill that way, never thought of him that way, which had been part of the problem when he'd confessed his feelings. But his voice *had* sent a shiver down her spine earlier, before she realized it was her old friend on the line. And twelve years had passed since she left Bill at Sheldon. He'd be thirty now. Thirty. Definitely a man.

What had he done in the past twelve years? He'd dreamed of a career in advertising. Had it happened? And had he found love? At thirty, he'd undoubtedly had relationships with women who hadn't known him as the nice guy of Sheldon High. And hadn't one of Bill's dreams been to be a young T-ball dad? Had raising his niece changed his plans? And how had he become her guardian?

So many questions. And Colette very much wanted the answers. She *had* missed Bill, more than she realized, until now.

"Lettie? You still there?"

"I'm here." And suddenly, she was very eager to see him again. Why had she waited so long?

"Do you know when you're coming to town?"

Amy ventured up from the pillow and flashed a knowing, sinister grin. "You're going out with him?" she whispered, her eyes growing wide.

Going out with Bill? The thought hadn't occurred.

No, that wasn't true. She was interested in connecting with Bill again. What girl wouldn't want to meet up with the guy who'd been her friend and confidant through those chaotic teenage years? Reconnect for old times' sake, not as a date or anything.

Amy, misunderstanding Colette's lack of a response, picked up the pink vibrator and dropped it in the bag. "Maybe you won't need it, after all," she mouthed.

Colette fought the urge to laugh. Although she did want to visit with Bill again, she didn't plan on it being *that* kind of visit. She simply had a curiosity to know what became of him—that was it. And there was nothing wrong with old friends getting together. Granted, it'd be better if she wasn't lying to him at the time, but that would only last a week.

"Oddly enough, I'm coming to Atlanta tomorrow,"

she said, grinning. It'd be fun to see Bill again. Shoot, after spending six agonizing months with no-words-above-two-syllables Jeff, she would thoroughly enjoy carrying on a decent conversation with a man. And maybe she could figure out a way to keep the lies from entering the dialogue. Somehow.

"Then how about tomorrow night? Are you free?"

"I believe so." Her stomach fluttered. Lord, what was she doing? And why did it feel more like a date than a simple meeting of old friends?

"Excellent," he said, a hint of eagerness in the single word. "I'll make the arrangements. Give me a call when you get in town."

"Sure." Colette smiled at Amy. Her sister's request had inadvertently helped Lettie find Bill again.

"How long will you be here?" he asked.

"Through the weekend," she said, while Amy nodded her approval.

"Do you have a place to stay?"

Okay. This shouldn't surprise her. Bill Brannon was the kind of friend who'd offer her a place to stay if she was coming to town. It didn't mean anything more than that.

"The company provides a hotel typically, but my sister lives in Atlanta, so I usually stay with her when I travel there."

Amy slapped both hands to her mouth, while her big round eyes bulged and her head did that slow I-can't-believe-you're-doing-this shake.

What'd she expect? If you lie for a living, you get pretty good. And the truth was, if Colette had been traveling for a company, the arrangements would have been made.

"Amy lives in Atlanta?" he asked.

She grinned, not surprised at all that Bill remembered Amy. He was that kind of guy, the type to notice a fifth grader, even when he was a senior.

"In the Norcross area," Colette said. "She works there."

She refrained from telling him the name of Amy's employer. It wasn't as if she were ashamed of the way her sister made a living. Designing sex toys was as worthy a job as any, in Colette's opinion. It beat the heck out of lying, hands down.

But she didn't want to insinuate Amy hadn't made the most of her life. She had, and Colette was proud of her for finding her own little niche in the world. Even if that niche involved pink, rainbow, light-up G-spot finders.

"She's got a great position in product design," Colette added, while Amy stifled her snort.

"I'm glad for her. She's a sweet kid."

Colette eyed the pretty brunette on the other end of the couch, a younger version of their mother, with long limbs, full lips, wide eyes. Much the same as Colette, minus the blond hair. And very much a woman—though if Bill thought of her as a kid, Colette wouldn't beg to differ. Amy would always be her baby sister, so "kid" fit.

"I'm pretty proud of her myself."

At that, Amy flicked her tiny nose in the air and smiled triumphantly.

"Tell you what, Lettie. I've never been one to beat around the bush," he said.

Colette sighed. "I remember." She could always count on Bill's honesty, his frankness.

"So I want to know. Are you planning to spend your evenings with Amy while you're here?"

His question sounded . . . suggestive? Her brows furrowed. Was there more to this reacquainting than she thought? And if there was, was that such a bad thing? What would it be like to have a real date with Bill? Could she even look at him beyond a friend?

Twelve years ago, Colette hadn't thought so. But things do change over time. Could she think of him that way? Was that even what his question implied?

She decided against asking him for clarification. "That's what I had planned, but I'd love to see you tomorrow."

"I'd love more," he said, erasing any doubts of his meaning and reminding her of his words on graduation night.

"*It's not enough.*"

She held her breath, then let it out slowly. Oh man, what had she done?

"You could still see Amy while you're here. But spend some time with me, Lettie. More than one date."

Her mouth fell open. He'd called it a date. Plain and simple, no punches held. Pure Bill. Tell it like it is.

A date. With Bill? More than that—a date, with Bill, while lying to him for his niece?

Fighting the increasing tension in her neck, she leaned her head back on the couch and closed her eyes. Had she totally messed up?

"Give me a chance to show you what we missed out

on back then," he said, his voice delving deeper, huskier. "What do you say, Lettie?"

Her eyes flew open. No punches held, indeed. "What we missed out on?"

"By not seeing if there could be more to it than friendship," he answered. Yeah, he'd always been confident, but this—well, *this* wasn't the Bill she knew back when.

Then again, he was older now. And so was she. What would it hurt to see if their potential for a relationship had grown in the past decade too?

What if it had?

A date? With Bill? She still couldn't quite grasp the concept.

Colette pondered what to say. Sure, she wanted to see Bill again, but a date?

He cleared his throat. "I can't tell you how much I regretted not trying to find you after you left town. I've gotta admit I was mad at first. And that cost me."

"What do you mean?" she asked, while Amy raised her brows and evidently tried to determine his end of the conversation.

"I didn't try to find you until after I finished college. I kept waiting for you to find me."

"I should've stayed in touch," she said, another tinge of guilt pressing heavily on her chest.

"Hell yeah, you should've," he said, then laughed, a richer, deeper laugh than she remembered. But like in high school, an honest-to-goodness Bill Brannon laugh warmed her completely.

"Are you wanting an apology?" she asked teasingly.

"I told you what I'm wanting. A date. For the record—I still believe you made a mistake back then."

"A mistake?" she asked, intrigued by the surplus of assuredness in his tone.

"By turning me down, of course."

Her laugh bubbled from her throat. "Modest, aren't you?"

"Just telling the truth. Admit it. You're curious, aren't you? Don't you want to see how good it could be?"

This was it. Yes or no. Could she even look at Bill Brannon like that? He obviously felt something in high school that she hadn't shared. What if that was still the case? Or what if, and this was the part that made her even more nervous, what if she did feel something for Bill this time? Wouldn't that ruin everything? Because she couldn't start a relationship, a real relationship, based on a lie. So she'd have to tell him the truth about Erika. And hurt Amy. She knew she wouldn't—couldn't—do either. Therefore, she should say no.

"I'd like that too," she said.

So much for self-preservation.

He exhaled, and she knew he was smiling. She couldn't say how, but she knew.

"Great. Then tomorrow night, we'll start getting to know each other again."

"I'm looking forward to it," she said, truthfully, for once.

"Good. Oh, and Lettie?"

"Yeah?"

"About that spot Jeff couldn't find . . ."

Her face flamed. She'd nearly forgotten the conversation he'd overheard. "Yeah?"

"Maybe he didn't know where to look."

CHAPTER 3

"Well?" Amy prodded. "Spill the goods. You know Erika's uncle?"

"Why didn't you tell me her uncle was Bill Brannon?" Colette asked, still shocked.

Maybe Jeff didn't know where to look?

Had Bill Brannon actually said that?

An overstuffed yellow throw pillow slammed into Colette's face and blinded her vision.

"What?" she asked, unable to wipe away the silly grin produced by Bill's parting words.

"Tell. Me. Now."

Where to begin? She decided on the key fact of importance. "I'm lying to him, for you and your friend."

Amy blinked, but quickly recovered, and seemed undeterred. "Sorry, but I made a promise to Erika, and I can't let you back out on your part now. Her uncle is way too overprotective, anyway."

Bill was an overprotective uncle. Guardian, Amy had said.

"I don't even remember him having a niece," Colette

said. "His sister was much older than Bill, but I don't remember Ginny having any kids."

"Erika's eighteen, so when you left Sheldon, she'd have been in first grade. You probably wouldn't have known her."

"Maybe not, but Bill remembered you."

Amy propped her arm on the back of the sofa and fingered the tip of her ponytail. "What can I say? I'm memorable."

Colette curled her feet underneath her on the couch, tapped the pile of sex toys and grinned. "You do tend to make an impression."

Amy laughed. "Funny, I don't remember him."

"You should. He was the guy I was closest to in high school." Then, when Amy nodded and smirked, Colette corrected, "Not like that. As a friend."

Amy snapped to attention. "Black hair?" she asked.

"Yeah." Colette watched Amy's expression change as she obviously put a face with the name.

"Wait a minute. Good-looking, right?"

Colette thought about it. Bill *was* good-looking, if she'd have been looking at him that way back then. "Yeah, I guess you could say that." Then she nodded. Who was she kidding? "Sure, he's good-looking."

"Holy cow, that hottie I remember is Erika's uncle?"

Colette sucked in a gulp of air, then started coughing.

"You okay?" Amy asked as Colette's eyes watered.

"I'm . . . fine," she said, brushing her tears away with the back of her hand. "You were in the fifth grade then, right?"

"Old enough to know a hottie when I saw one," Amy answered. She smiled broadly and picked up a penis ring from the pile of toys. "Did you know this little jelly circle makes a guy last up to three times longer? And we have them in six flavors now. This one's peach." She tossed it in her bag.

Only Amy could pronounce Bill a hottie, then move directly into the subject of penis rings, without batting a lash.

"Seriously," she said. "Three times longer."

"I had no idea," Colette said. "Maybe you should send some to Jeff."

Amy laughed so hard she snorted. "A minuteman, huh?"

"If that."

After plinking the last penis ring in the bag, Amy slapped her hands together. "I still can't believe it. Erika's uncle is that hottie from Sheldon. Can't believe I never put it together, but then again, I haven't seen him yet. Erika and I always meet somewhere when we go out."

"There's something about you calling him that—"

"What?" Amy asked, separating her remaining toys by color.

Did all sex toys come in shades of neon, or just hers? Colette decided now wasn't the time to ask, particularly with the subject at hand. "Bill. A hottie."

"You're saying you aren't thinking about it now?" Amy asked, though the question lost its potency when compared to the size of the fluorescent orange vibrator in her hand.

"I've never even kissed him."

Amy tossed a bottle of edible massage oil in her bag. Then she lifted it back out and removed the top. "Hey, try this new flavor. It's called wild banana." She held the pale yellow container toward Colette.

Knowing Amy wouldn't leave her alone until she tasted the stuff, Colette took the container, held her finger over the top, flipped it, then gave it back to Amy.

"Go on, Lettie, try it," Amy encouraged.

Resignedly, Colette put her finger in her mouth and tasted Amy's latest concoction. The sweet, tangy oil teased her palate. "It's delicious."

"It is, isn't it?" Amy tasted a drop, then closed the bottle and put it in her bag. She continued gathering her toys, plopping them in her shiny duffel.

"You called me Lettie." It had taken a moment for Colette to pinpoint the oddity in their conversation.

Amy stopped short, her fist clenching a fur-embellished pair of pink handcuffs. "I did, didn't I?" She seemed as surprised as Colette.

"You know I hate that name." She'd been "Colette" for twelve years. The name emanated everything she strived to be—mature, sophisticated, goal-oriented.

Tilting her head to the side, Amy looked skeptical. "Do you? Really? Or did you simply hate that it reminds you of Sheldon? It wasn't all that bad a place, you know."

" 'Lettie' sounds like a girl who lives for having fun and being reckless," Colette informed. But she *had* liked the way it sounded from Bill.

"Nothing wrong with a bit of reckless fun every now and then." Amy lifted a silver-bullet vibrator from her bag of tricks. "Speaking of fun, you ever tried this one? It has a remote control unit with three speeds. You can pulsate, vibrate or throb."

"Where do you come up with this stuff?" Colette asked, eyeing the tiny silver contraption, more like an egg than a bullet, in Amy's palm.

Smirking, Amy shook her head. "You've never been good at lying. Be thankful people on the other end of the line can't see your face." She rubbed the bullet between her thumb and forefinger, holding it at eye level in front of Colette. "You already have this one, don't you? And I bet you use it regularly."

Colette couldn't fight the tinge of heat creeping up her neck to settle in her cheeks. "It's one of my favorites."

Amy laughed, wiggling her arched brows. "I'm betting Erika's uncle may want a try at being your favorite."

"I can't even imagine sex with Bill." And the moment Colette made the statement, she did. A vivid picture of Bill Brannon, his dark eyes filled with desire, flashed in her thoughts.

Oh man. She swallowed and pushed the thought away. For now.

"Hopefully, you won't have to imagine it," Amy said, smiling wickedly, as though she had actually seen where her sister's mind had roamed. "I should've realized you would have known him at Sheldon. It never occurred to me that Erika's uncle could've been that guy I remembered."

Erika's uncle. Colette still hadn't learned everything there was to know about that situation. "You said he's her guardian?"

"Yeah," Amy said. "Her mother died when Erika was fifteen, and he took her in. She finished up high school in Atlanta and then we ran into each other a couple of months ago. She was a few years behind me, but I helped her when her mom died." Amy shrugged. "Erika needed someone who understood. Even though I hadn't lost a parent, I sure knew what it was like to barely have one around. I guess we kind of connected from that."

Colette wasn't surprised. Although Amy tried to pretend she didn't care about family relationships, or the lack of family she and Colette had growing up, she really did. And it would've been just like Amy to seek Erika out during that hard time and try to help the young girl cope.

"So she's been living with Bill for three years?" At twenty-seven, Bill had taken in a teen. Again, Colette wasn't surprised. He would have wanted to make certain Ginny's daughter had everything she needed, emotionally and physically, after losing her mother. That was Bill.

"Yeah. And she says he's great and all," Amy added. "Don't get me wrong. I think he's been a terrific uncle, but Erika says he's having a hard time realizing she's an adult. She said he'd hit the roof if he knew she wanted to spend a week with Butch."

Butch. Colette hoped the name didn't fit the man.

"But wouldn't it be cool if you and Erika's uncle hooked up? Who'd have thought that Erika using My Alibi could help you reconnect with an old flame?"

"He wasn't an old flame," Colette corrected.

"Did I say 'old flame'? I meant 'old friend'," Amy said, but her glittering eyes betrayed her words.

"Don't get any wise ideas about commitment here, Amy. If we do anything—"

"You mean if you have sex," Amy said, evidently enjoying the shock value of this conversation.

Colette remembered the way the sound of his voice had brought a response from her long-deprived libido. Yeah, it was definitely a possibility.

"Okay. *If* we have sex, that'll be it, pure and simple." She recalled his promise, and mumbled, "He hinted he'd find my G-spot."

Amy's green eyes sparkled as much as her embellished duffel, and Colette immediately wished she'd kept her big mouth shut about that little tidbit.

"Did he now?" Amy asked, withdrawing the pink vibrator from her bag and grinning. "So, Pinky here has nothing on Bill, huh?"

Might as well go for broke. She and Amy had never kept sex secrets in the past. Why start now?

"He said maybe Jeff didn't know where to look."

Amy curled her arms around her stomach, causing the misshaped vibrator to poke her side while she cackled with delight. "So, not only is Bill Brannon God's gift in the looks department, a sweetheart of a nice guy and has an ass like nobody's business, he also knows his way around a woman's body. Why would you want to go for someone like that?"

Colette scooped up the dislodged pillow and flung it at her sister. "An ass like nobody's business?"

Amy turned her head, letting her ponytail take the blow. Then she twisted toward Colette and winked. "Hey, I may have been little the last time I saw him, but I wasn't blind. Face it, sis. You should've hooked up with him years ago. I say, go for it. Burn up the sheets."

"Then accept the fallout when he finds out I'm lying?"

"He won't find out, unless you tell. And you'll only have to lie to him this once, I promise."

Bill stared at the sleek automobiles displayed on his computer monitor as though envisioning the new advertising campaign for Bentwood Motors. This was what he should have been doing, since his proposal was due by the end of the week.

Unfortunately, the words Alvin Bentwood conveyed as key phrases for his new slogan weren't foremost on Bill's mind. Lettie Campbell's confident words in gym class on her first day in fifth grade were, however.

"I can do it," she had said, eyeing the cheering groups of kids all eagerly participating in double Dutch.

The students at Sheldon Elementary had jumped rope double Dutch since the first grade, and admittedly were pretty damn impressive. Lettie, however, hadn't been exposed to Mrs. Wilson's favorite form of exercise for physical-education classes.

"You ever double Dutched before?" Bill asked, still intrigued by the pretty blonde who had made his preteen heart skip a beat that morning.

Lettie flashed a confident grin at the rest of the kids. Then she turned toward Bill, lowered her voice and whispered, "Can you tell me how—fast?"

Bill knew better than to laugh. He may have only been eleven, but he already knew girls didn't like being laughed at, and he wasn't going to ruin his chances of winning Lettie Campbell's trust.

"Come on," he said, and guided her through the gym

to the stage, where they practiced her footwork behind the thick velvet curtains.

Ten minutes later, Lettie Campbell—double Dutch extraordinaire—emerged ready, willing and able to give double Dutch a go.

She tripped on the rope during the first jump, but remained fearless. Snatching a quick look at Bill, she cleared her throat, tossed her blond curls and asked to start again. The second time, she got it right. And thanked Bill profusely afterward.

It was the beginning of a friendship that would last through high school. Bill had hoped that eventually their friendship would provide the basis for something that would last much longer. That hadn't happened when he told her how he felt on graduation night. Unfortunately, his ego had been too bruised to see that he simply needed to keep the friendship intact and give her time to think about the possibility of the two of them together.

But time had passed. He'd matured beyond the boy who'd been crushed at her rejection. Starting tonight, with their first date, he'd keep his promise . . . and show Lettie Campbell exactly what they'd missed out on back then. And what they could have now.

In high school, Lettie had seen him as a friend and all-around good guy, which was an accurate depiction. In fact, Bill was still the one that friends and family could count on, particularly now, taking in Erika when she should've been sent to live with his parents in Branson. But a teenager didn't want to be raised in a haven for the silver-haired. Besides, Ginny specifically asked Bill to take care of Erika when the cancer took its toll.

Ginny never thought she'd die so soon, merely three

months after she made the request. Or that he'd end up inheriting a fifteen-year-old when he was merely twenty-seven. But he had. And it hadn't been so bad. True, it was hell on his love life—having his niece, a striking young woman with every bit the sexual awareness her mother had at that age, under his roof. He couldn't very well expect her to abstain if he was playing bump-and-grind down the hall.

So he'd abstained too. For the most part. At least under his own roof. And, although the main reason had been because of Erika, Bill hadn't denied another possibility for his few-and-far-between lovers over the past few years.

He'd never had the one he wanted.

Tomorrow, that could change.

In the fall, Erika would move into her own apartment near the Georgia Tech campus, where she'd attend college. Then Bill would, once again, be on his own. This week he was getting a taste of that life again. Erika was out of town taking the training course for her summer job, a position that would help her pay for college textbooks.

Not that his niece needed help, with Bill footing the bill for everything, but Erika was headstrong and was determined to assist him with the finances, particularly since Ginny died without an asset to her name.

Erika. It thrilled him to hear Lettie verify his niece's new job was on the up-and-up. He'd thought it extremely odd a company would hire a girl fresh out of high school, then pay to send her to Florida for a training session, especially when she was only planning to work at the place through the summer. But he couldn't deny she was a smart kid. Smart and strong and determined. Much like Lettie was in high school.

Which wasn't a bad thing. Not bad at all.

It'd taken him a little longer to get his master's degree, since he tried to bounce his classes around part-time jobs and full-time parenting. But it had been worth it. Erika was ready to spread her wings and fly. And he had a chance to grab Lettie Campbell's attention again.

He'd nearly swallowed his tongue when he realized who was on the other end of that line. Lettie.

In high school, she'd liked the boys who were tough, confident and a tad wild. Bill never fit that part. But he could, couldn't he? Long enough to win her over? Surely, he could pull it off for a while, then ease her into the realization she'd fallen for her friend.

He'd heard her sharp intake of breath when he promised to find her elusive treasure. The one Jeff had failed to locate.

Whoever the hell Jeff was.

But she and "Jeff" were over. He'd heard that much in her conversation with her coworker. And from what he gathered, no one else was currently in the picture, since the other woman had offered something to help Lettie find her magic spot.

Bill grinned. His comment had "bad guy" written all over it. It had "the kind of guy that Lettie Campbell would want" written all over it. And she did want him. He heard it through the line. Her breath quickening on the other end. Her excited gasp when he'd made his claim.

"I'm looking forward to it," she'd said.

Little did she know, Bill had been looking forward to

it for much, much longer. And little did she know, he didn't plan on anything ending after one week. Because a week with Lettie Campbell would merely whet his appetite. A lifetime was more like it. He wanted her. Had wanted her for as long as he could remember.

Now he'd have her.

$\mathcal{C}$HAPTER 4

$\mathbf{A}$my Campbell typically didn't make personal calls from work, but this was an emergency. What would Erika say when she found out her uncle and Amy's sister were old friends? And when she found out they were having a date—tonight?

She picked up the phone and dialed, then put the receiver down when her door opened and Wallace Baker barged in. His Albert Einstein–style white hair spiked out in even more directions than usual, and his wire-rimmed glasses barely balanced on the tip of his nose.

"Wallace, you really need to knock before entering my office."

"I did. You didn't hear it?" He nudged his glasses upward with a knuckle and looked genuinely confused as he glanced back at the door. "I mean, it wasn't locked, so I came in, but I did sound off as I was coming."

Amy held back her laugh. He really should watch his word choice, particularly while working at a sex toy company. She tried not to think of the man, over thirty years older than herself, sounding off while he came.

"Next time, if you'd wait for me to tell you to come in, that would be better."

Wallace had only been at the company for two weeks. He was a perfectionist, which was why she'd hired him. Plus he could see the big picture, understand the potential of what Adventurous Accessories could be and was eager to help her achieve her goals. Moreover, he was an honest-to-goodness genius, and you could never go wrong with a genius on board. Or so she'd thought.

Sometimes, however, he was too eager. Like now. As in entering her office on one of those knocking-as-he's-opening-the-door kind of things. What if she'd been testing a product? True, she never tested the vibrators, nipple teasers or love potions while in her office; Adventurous Accessories had private rooms for that kind of thing, and as project lead, she had her own suite. But still . . .

"I can do that," he said, nodding. "Just wanted to let you know Pinky didn't pass the trial run."

Amy's jaw dropped. "What do you mean?"

"Can I sit?" He pointed to one of the two leather chairs facing her desk.

"Of course." Dang, was he a "Mother, may-I?" guy about everything? Lord knows, if she ever did want a man in her bedroom, she wouldn't want him asking questions throughout the process. She'd heard of the type.

Do you like this? How do you like that?

Try it and see what the woman likes, Bozo.

But Amy didn't have to worry about those occurrences, the ones her friends described whenever they went barhopping and talked about bedhopping. She used the toys, got the job done and didn't have to worry about how she looked in the morning. It was a foolproof system, and she liked it.

Moreover, she liked her newest toy more than any other. Listening to Wallace's claim, she was floored. She had one of the Pinky demos at home and had even offered it to her sister because it was so good at hitting the mark every time.

It failed?

"How many test subjects?" she asked, grabbing a pen and paper.

"Thirty."

Amy frowned. That number was large enough to get a general idea. "And what was the percentage?"

He cleared his throat and pulled a folded paper out of his shirt pocket. "Twenty percent positive response."

Six women out of thirty? That was it? But it had found her bull's-eye every time. Multiple times, in fact.

"I . . . have a theory," Wallace said, "but I'm not sure if it's one you want to hear."

"I'm listening," she said, her brow furrowed. "Any theory that could potentially help our company and our products is one I want to know," Amy clarified, though she cringed inside. Did she really want to hear anything negative about Pinky? It was her creation, the one that would catapult her to fame in the sex toy industry. And it only worked 20 percent of the time?

What was up with that?

"Well, it's been my personal experience," he said, his face tinting a tad from peach to pale pink, "that some women require manual stimulation as well."

Amy blinked. "This is manual stimulation, Wallace.

It's a toy. A do-it-yourself for the woman who doesn't need, or want, a sexual partner."

Another clearing of his throat, a finger crooked in his shirt collar, and his hue altered from pink to red. "What I meant was, some women may not be able to simply use a toy. Some may require a toy *and* a partner."

"Why?" Amy asked, stunned by his so-called-theory. Had he tested it? And if so, on how many subjects?

He straightened in his chair and his color shifted closer to normal. "Adventurous Accessories does promote its products as enhancements to a couple's lovemaking. Maybe Pinky is more of an enhancement to the act, rather than the sole instigator."

"But my entire concept was for something that stimulates the G-spot without a partner," she said, not embarrassed one iota talking about sex. She'd grown up in the same house with Wanda Campbell, after all.

"I know. That's why this was so difficult to bring to your attention. But, in truth, if you market it as a solo act, and then it doesn't live up to the claim, Adventurous Accessories will take the heat for it." He inhaled deeply, exhaled loudly, as though immensely relieved to have made his point.

Amy considered the possibility and knew he was right. Dang it.

"Okay. Change the marketing angle. But include a teaser that it can keep you happy while your partner's away too," she added, determined to suit women who were like her as well.

Women like her. Which was . . . what? Toy savvy? Men haters? No, she didn't hate men. She just didn't need one.

Self-sufficient. Yeah, that was it. And that's what she'd continue telling herself.

"Anything else, Wallace?"

"No, that's all."

"Fine. Try to get something worked up by tomorrow morning's staff meeting. We'll go over it with the team then."

"Will do, boss." He stood and made a quick exit.

"Boss," she repeated, grinning as she crossed the room and locked the door. Privacy should be easier to come by in her business. She returned to her desk, snatched the phone and dialed.

One ring . . . two . . .

"Hello?" a husky voice answered from the other end. No doubt Butch had been sleeping.

"Can I speak to Erika?" Amy punched the speaker's button, dropped the phone in the cradle, then tapped her computer keys to view the latest product statistics while she spoke to her friend. Her orange stallion vibrator was slowly but surely making its way to the top of the line and had crept past the fuzzy navel massage oil in sales. Cool.

"Hang on. She's walking on the beach. Want me to yell at her?" Butch sure didn't sound like the romantic picture Erika had painted in her James Dean description.

"If you could see if she's nearby, that'd be great. You don't have to yell—"

Amy didn't get a chance to complete the sentence. Butch evidently didn't mind yelling. At all. She winced while he bellowed her friend's name so loudly she was surprised she didn't hear it in stereo, echoing all the way from Tybee Island to Atlanta.

She listened to the two of them snap at each other, then heard the receiver clang as if dropped to the floor. "Erika?"

"I'm here. Hold on. Butch, where are you going?"

"Beer," he answered.

The unmistakable sound of a slamming door overpowered the line.

"Sure. Why should today be any different?" Erika sighed into the phone. "Hello?"

"It's me," Amy said, turning away from her computer screen.

"Hey!" Erika's voice took on an entirely different tone than a moment ago with Butch, as if she were actually pleased to talk to Amy. "How's it going? Everything's okay with Uncle Bill and the alibi, right?"

"I've got a couple of things to tell you," Amy said, "but first tell me if everything's okay there. I thought you said he was your dream guy? The one you wanted to spend your life with?"

"Yeah, I said that."

"That wasn't what I heard," Amy informed, as if Erika didn't know she'd caught every word of their heated little exchange. "What gives?"

"Oh, it'll be fine. I've never been around him when he's drinking quite so much. And he's a little . . . different around his buddies. It's biker week here, you know."

"I didn't know." Amy frowned. "Biker week" didn't sound very romantic.

"Yeah, they stop off at Tybee Island, then head on up toward Myrtle Beach for the big bash."

"Are you going to that too?" Amy asked.

"Somehow I think he'll be okay without me. . . ." Her voice trailed off.

"Have you met someone else?" Amy asked.

"No. I'm still crazy about Butch, even if I'm having a time trying to figure him out. Being with someone around the clock isn't quite the same as dating. But everything's going fine, really."

"Is it your mom?" Amy asked. Erika had been very emotional since her eighteenth birthday, appearing to miss her mother even more than before. Therefore, Amy didn't want to do anything to upset her. She had been so excited about the chance at a romantic getaway with her true love. Unfortunately, Amy didn't hear any of that excitement in Erika's tone now.

"I'll be all right," Erika said. "Let's talk about something else. Was your sister okay with me hiring her? She didn't mind, did she? I mean, she shouldn't, right? It's just another client, nothing really out of the ordinary from her regular job."

Evidently, Erika didn't want to touch the subject of her mother, and that was fine. Amy was smart enough to let her friends talk when they wanted to talk, and be quiet when they wanted to remain quiet.

"Amy?" Erika asked, reminding Amy that she'd been silent a few seconds too long in this conversation. "She's okay with the alibi thing, right? I really don't want my uncle knowing where I am; he'd freak. This is just another client for her, right?"

Amy mustered up her courage. "Not exactly."

Erika opened the top dresser drawer and eyed her clothes, folded in neat little stacks. Then she turned to see Butch's suitcase, with every stitch of clothing, primarily leather, piled on top. Sliding her hand beneath the bottom pair of jeans in her drawer, she found the pointed edge of an envelope and eased it free.

Propping the phone in the crook of her neck, she sat on the bed. Then she carefully withdrew the paper from the envelope.

"Erika?" Amy said on a huff. "Didn't you hear what I said?"

"No, to be honest, I didn't. Tell me again." She liked Amy, and she loved that she'd run into her in Atlanta. It'd been a long time since she'd been around someone who knew about her past, who understood where she came from.

Amy had been her "big sister" at Sheldon High. When the middle-school kids prepared to move to high school, the faculty assigned a senior to help them learn the ropes. She had been blessed to meet Amy Campbell through that pairing. Even more because Amy had been there, and had truly cared, when her mother died.

Erika unfolded the letter, scanning the words in her mother's familiar curly script. She swallowed past the thickness in her throat.

"Your uncle and my sister knew each other in Sheldon. I can't believe we didn't think about that possibility."

Erika blinked past her tears. "What did you say?"

"They knew each other before."

Erika pulled her attention away from the letter, blinked a few more times, then forced her mind to concentrate on the implications of Amy's news. Uncle Bill knew Colette Campbell. Okay, that wasn't such a bad thing, was it? As long as they didn't recognize each other's voices on the phone, what would the harm be in . . .

"Amy?"

"Yeah?"

"How did you find out that they knew each other?"

"It wasn't that hard. She called him, gave him her name—"

"She uses her real name for My Alibi?" Erika asked, and the pieces clicked into place.

"There's no reason not to; none of her clients have known her before."

"Didn't she recognize his name on the application?"

Oh God, this wasn't good. He'd never understand why she wanted a week with Butch. Uncle Bill had been adamant that she finish college first, before chasing after love, the way her mother did.

She let her back fall to the bed and clutched the letter to her chest. Her mother had no regrets, and neither would she.

As long as she didn't hurt Uncle Bill.

"I think she was paying more attention to the client information than the contact, particularly since you said he wouldn't be home."

"He was home? She actually spoke to him? She was supposed to leave a message." This couldn't get any worse. Oh God, she'd promised her mother she'd be good for Uncle Bill. It was the last thing Erika had said to her before she died. But then, there was the letter. . . .

"She would have, but he answered the phone."

Erika closed her eyes. This was not happening. It wasn't. She'd followed her heart, just like her mother had said to do in her letter, and pursued true love. It was supposed to go perfectly. She'd spend a week with Butch, fall in love for life and maybe even come back with a ring on her finger. Wasn't that the way love went?

Admittedly, the first day with Butch left plenty to be desired. And now Uncle Bill knew? But if he knew, why hadn't he called?

"Did your sister tell him about me? The truth about where I am?"

"No. In fact, she's giving your case to another My Alibi representative today. That's what I wanted to tell you."

Erika breathed a little easier. "So he doesn't know? I'm okay?"

"He doesn't know," Amy soothed. "And he won't find out, or at least I don't think he will."

"What do you mean you don't think he will?"

"Your uncle asked my sister out, and they're going on a date. Tonight."

Erika sat straight up in the bed. "Get out!"

Amy's laugh relieved the tension pulsing through the phone. "Seriously."

A flurry of emotions battled within Erika. True, she didn't want Uncle Bill to find out she lied. But another part of her wanted him to find true love too. He'd dated over the past three years, but rarely did he ever take a girl out twice. The interest simply wasn't there. Plus some women were turned off when they saw the teenage girl living under his roof, or when they had to call it an early night because he didn't want to leave Erika alone.

What if Colette Campbell was his true love? The one who could fulfill his dreams, the way her mother described in her letter. Wouldn't her mother have wanted Erika to help make his dreams a reality too?

She placed the paper against the comforter and smoothed out the wrinkles, then silently read the last lines:

I'll never regret chasing the dream, following true love. Don't you regret it either. Chasing my dream gave me what I treasure more than anything—you. Everyone deserves a chance to have something, or someone, that makes them feel complete. That's the reason we live, isn't it? To find completeness. I want that for you, Erika. More than anything, I want you to find happiness—to find love—and to feel complete.

Erika swallowed thickly, looked out the window and saw Butch ambling up the sidewalk. Was he her true love? Right now she wasn't so sure. But she wasn't going to back down from chasing this dream. Not yet.

"Amy?"

"Yeah."

"Tell me what you think about all this," Erika said, folding the letter and sliding it back in the envelope.

"I'm sure Cassie, the girl who is taking over your case, will do a great job as your alibi," Amy said.

"I'm sure she will too," Erika said, quickly crossing the room to put the envelope back in the drawer. "And I'm betting it all happened for a reason. I ran into you. You told me about the alibi agency. Your sister ends up calling Uncle Bill. Sparks fly."

"I want that for you, Erika. More than anything, I want you to find happiness—to find love—and to feel complete."

"The two of them are meant to get together, and it's going to be wonderful," Erika continued, pushing the corner of the envelope under her folded jeans, then easing the drawer shut. "And I believe there's a reason I came to Tybee Island too. I'm chasing my dream, and it's going to be wonderful."

Butch punched the door open, stormed in and dropped the beer on the counter. "I wanna make up."

"I've gotta go, Amy. Everything's going to be fine. For everyone."

CHAPTER 5

Did coffee in the afternoon qualify as a date?

Colette didn't think so, but she wasn't certain. Maybe sharing a coffee was all Bill had in mind when he said they should get together while she was in town.

However, she thought with a smile, *guys generally don't locate your G-spot over coffee.*

She laughed out loud, then waved away the stares of her fellow passengers on the MARTA train.

"Our next stop is Midtown. Midtown is our next scheduled stop," a woman's computerized voice cracked repeatedly through the intercom system.

Her stomach quivered. Funny that Bill had suggested they meet at Jitters for a break from work, since "jitters" accurately described her present state.

And why? This was Bill, after all.

But this was also Bill, twelve years older than she remembered. How had he changed? How had she? Would he even recognize her now? In her opinion, she still looked fairly close to the girl from high school. Her hair was shorter than he'd remember, and her attire was different now. She glanced at her navy pantsuit, practical pumps and silk chemise. Not exactly the look-at-me–type thing she wore back then. Would he take one look and realize she wasn't the impulsive girl he'd befriended before? That she'd settled down and actually grown up? Did she want him to see her as settled?

The train screeched to a halt.

"Midtown," the voice announced, and the doors slid open.

Colette swallowed, stood and took a deep breath before exiting. Jitters was a half block away, so she had a little more time to gather her composure before she saw . . .

Have mercy.

He casually leaned against one of the columns in the station. His jet-black hair was shorter on top, different than she remembered, but a tapered cut that befitted a successful businessman. Navy suit. Red power tie. Thick dark brows. Eyes the color of chocolate.

Had he always been that tall?

Her stomach pitched. She'd never been nervous about seeing Bill in the past. But she'd also never really "looked" at Bill in the past. Not the way she was looking now. The way she'd look at a hot, hunky, successful man in a gorgeous suit, totally worthy of a *GQ* cover, with a lean, fit frame, who was giving her a smile that was . . .

Real.

Excitement pulsed through her, and she laughed. This was her old friend, and she'd missed him.

"I thought we were meeting at the coffee shop," she said, quickening her pace until she reached him and wrapped her arms around his neck.

Lord, did he always smell this good?

Laughing, he squeezed her tight, lifting her from the floor in a big bear hug, then gently placed her heels back on the concrete. "Good to see you, Lettie."

"You too." Her feet may have been on the ground, but her head was still floating, particularly when she looked into his eyes. They were alive with anticipation, and didn't hold an ounce of the pain that she'd witnessed the last time they'd been together. God, how she'd hated hurting him before. And, man, how she'd missed looking into those eyes.

Bill held her there as the train pulled away. "You okay?"

Could he tell she was trembling?

"Yeah. Just can't believe it's been so long."

"Me either. But never again. Deal?"

"Deal."

"I know we said we'd meet at Jitters, but I was eager to see you," he said.

"I was eager too."

"Come on, I'll show you the way." He guided her through the station. "How was your flight?"

Without warning, she gulped air and started coughing. Lying was going to be even tougher when she was this close to Bill, with his palm against the small of her back while they made their way down the street.

"You okay?" he asked again, and stopped walking.

Colette nodded. Oh yeah, she was great. At the moment, she was lying to her old best friend, whose mere presence, by the way, was making her uterus do a happy dance. And why was that? It hadn't been that long since she'd had sex—even if it wasn't anything to write home about—but there was something about looking at Bill, and knowing that this was the guy who'd known her back when, that had her seeing visions of . . . naked Bill.

Bill, who was currently on the receiving end of a My Alibi lie.

Yep, she was super.

"I'm fine," she said, her eyes watering.

He withdrew a handkerchief from his back pocket, then gently wiped her tears away. "Better?"

"Yeah." Why didn't it surprise her that Bill kept a handkerchief in his pocket? And why did she think he probably kept it for times like this? For wiping away tears. Had he wiped away his niece's tears during the last three years? Colette looked at those dark eyes, at the mouth frowning slightly at the corners as he brushed the last teardrop away. Yeah, he had wiped all of Erika's tears away. That was just the kind of guy he was. The kind of guy he'd always been.

"Thanks."

He grinned, and she realized something else. She'd missed his smile too. "Think you can handle a cup of java now?"

"Sure. I only get choked breathing." *And listening to you ask about a flight that didn't take place.*

"Good. Because we're here." He pointed to a small coffee shop, its exterior completely covered in cobblestone and its windows bordered in red-and-gold stained glass. A crimson awning with the Jitters logo—a tall, steaming coffee mug—balanced above the door.

Colette had heard of the locally owned shop, but she'd never ventured to Midtown to try it out. Matter of fact, she rarely left Marietta during the day, which would prove an advantage now. She could honestly experience Jitters for the first time . . . with Bill.

"I come here every afternoon," he said, then shrugged. "Hey, if you've gotta have a vice, I figure coffee isn't such a terrible one to tack onto your day. I remember you had to have a candy bar every afternoon before sixth period at Sheldon. Still need your daily chocolate fix?"

She shook her head. "I guess not." It'd been years since she'd given up her afternoon ritual. She'd replaced it with a morning ritual, but that didn't have anything to do with chocolate. And she wasn't about to share that little secret with Bill.

"Guess we have changed." He opened the door and waited for her to step through as a bell-laden ribbon announced their entry.

"Hi, Mr. Brannon," a young waitress asked, her broad grin overpowering her pixie face. "You're running a little late for your afternoon caffeine fix, aren't you?"

Bill laughed. "I was waiting for my friend. Maria, this is Lettie Campbell. Lettie, meet Maria, the best waitress in Atlanta."

The young girl giggled. "He just says that because I give him extra whipped cream." She reached for two menus from a wooden bin by the door, but halted when an older waitress hurried toward them from the rear of the restaurant.

"Maria, you're going to be late for class," the woman scolded. Frowning, she took the menus from Maria's hand.

"Sorry, Mr. Brannon," Maria said. "You're getting Mama today."

The white-haired woman glared at her daughter. "Go to school, Maria."

Maria shrugged. "Nice to meet you, Lettie. And I'll see you tomorrow, Mr. Brannon." She gave her mother a smile that said she wasn't bothered at all by the older woman's disapproval, then she headed out the door.

"That girl," the woman muttered. She turned toward Bill. "Would you like to sit inside or on the patio?" She wore a red T-shirt and black pants, and had a short pencil tucked behind one ear. She was dressed like a teen, but Colette would guess Maria's mother hadn't seen her teens in a good forty or fifty years.

"Up to you," he said, smiling at Colette.

"Patio."

They followed the waitress while Colette tried to recall the last time a man had opened a door for her, or asked her where she'd prefer to sit.

She couldn't remember.

The patio was small, with five circular wrought-iron tables decked with crisp white tablecloths and thick red candles.

"Your menus," the woman said, dropping two thick folders on their table, then leaving.

"She seems to be having a bad day," Colette said, as the woman barreled through the restaurant.

"Nah, that's just the way Rita copes. She's been grumpy ever since Maria started back to college. Rita's convinced if her daughter gets her degree, she'll leave town."

"You know them well?" she asked.

"Just from my daily cup of coffee. Sometimes Rita

feels like talking; sometimes she feels like throwing something."

A loud crash sounded from the kitchen.

"Looks like today is a throwing something day," he said, winking.

Her heart skittered in response to that wink.

"I'm glad you could take a break from work," he said. "I thought that would help us get past—" he leaned forward and lifted his palms—"this."

"This?" she asked.

"The awkward stage of seeing each other again after so long. You're still as beautiful as I remember, by the way."

Heat bristled against Colette's cheeks, and she didn't know how to respond. He was right—this was awkward. But fun. She scanned the menu to keep him from seeing her face.

But Bill Brannon had always been a master at reading her; evidently, that was still the case.

"You've definitely changed," he said.

She jerked her head up. Did he know she was a professional liar? "How?"

"The old Lettie wouldn't have gotten embarrassed just now. In fact, you'd have put on a fake pout because I didn't say you were *more* beautiful than I remembered; then you'd have punched me and told me not to get any ideas about stealing half of your Snickers in the afternoon."

"True," she admitted, while a surge of relief washed through her. "But it wouldn't have mattered. You'd have taken half, anyway," she said, really enjoying the stroll down memory lane.

"What can I say? I took what I wanted."

"Did you?" she asked, unable to resist. "Always?"

His chair squeaked as he scooted forward, placed his elbows on the table and clasped his fingers under his chin. "No, I didn't, or I wouldn't have let you leave Sheldon that night. But, like we've already determined, we've changed."

"So you're saying you take what you want now?"

A deep dimple pierced his left cheek with the wideness of his smile. "Definitely."

She mentally attempted to slow her pulse. Lord, she felt light-headed, but she didn't want to stop this insightful conversation. Particularly not with this latest Bill Brannon admission. "And what is it you're wanting right—"

"Take your order?" Rita said, halting Colette's attempt to see how far he planned on this "thing" going.

Bill winked at Colette, and once again, sent her heart racing. "Go ahead."

"No," she said, handing the menu to Rita. "You tell her what I want," she challenged.

Rita turned back to Bill and smiled. It was the first smile she had seen from the woman, and it stretched from cheek to cheek. "There's forty-two choices," Rita said, intensifying the pressure.

Colette laughed. "Pretty good odds, *if* you still know me."

With his eyes never leaving Colette's, he handed the menu to the waitress. "She'll have a Snickers mocha latte with extra whipped cream. And I'll have the same." That dimple flashed again, and she fought the way it made her tongue want to lick it. Lord help her, this was

Bill. But granted, this was a grown-up, confident and definitely male version of the brotherly friend from high school.

How did she ever look at him as a brother type?

"Well?" Rita coaxed.

"I'd have ordered an espresso," Colette said.

The smile on the older woman's face would rival any beauty queen's. She cocked her hip and looked pointedly at Bill. "Looks like you were wrong—"

"But," Colette interrupted, "after hearing you have—what was it called again?"

Bill's look of triumph was priceless. "A Snickers mocha latte."

Rita shook her head. "*Hmph*. I suppose you want the extra whipped cream too, right?"

"Definitely," Colette said.

The frustrated lady left.

"Guess I've got some catching up to do, to figure out everything about you that's changed since graduation," he said.

"And I've got plenty to learn too. Like your niece. She's living with you now?" Colette asked.

She'd have to choose her questions wisely, so he wouldn't know that she already had his address, his typical work schedule, cell phone number and work number on an information sheet at her office. Lord, this lying business sure was easier when you were doing it to strangers.

His smile faltered. "Do you remember my sister, Ginny? She was eight years older than I was, so you may not."

"I remember her. Black hair, very pretty."

"Yeah, that's Ginny." He accepted his mug from the waitress and took a sip, then watched her do the same. "You like it?"

She nodded. "It's delicious."

What was the appropriate thing to do? To say? Did he want to talk about Ginny and Erika, or would he rather not? Way back when, she could tell when Bill wanted to talk, what he wanted to talk about and when he'd rather remain silent. Now, though, she didn't have a clue. And that realization stung. They really did have a lot of catching up to do.

He continued sipping his drink, but finally placed it back on the table. "We lost Ginny three years ago to cancer, and Erika needed a place to live."

There was a lot he wasn't saying in the statement, but Colette assumed he didn't want to get into the details now, so she played it as safe as possible. "I'm sorry about Ginny, but I'm not surprised you took Erika to live with you."

He gave her an easy smile. "She's a good kid, and I was at a point in my life where I could take care of her."

"Not exactly what most single men do, though, is it?" she asked, and took a big sip of her drink. The caramel and chocolate met her stomach and made her feel nearly as good as the dimple in his cheek.

"No," he admitted, "it wasn't what I'd planned either, but I wouldn't have it any other way. And besides, if it hadn't been for Erika making that trip to Tampa this week, we might have never crossed paths again." He flicked thick dark brows and finished off his mug.

Colette still had half a cup of latte, but she couldn't drink any more.

"Full?" he asked.

"It's more filling than an espresso."

"I'll say. So, how long before you need to get back?"

She glanced at her watch to stall for an answer. At My Alibi, her hours were her own, particularly since so much of her work was done at home. But he thought she worked at a computer graphics company.

"I've got another half hour," she said; then, when he looked surprised, she added, "I didn't take lunch."

"Then why don't we walk a little farther down the street? I want to show you something." He stood, left his cash payment on the table and moved behind her.

Colette hadn't had a man withdraw her chair in a very long time. If ever. She didn't think she was necessarily into that kind of thing, but right now she'd beg to differ. She was very, very into it. "Thanks."

"No problem. This way," he said, taking her hand and leading the way through the patio exit.

"Are we going to your office?" she asked.

"No, but we can stop by there if we have time. It's that building, twentieth floor." He pointed to one of the large high-rises.

"I always knew you'd do well. An advertising executive, right?"

He stopped walking, tilted his head. "How'd you know?"

"One, it was your dream. And two, that's what your assistant said when I called the number you gave me this morning."

"Can't hide anything from you, can I?" he asked, squeezing her hand.

Her breathing hitched, but she pulled it together. How

long could she hide something from him? And how would she live with herself if she did?

"Bill, I need to tell you," she started, but stopped when he put a finger to her lips, then eased it away.

"Wait. I deserve a chance to guess too."

"Guess?"

"About whether you've achieved your dream."

That wasn't even close to what she'd been about to say, since she was going to tell him about My Alibi and Erika. But that wouldn't have been a wise move. Not yet. Amy had asked her not to say anything, and if she were going to tell him about Erika, she'd need to talk to Amy first.

"My dream?"

"I know you're working for a computer graphics company. Are you doing that so you can perfect your technique with computer-generated designs?"

"Designs?" she asked, bewildered.

"That's all you talked about in high school," he reminded. "Designing your own clothing line and opening a boutique in a big city. Is that still the dream? And if it is, I bet your current job is helping you get closer to the goal."

Her current job was helping her get closer to the goal of owning a boutique. But she'd fine-tuned the dream a bit to designing beautiful, yet sensual, lingerie, rather than general clothing. And she hadn't ever thought of producing computer-generated designs. What would be original about that? However, his logic did play true, since he believed she worked for Integrated Solutions.

"I am saving money for a boutique," she admitted. "And I'm getting very close to having what I need for start-up." She couldn't deny the pride at telling Bill her goal was in sight.

"I knew you would," he said, starting to walk again. "That's what you deserve, everything you ever wanted."

Oh man, was he ever killing her with his positive comments! If she did get everything she deserved, it probably wouldn't include fulfilled dreams. A nightmare would be more like it.

"Here we are."

Colette looked up to see a long brick building and a huge playground hopping with kids. "What is it?"

"A community recreational center. The manager is a friend of mine, and I come here a few times a week to visit. He hosts a program for the inner-city kids during the summer, when their parents are working and they need something to do."

Tiny boys and girls climbed on teeter-totters and monkey bars. Older girls played kickball and a group of teen boys played an aggressive basketball game on a blacktop court. All of them were laughing, exercising, having fun. And all of them reminded her of those carefree days of high school, the last time she and Bill had been together.

"I can see why you wanted to show me this place. It's nice that your friend is doing something for these kids."

"I know, but this isn't what I wanted to show you. That is." He indicated a group of girls in one of the shady spots by the big building.

Long black loops arced through the air in the midst of the chanting group. Leave it to Bill. . . .

"They're good," she said. It'd been a long time since she had seen anyone jump double Dutch. But she remembered the fun, could practically feel the excited energy pulsing through the stomping, jumping, chattering girls. And she could feel more too. The memory of that day when a determined eleven-year-old helped her fit in by teaching her how.

She looked at Bill.

He looked at her.

"Thank you."

He didn't ask why; he knew. Putting one finger against her chin, he tilted her head and moved closer. . . .

"Hey, Mr. Brannon!" a girl twisting one side of the ropes called.

A deep sigh echoed from his chest, and he turned toward the sound. "Hi, Regina."

Colette laughed. Businessman, guardian and fan of double Dutch. There were many sides to the man he'd become, and she enjoyed seeing each of them.

"You do come here often, don't you?"

He shrugged. "I was always an admirer of talented rope turners."

"Mr. Harris is inside!" Regina called again. She was missing her front teeth, which made her "inside" more of an "inthide."

"I'm not here to see him," Bill admitted. "I just wanted to show my friend how talented your group is. She knows how to double Dutch too."

"Really? You wanna jump now?" Regina asked.

Colette examined her pantsuit and navy pumps. "Probably not today," she called back. "Maybe another time, though."

"Gotcha!" Regina said, then turned her attention back to the twirling of the ropes.

"I should get you to the train if you're going to make it back to work on time," he said, waving to the kids.

They walked away, while Colette pondered their afternoon. Was this their date? Did she want it to be?

No, she didn't. She was only beginning to understand, and appreciate, Bill Brannon. Not merely the friend, but the man. And she didn't want it to end.

Unfortunately, he hadn't said anything else since they left the rec center, and she had no idea if he planned on their "date" ending when they reached the train.

He'd hinted that they would have more—a G-spot-finding more—in their conversation last night. Had that merely been a joke, to make her feel less uncomfortable about the steamy conversation he overheard? That'd make getting out of this lying issue much simpler, wouldn't it?

But it wasn't what she wanted. Not anymore.

She wanted Bill.

"I really enjoyed our date," she said, entering the MARTA station. She was fishing, but she had to know. If this wasn't their date, he'd tell her.

She turned, waited.

Lord, had he always had that dimple? Because she couldn't imagine having all of those heartfelt, and somewhat intelligent, conversations with him in high school and ignoring it. And that smile . . . that smile would make any woman in her right mind swoon.

"Lettie," he said.

"Uh-huh?"

"Wait here."

She blinked. Wait here? Before she could protest, he turned and shuffled between a crowd of passengers trying to jockey their way into position for the next train. She squinted, but lost him in the mass of people.

"Wait here"?

Frowning, she checked her watch. She really should get back to work and make sure Cassie was set on taking Erika's case, as well as pick up her assignments for the night. Okay, so she hadn't got the response she wanted from her "enjoyed the date" remark. That was probably better, anyway, right? Now she wouldn't have to worry about lying to Bill. Cassie would handle the remainder of Erika's week, and Bill would assume Colette would return to Tampa. Case closed. End of semidream of having something beyond friendship with Bill Brannon.

However, she had no doubt she'd be having new dreams now. Dreams where she vividly saw his face when she tested one of Amy's toys.

God help her, she wanted him, and she hadn't told him. Maybe *that's* what she should do. When he came back, she'd tell him what she wanted.

That's the Lettie Campbell he knew in high school. So it wouldn't surprise him if she merely reminded him that they were mature adults who might enjoy each other's company at a more intimate level. Intimate. With Bill. She'd never have thought of it before and, in truth, she wasn't thinking "intimate" now.

She was thinking, *sweaty* and *steamy*.

Was the MARTA station getting hotter?

"For you," he said, his words feathering against her neck.

She turned and ended face-to-bloom with an exquisite pink rose. Inhaling, she let the sweet scent calm her nerves. Surely, he was thinking about more. There was that G-spot comment, right?

"It's beautiful. Where did you get it?"

"There's a vendor outside, and I thought it was the perfect flower to let you know how much I'm looking forward to our date."

"Looking forward to it?" Oh yeah, here goes that uterus happy dance again.

"You didn't seriously think an afternoon coffee would be enough, did you, Lettie?"

She shook her head. She'd sure hoped not.

"You do want more. A date. With me," he said.

It wasn't really a question, but she nodded anyway. There was no way she could form words.

"Good," he said, brushing the petals down her cheek, "because I want to get to know you, Lettie. Even better than before. And I plan to start tonight."

Another nod was as good as she could do, given where her mind had headed, to visions of hot and heated, ready and willing, Bill.

He guided her to the train. "Here." He placed something in her hand. "It's my card. E-mail directions to Amy's apartment, okay? Pick you up at seven?"

"Seven's fine," she said, and was glad her excited libido had handed over the reins to her voice.

"Next stop, North Avenue. North Avenue, our next stop," the intercom voice announced as Colette looked through the tram windows to watch Bill Brannon disappear.

"That's a beautiful rose," a woman said from the seat across the aisle.

Colette looked at the flower, inhaled its scent again, then closed her eyes as a hint of a memory emerged.

She couldn't put her finger on it, but she decided to let it go. She'd relish her afternoon for now and look forward to tonight, and her date. A date with an old friend and, perhaps, a future lover.

CHAPTER 6

I labeled both phones with the corresponding company names, as well as the names of my clients. I'm only responsible for two tonight, so it shouldn't be that bad." Colette handed the cell phones to her sister and pointed to the white stickers identifying pertinent information. "I hate asking you to do this." She fiddled with the straps on her dress. "Maybe I should cancel this thing with Bill."

"This 'thing' is a date," Amy said, "like he told you this afternoon when he gave you this rose." She leaned over the kitchen table and stuffed her nose in the center of the flower. "I guess that'd be one of the perks to going out with a real guy, instead of merely taking advantage of toys."

"What's that?" Colette asked.

"Flowers."

Colette laughed. "That's one way of looking at it. But we're simply having dinner, a show and sex." He'd confirmed the dinner and show when he responded to her e-mailed directions. The sex, of course, was a given.

Amy didn't bat a lash. "Exactly. Dinner, a show and sex. In other words, a date. And if you so much as try to cancel, I'll kill you. Don't you think I can handle being an alibi for a night?" She tucked the phones in the side pocket of her purse.

"I'm sure you'll do fine, but humor me one more time, please."

Rolling her eyes, Amy put a clenched fist to her ear and deadpanned, "Hello, this is Amy with"—she eyed the back of one of the phones—"Century Pharmaceuticals. Can I help you?" She withdrew a tiny notepad and pen from her purse, tilted her head as though propping her imaginary phone on her shoulder, then pretended to write a number on the page. "Certainly. I'll be happy to give Mr. So-and-So your message, and I'll ask him to get back to you as soon as possible. Have a great night."

A grin tugged at the corners of Colette's mouth, but she held it in check. Her sister was quite good at prevaricating over the phone. "Then what?"

"Then I call the cheating culprit and let 'em know they need to check in with the cheatee. No sweat."

"But I'm asking you to lie." Colette hated her job more by the minute, especially now, dragging Amy through the muck too.

Amy made a large production out of clearing her throat. Then she placed a palm against her chest and confessed, "As shocking as this might come to you, it wouldn't be the first time I've fudged the truth." She grinned, and one deep dimple winked from her right cheek.

Funny how Amy's dimple had never reminded her of Bill before, but after this afternoon, and most certainly after their date tonight, Colette suspected she'd never see another dimple again without remembering his.

"Tell me, though, what do I have here? Married or single?" Amy pointed to the phones protruding from her purse.

Colette indicated the slim red one. "I'm glad you asked. This one is an, um, unusual case."

"I'm all ears," Amy said, wiggling her brows. "Is it kinky?"

Colette laughed. "Yeah, I guess you could classify it as kinky."

"Cool. Spill."

"It's a married couple in their fifties who don't want their grown kids knowing where they are this week. They told them they're vacationing in Florida."

"But they're really . . ." Amy prodded.

"Oh, they're really in Florida, but they're at a couples resort."

"Why would they want to hide that?" Amy asked, obviously disappointed the story wasn't juicier. "Shoot, that's kind of sweet, and I'm sure their kids would love it."

"I didn't tell you the name of the resort," Colette teased.

"And?"

"Love Beach," Colette said, then laughed again at her sister's dropped jaw.

"Get out! The nudie sex-therapy place?" Amy picked up the phone and eyed it with a whole new appreciation. "You know, a lot of our product testers go to that place. Actually, I could use an older couple that takes an occasional walk on the wild side to try out some of my newer items."

"Oh no you don't," Colette warned. "You are not about to start fishing for sex toy testers from my client base. Promise me, Amy."

"They'd probably like it."

Colette grinned, but shook her head. "Uh-uh. Don't go there."

"All right," Amy said in a semipout. "But if you change your mind, I really could use an older couple's opinion on the two-person vibrator."

"Two-person vibrator? Surely, if you brought that home, I'd remember."

"Oh, you'd remember, all right. But it hasn't left the lab yet. The prototype is at the office, but it's way cool. Or, I should say, way hot. That's the problem. If they use it with gusto, it melts. Or at least it did for the couple who tried it."

Colette's jaw dropped this time.

"Don't worry, no one got hurt, and I think I've got the problem fixed. We're using a more durable plastic, but it's a little harder for the male to climax. Before, the vibrating penis ring kind of held on like a turtleneck. Now it fits more like a vise." She shrugged. "Then again, generally they don't mind it lasting a bit longer, right?"

"Right," Colette said. Then, because she couldn't resist, she added, "How exactly do you bring these issues up at your weekly staff meetings? You're still the only female on the team, right?"

"There are several teams, depending on products. But I'm the project leader for ours," Amy said with pride.

"So I guess you'd say I run the show. And yeah, they're all male. What about it?"

"Just picturing you standing in front of a bunch of men and telling them the next topic is the melting vibrator that can be fixed as long as the guy doesn't mind waiting awhile before he comes. Or something like that."

"That's pretty much how I told them," Amy said, apparently impressed. "In more technical terms, of course."

"Of course," Colette said, stifling her laugh.

Amy, however, didn't hold back. She giggled until she snorted. "Believe it or not," she said between chuckles, "I've never cracked a grin in there. And every guy on the team is older than I am, so it'd be kind of odd if I lost it. Besides, it's serious stuff."

"I'll say. And I bet those men would agree, particularly when it involves a toy melting on their penis."

Amy held up her palm. "Wait. It gets better. The guy who melted it is one of our models, so he really didn't mind the warm plastic. Guess he's used to wet plastic on his part."

Colette was quite familiar with the models Amy used for her toys. Men who were paid to let the company produce a penis mold from their anatomy. Still, she wondered what kind of guy would take a job as a penis model.

Amy unzipped the bag and withdrew a vibrator as long as her forearm. A very thick, very pink vibrator.

"No way," Colette said, her mouth going dry.

"Well, I admit, we embellished a little, but he was pretty darn close."

"The same guy who melted the two-vibrator deal?"

Colette asked, still eyeing the oversize toy in her sister's hands.

"Yep. This is his personal one. Seems like we should have him autograph them or something, huh?"

"And a guy with *all that* melted your toy?"

"Looked like purple butter by the time he and his girl-friend had finished. But they both agreed it got the job done."

"His girlfriend goes along with his testing sex products?" Colette asked, watching Amy plop the toy, modeled after a real man—*have mercy*—back in her bag.

"Actually, I'm not so sure they're more than just sex partners, come to think of it. They come in, get the job done in one of our privacy suites, then head their separate ways."

Colette peeked in Amy's bag at the huge length of plastic penis. "Goodness," she whispered, amazed at what Amy's company went through in order to make sex more enjoyable. Then again, her products really were incredible. Not that Colette had tried the two-person ones. Yet. She wondered if Bill . . .

"What about this one?" Amy asked, taking Colette's thoughts away from melting two-person vibrators and Bill Brannon. For now.

"What?" she asked.

"This one? Married or single?" Amy indicated the other phone in her purse.

Colette noted the trim black cellular. "Married. Supposedly, he's at a pharmaceuticals conference in New Orleans, or that's what he told his wife."

"But where is he?" Amy asked, lifting a curved brow.

"Oh, he's in New Orleans, but he's got an eye for

Bourbon Street ladies. Evidently, he needs a stripper fix every two months. By the way, if he calls tonight, have him take a tie to the My Alibi satellite office in New Orleans. He knows the address."

"He's leaving the tie behind to prove he was there, right?" Amy asked.

Colette nodded. "The satellite office will mail it to his home next week."

"Sounds like he's a regular customer."

"Most of them are," Colette said. "Once a liar, always a liar."

Amy tapped the black cellular back into her purse. "I don't have to stay here, do I? I mean, I can go out and take the phones along in case your clients get any calls, right?"

Colette barely comprehended Amy's question. Instead, she concentrated on her own statement. Once a liar . . .

She'd lied to Bill.

That tiny spot beneath each ear, the one that burned right before she cried, started to tingle.

"Colette?"

"Yeah."

"Don't do it," Amy warned.

She swallowed past the nagging burn. "Do what?"

"Talk yourself out of it."

Colette crossed the room and sat at the kitchen table, straightened the frayed edge on a woven bamboo place mat. Amy had given her the mats when she'd first rented the apartment, claiming they were supposed to bring good luck.

Yeah, right.

Amy scooted to the other side of the table, sat down and grasped her sister's hands. "It's not like that."

"Like what?"

"You aren't lying to him anymore. You gave Erika's phone to Cassie today."

"He thinks I live in Tampa. Last time I checked, that's a lie."

Amy released her hands and smothered a laugh. "Okay, so don't talk about where you live."

"He also thinks I work for a computer-graphics training company."

"Or where you work," Amy added.

"Or wait," Colette said, "here's a wild thought. I could tell him that his niece is on Tybee Island."

Amy straightened in her chair. "That would kill her." Her voice didn't hold even a hint of anger, but it was filled with concern for her friend. "She doesn't want to hurt her uncle. She loves him. But she loves Butch too. Come on, you said you would do this for me."

"That's before I knew her uncle's name."

"It's one week. After that, when Erika gets back, we can talk with her about telling him the truth. Or not. I just don't want to ruin her trip by calling her now, or by telling Bill before she has a chance to prepare. You did promise me," Amy reminded.

Colette ran the corner of the place mat between her thumb and forefinger. "There's a simple solution to all of this, you know."

"What's that?"

"I could call him, tell him I can't do the dating thing and be done with it."

"Don't you dare," Amy warned. "I'd never forgive

myself if you threw this chance away over me. You don't have to cancel. Just let Cassie do her job with Erika, go out with Bill and have a great time."

"Besides," Colette added, still in her own side of the conversation, "you said you have plans. And if you have a date, or if you'd rather not fool with taking care of my clients, I'm sure he'd be willing to postpone."

"Nice try. I'm going to Cowboys with Brenda from the office, but I'm perfectly capable of taking a phone call or two while we're there. Geez, I can't remember the last time I saw you so shook up." She squeezed Colette's palms. "I'm beginning to think there's more to this attempt to stop the date. You're nervous, aren't you? It's Bill. The old friend you knew in high school. And the one who promised to find your G-spot this week, without the aid of toys. Remember?"

"And you're saying this to keep me from being nervous?"

Amy stood from the table and headed to the refrigerator. She withdrew a bottle of water and took a long swallow. "I'm saying it to let you know you'd be crazy to let this opportunity, and Bill Brannon, pass you by." She took another sip, then placed the bottle back in the fridge.

"I've gotta admit, I've been thinking the same thing, particularly after this afternoon. He's still that same sweet Bill, the guy I could talk to forever." She attempted to hold back her smile, but failed, and it burst free. "But there's a huge heap of sexual tension that didn't exist in high school."

Amy licked the leftover moisture from her lips. "My bet is that it was there all along on his end. You were just so happy to have a great friend back then, you didn't let yourself see there was more there than meets the eye."

Colette drew a breath and prepared to tell Amy that there had definitely been more on his end back then, but Amy's words halted her attempt.

"Didn't you say he's picking you up at seven?" She turned and glanced at the digital clock on the microwave.

Colette followed Amy's gaze. "Is it seven?"

"Ten till," Amy said.

Ten minutes. "Okay. I can do this, right?"

"Right." Amy nodded her head for emphasis.

"Then I better head down. He's supposed to pick me up outside your building."

"*My* building?"

"I live in Tampa, remember?"

"Right." Another shrug. "Maybe I'm not as good at this lying business as I thought."

"Which is precisely why he's picking me up outside. I didn't want him to see you try to pull this off."

Amy straightened her back, crossed her arms beneath her chest. "Am I that bad?"

"Put it this way. You'll do fine over the telephone, but I wouldn't want my contacts seeing your face while you're feeding them a line of bull."

"Then I must take after you," Amy said.

Colette laughed. "Yeah, you do."

"Either way, you need to go." Amy unfolded her arms and made a shooing motion toward the door. "Chop, chop."

Nerves writhed like snakes in Colette's stomach. She

stood firmly by the table, her feet refusing to budge. "Do you think I'm making a mistake?"

Amy crossed the room and stood face-to-face with her sister. Placing her palms on Colette's shoulders, she shook her head. "No. In fact, I believe you are positively *not* making a mistake."

"So, why do you look like that?"

"Like what?" Amy asked.

"Worried."

Amy's dimple deepened with her smile. "I'm not worried. I'm anxious."

"Anxious for what?" Colette questioned.

"To see my big sister take a chance at finding Mr. Right. Or at least Mr. G-spot."

"Somehow I don't think the proper method for finding Mr. Right, or Mr. G-spot, for that matter, includes ly—"

"Nope," Amy interrupted. "I won't hear it. Not again. You're a woman on a mission." She turned Colette and steered her toward the door. "Now go have fun," Amy instructed, sounding more the older sis than the younger, as she firmly pushed her out of their apartment.

Colette took a few shaky steps toward the elevator and wished she hadn't worn stilettos. It seemed the thing to do, since he'd seen her as a practical businesswoman earlier today. She didn't want him thinking of her as practical tonight. But she hadn't owned a pair in years. She'd bought these after work this afternoon and still hadn't broken them in. Which meant the night would probably end with several blisters on her heels.

She frowned. Tripping, or flat-out falling, wouldn't do much for her sex appeal.

Running her hands across the front of her dress, she experienced a last-minute surge of panic. Should she have worn something this short? This sheer?

This red?

"Amy?"

"You look great," Amy called from the doorway. "And one more thing."

"What?" Colette stepped into the elevator and wondered if Amy had changed her opinion. Would she tell her not to go? That she shouldn't get her hopes up?

Would Amy tell her that now? In time for her to turn tail and haul her butt back inside the apartment?

She held her breath and listened for her sister's final words.

"I won't wait up. Lettie." Amy's giggle trickled down the hall as the doors slid shut and Colette's nerves, once again, took control.

CHAPTER 7

With their fifth-floor apartment, a ride down the elevator as the only occupant normally gave Colette a chance to relax and think. Now, however, the creeping of the old machine added to her anxiety, reminding her of the Tower of Terror ride, where the sucker crept its way to the top, then plummeted in a mind-boggling free fall.

Oh boy, was she ever gonna fall! And probably land smack-dab on top of her lying heart.

"Come on, Lettie, get a grip," she mumbled as the big box slugged its way toward the first floor.

Lettie. She'd said the name. Out loud. If only to the four walls surrounding her, she'd said it, nonetheless. Amy had said it too, but this time, it hadn't sounded wrong.

Why not?

Because that's the way Bill thought of her: as Lettie, the girl ready for anything, and afraid of nothing.

The elevator jerked to a halt and the doors rattled open, beckoning for a confident woman to emerge and take what she wanted.

Colette tossed her head, flipped her hair, then ran her hands down her skimpy dress. Her fingertips brushed the top of bare thighs, shaved and lotioned and ready to be caressed. By Bill Brannon. Along with every other part of her anatomy.

Bill Brannon. The man she'd always seen as a friend. But this afternoon, the man who'd reconnected with her emotionally, and had stirred a tornado of desire physically. With his smile. His words. His touch. That pink rose.

The man who wanted her back then. And, from all indications, the man who wanted her even more now.

She moistened her lips, lifted her shoulders. Why shouldn't she be confident? Wasn't that what he expected? And wasn't that the real reason she'd chosen the flaming minidress, thin and backless, making no secret of its silk fabric teasing her nipples?

Colette—correction—Lettie Campbell was a confident, desirable woman, and he knew it. Wanted it.

Anticipated it.

She placed one high heel in front of the other and pranced across the lobby, the same way she'd strutted through Sheldon High's halls when Bill Brannon, and every other male, watched her pass.

Exiting the building, she paused for a moment to let the cool night air kiss her skin, then flashed an I-want-you-now smile at the sexy hunk of man leaning against the side of his car.

Have mercy, he looked even better than he had this afternoon.

The black Camry spoke volumes about the guy leaning against its shiny frame. For one thing, it wasn't a tiny sports car. For another, it wasn't red. And everyone knew the truth about guys who drove tiny red sports cars.

Compensating.

Bill, obviously, had no reason to compensate. Which made her smile even brighter. No problem with confidence now. With one look, Bill Brannon made her feel like she could move mountains. By the way his dark brows flicked and those mocha eyes drank her in, she'd bet she was moving his mountain right now.

Not bad, Lettie.

His eyes performed a thorough perusal, starting with the loose waves on her head to the red heels on her feet, and pausing at several key intervals in between.

Heck, she knew appreciation when she saw it. And right now, Bill Brannon was thoroughly appreciating her.

Lettie sashayed down the concrete path, heels clicking with each step toward his car. Then she stopped, shifted to one side and placed a hand on her hip. "Well?"

One corner of his mouth tipped up. "Well."

Gathering more courage by the second, she shifted her weight again and watched his eyes focus on her chest, where the silky fabric shifted in direct correlation to her move. The halter of the skimpy dress plunged dramatically, and Lettie knew he could see the entire swell of her right breast, save the nipple. "Well, you saw me in business mode today. Tonight, you see me in play. Have I changed that much in twelve years?"

That firm jaw seemed to clench a little harder. Eyes deepened to match the darkening sky. "Hard to say. Turn around."

"Turn around?" Her heart plunked a happy rhythm in

her chest. The sexual chemistry had been palpable between them this afternoon, but they'd still maintained that friends-meeting-again aura that had enveloped them from the moment she'd hugged him by the train. Right now the chemistry was still there, but it had ignited to near combustion level. Zinging between them, and setting her body on red alert for more.

Lettie could hardly wait.

"Yeah," Bill said, his voice husky and demanding. "Turn. Around. And do it slowly, Lettie. I don't want to miss any details."

Once again, his use of her name sent a shiver down her spine.

Peachtree Industrial, where her apartment was located, was a busy street at any time of day, particularly now, when most of Atlanta was still en route to and from after-work activities. But in spite of the cars idling at the stoplight by the parking lot, Lettie did as he asked.

She turned. Slowly. And let him look his fill.

When her back faced him, she tossed a glance over her shoulder, knowing the combination of backless dress and come-get-me look would have the desired effect. "So, what's the verdict?"

The thick cords of his neck shifted as he swallowed. "You're as stunning as ever. Even more than back then."

She finished her turn, cocked her hip once more, then grinned at his focus on her breasts. "You like the dress."

"The dress is fine, but what's inside it—yeah, I like that a lot."

"Good. Then it's my turn."

"Your turn?" he asked.

"To see if you've changed."

"I see." He took a small step forward, braced his legs apart and, like she had done, let her look her fill.

Lettie gave him a dose of his own medicine. Starting at his gorgeous face, she examined every mesmerizing feature.

Had his lashes always been so thick? Perfectly framing eyes that looked like melted chocolate?

Yeah. They had. But she hadn't remembered how easy it was to get lost in them, to want to kiss each lid and feel those long wisps against her lips.

Her feminine center quivered.

She cleared her throat and controlled her breathing, which had converted to short, eager gasps as she gaped at this fine male specimen. And imagined him up close and extremely personal.

Following the path from forehead past a straight, determined nose, she stopped when she reached his mouth. Full, totally kissable lips tempted her to stop this inspection and get the show rolling. Especially when that devilish dimple winked at her wickedly. But fair was fair, and she wanted to look.

Lettie continued ogling, down his corded neck, across broad shoulders to biceps that pushed for recognition against a stark white shirt. She envisioned her hands curling to hold on to those big muscles like lifelines as he hovered above her naked body, driving inside her, taking her where she desperately wanted to go.

There was no hiding where her thoughts had headed; she was practically panting. But she wouldn't stop now. She couldn't, anyway. He looked too dang hot for her to quit a personal inspection, though she totally planned to investigate later—without the encumbrance of clothing.

The hint of black hair peeking from the V in his shirt, where the first two buttons were undone, beckoned her to follow its path. Her fingers itched to do exactly that. And venture lower.

Much lower.

Lettie studied the way his black pants hugged his hips, caressed strong thighs. She could only imagine what the soft fabric was doing against that luscious behind, the one Amy had christened, "an ass like nobody's business."

Rather than laugh out loud at her sister's comment, she licked her lips. "Turn around."

He grinned.

"Turn. Around."

His smile, if possible, grew even more . . . cocky. And dang if it didn't make her wet. He knew he looked good, from every angle. And, as he turned to verify that fact, there wasn't a thing she could do but agree.

"Want me to spread 'em so you can frisk me?" he asked, placing his palms on the side of the car as if he were totally up for a game of cops and robbers.

She thought of the furry handcuffs in her apartment. How long would it take to get them? Too damn long. But another time . . .

Oh yeah.

He turned toward her, and another flick of those dark brows made her nipples harden. Reaching out, he placed a warm hand on her waist and pulled their bodies together.

Generally, her five-foot-nine frame put her nearly eye-to-eye with most men. Occasionally, when she wore heels, it put her a tad above them. But Bill Brannon had a couple of inches on her, even with the stilettos, so she tilted her head to look at his gorgeous face. "Back then, I should have—"

He brought one hand to her face, letting his fingertips gently brush her cheek while he traced her lower lip with the pad of his thumb. "Yeah. You should have. We should have. But we didn't. Not then."

The long fingers at her waist slid to her back, then pressed her body even closer to his. "Bill." Her mouth tingled, moving against his thumb.

His eyes flashed a hint of warning and he pulled his thumb away, sliding it down her throat until it paused at the base, where Lettie knew her pulse hammered.

"We should've done a lot of things differently back then," he continued.

A horn blasted from the busy street and reminded her they'd yet to step foot in his car. But Lettie's body was on fire, pressed against his, and she wouldn't care if all of Atlanta watched.

This was where she wanted to be.

"We should've definitely done this, back then." He brought his mouth to hers with hungry urgency, taking it as though it were his alone to claim.

His tongue swept inside, tangling with hers in a wild, stroking dance, a mating simulation that had her hips undulating in perfect harmony with the fluid thrusts of his tongue.

Whistles and horns, and a couple of encouraging cheers, echoed in the distance, but her blood pumped too feverishly to decipher the interruption.

Bill's large hand moved against her back, then dipped beneath the pool of fabric at the base of her spine.

She curved instinctively against his masterful touch, her breasts aching, her womanhood burning—hot, wet and ready.

Pulling his mouth from hers, he worked passionate kisses along her jaw, nudging her hair out of the way as he claimed her lobe and sucked it hard.

"What do you think, Lettie?" His voice was so thick, so raspy and so undeniably aroused, she wasn't sure whether he'd said the words. Or growled them.

"Th-think?"

"Shouldn't we have done this, back then?" The hand at her spine moved lower still, one finger toying with the top of her thong.

"Oh yeah," she managed, her head spinning.

Oh yeah. Definitely.

She rose on her toes and pushed her hips forward, pressing her heat against the hard length between his thighs. Twelve years ago, she'd never dreamed of sex with Bill. Now the thought of waiting five minutes to climb on top of him seemed near impossible. "Bill?"

"Yeah."

"Do we have to go to dinner first?" She was so ready, and the bulge in his pants said he was too.

His laugh rumbled against her neck. "Is your sister home?"

Dang, she should've asked Amy to head out early, just in case. But who'd have thought they'd start the date with a grope fest in the parking lot? "Yeah, she's home."

"Then we'll go to my place."

"How far?"

He shot a glance at the headlights moving down the

busy street. "A good half hour's drive, if we don't have a lot of traffic," he admitted. "I'm in Paulding County."

"I can't wait that long," she said, and she meant it. He had her hotter in five minutes than Jeff had managed in six long, boring months. If she didn't come soon, she'd scream. Heck, if she did come soon, she'd scream.

Either way, she needed to scream.

Soon.

He opened the door, then helped her in. "Trust me, Lettie. I'd never make you wait."

Bill rounded the car and climbed inside in record time. No small feat since his dick had been in complete agreement with his parking lot X-rated production.

Hell, he'd always taken special care to monitor public displays of affection, never wanting to embarrass a woman by cuddling her in front of a crowd. But tonight, he'd cast aside all thoughts of political correctness and moved right on to *what* he wanted. *Who* he wanted.

Lettie.

In high school, she'd thrived on attention, doing something risky, causing a scene. She'd leaned toward guys who broke the rules. Sure, they'd grown up since Sheldon High. But he suspected that Lettie still enjoyed a bit of rule-breaking, every now and then. And, from the look of her in that business suit this afternoon, he also suspected that perhaps she hadn't broken any in quite a while. She'd looked very together and very settled. That was fine, for her professional realm.

However, Bill didn't want her seeing him as a mere professional acquaintance. And he wanted to be the one to rock her steady world and remind her that he understood the sensual side of her too. Given she showed up

for this date in a dress that said she was ready for anything, he'd say she wanted something beyond the norm.
And what Bill had in mind was anything but normal,
particularly for him, a guy who generally stuck to the
rules.

Their heated exchange in the parking lot should've
alerted her that he wasn't kidding about finding her elusive treasure. Cranking the engine, he couldn't help but
feel exhilarated by what he'd done, starting foreplay in
front of a honking, yelling and—if he heard right—
cheering audience.

From the way she'd climbed up his body during the
scene, Lettie had loved it.

Good. Because he planned to push his nice-guy, best-
friend image right out of the picture, at least until he had
her attention. Starting with the drive home.

"Are you ready?" he asked, steering out of the parking lot.

"More than you can imagine."

He entered the line of traffic, then stole another look
at Lettie while he waited for the light to change.

In high school, she'd been like the photograph of a
pretty girl that a teenage boy snatched out of a calendar
and pinned to his wall. A girl he'd look at every day,
dream about every night.

Now she'd catapulted from calendar girl to centerfold
queen. It'd taken every ounce of willpower he possessed
not to attack her on the spot when she waltzed out of
Amy's building, looking every bit the sex goddess in that
barely there red dress and high heels.

Her hair had been long and silky in high school. Now
it was short and wild, with wisps curling out in all direc-

tions, caressing her face, brushing her neck and framing those green bedroom eyes. Red gloss accentuated full lips and tasted like strawberries.

Hell, how many women wore flavored lip gloss past high school?

Only the ones who planned on being kissed, he realized. And kissed well. Which he'd done. And would do again.

Her breasts seemed larger than he remembered as they hovered beneath the two wisps of fabric centering each full mound. But, even though they may have grown, they were undoubtedly real. There was nothing fake or enhanced about Lettie Campbell. The genuine jiggle that teased his senses when she strutted out of the building had proven it.

Plus he'd watched those firm little buds peak and harden when he told her, commanded her, to turn around. Those hard points told him what he'd suspected all along. Lettie liked guys who took control—and right now she liked the one driving this car.

He'd feared he wouldn't be able to pull it off, being tough and assertive for Lettie Campbell. But anything that involved having Lettie was worth it, even if it meant he wasn't being completely honest. Eventually, he'd tell her the truth, that he'd love nothing more than to treat her like a queen, the way she deserved to be treated.

But first, he'd treat her the way she wanted. Like a hot little plaything made for his personal enjoyment.

He turned onto the interstate and rolled the windows down. The rush of wind and the noise from the surrounding traffic would intensify his next attempt to remind Lettie there was much more to what they could share than friendship.

He moved to the HOV lane, away from eighteen-wheelers and other tall vehicles. Sure, he'd planned to do this, after dinner and a show. Much later in the evening, when the traffic had died down considerably.

Accelerating, he attempted to space himself an even distance from the other cars on the road. He wanted to thrill her, not embarrass her. But he would thrill her. Thoroughly.

CHAPTER 8

Lettie watched her window slide down, then blinked her eyes at the onslaught of warm air whipping through the car. He said he wouldn't make her wait long, and she believed him. But she hoped they got there fast. Because she was so ready to *get there*. Fast.

"This feels wonderful," she said, leaning her head back against the leather headrest and letting the wind wash over her. The air fanned her chest, penetrating the flimsy fabric and tickling her already-aroused nipples. God, she hoped he didn't plan on driving very far.

She closed her eyes and fought to gain control over her itching-for-sex body. Surely, she could make it until they got where they were going. Though right now, she knew a few slides of her fingers against her drenched panties would do the trick.

It wouldn't take much.

But she'd been taking care of business herself for entirely too long, and she wanted—needed—a male-induced orgasm. Was that too much for a healthy twenty-nine-year-old female to ask?

Evidently, with Jeff, it had been.

With Bill, however, Lettie believed she could ask him anything, and he'd rise to the occasion. Literally. But the first thing she wanted to ask was how much longer they'd be on this highway.

"Where are we go—"

Her words stalled in her throat and her eyes popped open as his fingers slid beneath the left side of her halter and captured a nipple. "Oh."

Bill's eyes focused on driving down the road, while his hand focused on driving her crazy. Pulling the soft strip of silk toward him, he exposed her breast completely, the bulge pushed out farther by the bunched sliver of fabric.

"I, um," she said, then cautiously surveyed the traffic on the interstate.

"Do you want me to stop, Lettie?" Still staring straight ahead, he continued to drive, as though he weren't baring her body on a six-lane interstate.

"No." And what a no-brainer that was. She'd rather stop breathing than have him quit now.

Forgetting about the potential for voyeurs, she dropped her gaze to her chest, where Bill's thumb and forefinger pinched and rolled the exposed nipple.

Yeah, it was dark out, but the lights from the interstate spilled into the car, making the pale pink nipple appear even more boldly presented. As if it were spotlighted. For Bill.

"You didn't wear a bra." His fingers continued rolling and pinching, squeezing and kneading, while her uterus twitched to get in on the action.

He turned his head slightly and glanced at the breast on display.

She wet her lips. He'd known from the moment he saw her walk out of the apartment building that she was braless. Particularly after he'd insisted on a thorough examination to see if she'd changed. And if that weren't enough, he couldn't have missed her high beams pushing against his shirt when he'd pulled her body to his.

But he wanted to talk about it now. Maybe pointing out that she'd deliberately chosen a dress that left no option for a bra turned him on. And if so, she was ready to play this game. Ready, willing and able to turn Bill Brannon on.

Feeling bold, Lettie twisted in the seat and allowed him better access to her chest. Then she slid the other strip of fabric aside, so both breasts were blatantly bare and pushed together, while Atlanta rushed by in a swirling commotion of wind and noise.

Her blood pumped madly at the wildness, at the spontaneity, at this side of Bill Brannon. It was exhilarating. And maddening.

She wanted him. Now.

"Bill."

"Yeah." His hand ventured to the other breast, pulled at the nipple.

"How much farther?"

"I promised I wouldn't make you wait, didn't I?"

"You did, so I was wondering—"

"I forgot to tell you the rule," he interrupted, ignoring her question while his attention turned back to the road ahead.

"Rule?"

His mouth twitched, as though fighting a smile; then his cheeks lifted and he set that gorgeous smile free. "Damn, you're hot, Lettie."

She leaned across the seat, kissed the solid line of his jaw. He was playing a game and enjoying it. Needless to say, she couldn't wait to find out how she'd get to participate in the fun. "What kind of rule?"

He cleared his throat. "For riding in my car. I've got one rule, and right now you're breaking it."

She blinked. Was he serious? Bill Brannon? One of those weird-about-his-car kind of guys? And she'd been so certain he wasn't when she viewed the no-reason-to-compensate Camry.

"What rule am I breaking?"

"The rule about girls who don't wear bras."

She smiled. Oh, this had nothing to do with his car. And everything to do with them. Bill Brannon *had* changed. Or come out of his shell. Or something. But he was definitely, positively taking their relationship to a whole new, wonderful level.

Her pulse soared and her nipples burned. Tonight promised to be fun.

She shifted closer, put her lips to his ear. "You have a rule that only applies to girls who don't wear bras?"

"Doesn't everybody?" His rolling laugh bubbled down her skin, making her tingle. Everywhere.

"No, everybody doesn't. But I don't want to break your rule, and I'm obviously not wearing a bra."

"I'll say you aren't." Still grinning, and looking sinfully sexy in the process, he caressed the breast in hand.

"So what's the punishment? For a girl who blatantly breaks your rule?"

"The punishment fits the crime," he said, his throat pulsing as he swallowed. "Girls who don't wear bras . . ." He paused, while Lettie held her breath.

When he didn't complete the sentence, she exhaled, dying to know what he had on his mind. "Girls who don't wear bras . . ." she prodded.

"Can't wear panties either."

Even with the speedometer creeping steadily higher, the wind whistling around them in a steady, rolling *whoosh,* and the sounds of Atlanta at night penetrating the car, Bill heard Lettie's gasp.

Hell. Was his rule over the top? Maybe commanding her to remove her panties wasn't exactly what the doctor ordered for a first date.

He kept his eyes peeled on the road ahead. If he looked at her now and saw shock, or revulsion—or worse—embarrassment, it'd kill him. He did not want to hurt Lettie, didn't want to humiliate her. Matter of fact, by the end of the week, he hoped to woo her into thoughts of long-term commitment. Instead of ordering her to remove her clothes.

Damn. Had he messed up?

Her lips had been nuzzling his neck when he stated the totally-beyond-first-date-etiquette rule. Now she'd retreated to her side of the car, taking those delicious lips, and everything else, with her.

He took a breath. Time to fess up. Bill Brannon had no clue how to be that assertive. That commanding. That bad. But before he could speak the first word of an apology, she spoke.

And blew him away.

"Let it never be said," she said throatily, lifting her

hips from the seat, "that Lettie Campbell doesn't follow the rules." Then, as Bill fought to keep the car within the lines, and fought even harder to watch the show, Lettie lifted her skirt to her waist.

Bill had never been one for bragging, hadn't been the kind of guy who'd make some unbelievable claim about how much weight he could bench. But right now he'd swear he could lift a car. With his dick.

"So I need to remove these?" she purred, running a finger along the top of a red satin triangle between her legs.

He nodded. That was all he could do at the moment.

She smiled like the vixen she was and slid the panties down.

Bill caught a glimpse of heaven, a completely bare, shaved and slick version of heaven. "Lettie." Then she slid her skirt back in place and lifted the tiny scrap of red fabric that had been, one second ago, exactly where he wanted to be.

"You did want me to take these off, didn't you?" She reached for his wrist and placed the wet fabric in his palm.

Wet. For him.

"I'm keeping these," he informed, squeezing his fist around them, then pocketing the sexy wisp of clothing.

"I'd be disappointed if you didn't." She ran a finger along his jaw. "Now that I've paid the fine, what happens next?"

Bill turned his head slightly and sucked on her extended finger. "I have to examine the evidence, make sure you conformed to the rule. Completely. Raise your hips, Lettie."

Her eyes widened; then her lips curved, and she did as he asked.

With one shove, he pushed her dress up to her waist. "Now lower your hips and spread your legs."

Evidently, his foot had eased off the gas as he'd been enthralled with undressing his sexy passenger, because an eighteen-wheeler started past them on her side.

"Bill?" she said, her head turning toward the approaching vehicle, and a tinge of panic in her tone. Then she twisted her shoulders to hide her breasts from the man's view.

Bill grabbed the edge of the skirt and pulled it down, holding it in place until the trucker passed. Then, as soon as the intrusion was gone, Bill set the cruise control with one hand, while the other edged the skirt back up. "I told you I wouldn't make you wait."

"That's right. You did." Her voice was raspy, sexy, needy. She needed what he'd give her. And God knows, he needed to give it.

"And I keep my promises."

His hand slid between her legs, found the slick source of those damp panties held captive in his pocket. She was so open, so accessible, shaved and smooth and wet. He brushed the soft folds with his knuckles, then gently glided a finger into her slippery, hot center.

Lettie's back arched, legs spread wider, as she pushed toward his sweet invasion. She clenched around him, held on tight, in spite of her drenched heat.

Hell, he hadn't considered how hard it'd be to keep his eyes on the road, or at least one eye on the road, while touching Lettie Campbell. Damn near impossible. But he wasn't about to stop driving now. He had no doubt her excitement had been heightened by the situation. And he sure as hell wasn't going to stop touching her. Ever.

"Please," she urged.

Bill glanced toward his passenger, the woman he'd wanted more than any other for the majority of his life. Her mouth opened in a silent plea. Back arched and breasts thrust forward, letting the wind kiss those perfect pink-tipped nipples. Nipples that Bill would personally lick, kiss and suck before the night ended.

He withdrew his finger, added another, then delved them both into her dripping passion, steadily thrusting in and out, in and out, while she jerked beneath him.

"Bill." His name was a whimper on her lips. A pleading request that he would fulfill.

He'd wanted to make her wait a little longer, build up to an explosive climax she'd never forget. But the way her thighs had tightened, flexing for the touch that would send her soaring, he knew he couldn't make her wait any longer.

His thumb moved up her tender folds to her swollen clit.

Lettie hissed through her teeth.

"Is that it, Lettie? Is that what you want?" He knew he'd found her secret spot, and he caressed it fervently as he waited for her response.

When she didn't answer, Bill stopped, holding his thumb steady on her aching nub. It pulsed beneath his touch, so ready to push her into a frenzied climax.

"N-no," she pleaded. "Please, Bill."

"Please what? What do you want?"

His dick pushed against his pants, as though wanting to help her give the right answer.

"I want—"

Bill pushed his fingers deeper, pulled them out, plunged them in again, while she flexed around them. "What do you want? Tell me."

"Make me come."

While those might not be the three words he wanted to hear most from Lettie Campbell's luscious mouth, they sure as hell weren't far behind.

"With pleasure." His fingers continued pumping, while his thumb joined in, softly circling her tender cleft, then gradually increasing pressure. Faster and faster, harder and harder . . .

Her hips jerked off the seat as she screamed into the wind, while the depth of her passion soaked his fingers.

Then, as her body shuddered through the aftermath of her climax, Bill eased his hand away from her center and, while Lettie watched with sex-glazed eyes, he sucked her essence.

Shifting in her seat, she leaned against him. "Bill?"

"Yeah."

"I want you."

Lettie definitely had a way with three-word sentences. Particularly the ones that put an up-periscope in his pants. Who was he kidding? His dick had been on red alert since he'd glimpsed that dress. Those eyes. Mouth. Legs.

"How far are we from your place?"

His laugh echoed through the car.

"What?" Lettie asked.

"We passed it ten miles ago."

She nipped his ear, cuddled close, her bare breasts pushing against him. "I swear, Bill, I'd never dreamed."

"Dreamed what?"

"That you were so bad."

"Lettie Campbell, you ain't seen nothing yet." He steered up an exit ramp, then crossed over the interstate to head back toward home, and hoped his words conveyed his confidence in his ability to be bad. So far, she seemed convinced. Then again, giving her a screaming orgasm while doing eighty in the HOV lane qualified as pretty damn bad, if he did say so himself.

Now he had to prove his wildness in the bedroom. Without a car, the wind and the traffic adding to the appeal. Sure, he knew his way around a woman's body. He'd even wager he'd find that spot Jeff had missed during Bill's first tangle with Lettie in the sheets.

However, he wasn't all that certain what was different about a bad boy having hot and heated, wild and wicked, sex in the bedroom . . . and a good boy doing the same thing?

Because deep down, Bill Brannon knew he wasn't bad; he was good. And deep down, he knew he wasn't bad in the sack; he was good.

Damn good.

In a matter of minutes, he pulled in his driveway and prepared to head inside and continue being bad. But he quickly learned that being wild, being bad, didn't take much effort on his part, not with Lettie so willing to aid in his corruption.

His hand had barely grasped the door handle on the car when she stopped him in his tracks with, once again, three potent words.

"Do me here."

He turned toward her, surprised to find her hands already at his waist, fumbling with the button, then sliding the zipper down.

"You need this, don't you?" he asked as she jerked his pants down and curled shaky hands around his erection.

"You have no idea," she whispered, pushing his boxers down as well. Then she stalled her frantic attack and raised her eyes to his.

The light from his porch illuminated her pale blond hair and let him see the urgent desire in her eyes. But it also identified something else in her gaze—a question. And he'd die before he let her believe there was anything one-sided about what was happening here. "I need it too, Lettie. This. Here. With you."

Her smile warmed his heart. "You have protection, right?"

"Oh yeah." He withdrew the foil packet from his pants. "Lettie."

"Yeah," she said, her eyes never leaving his hands as they rolled the latex down the length of his penis.

"Are you still as limber as you were in high school, when you did all those cheerleader stunts?"

She laughed out loud, climbed across the console and eased a long, slender leg down the edge between the door and the seat. Her hot, slippery center found his aching penis and slid down his length, enveloping him like a glove.

"What do you think?" she asked, easing back up, then taking him in again.

"Hell. Yeah."

He'd never been with a woman whose intimate femininity was so bare, shaved and slick and ready. And he'd never been with a woman who made his world spin, urging him to delicious heights of ecstasy as she took control.

He clamped his mouth over one nipple, pulling and sucking and licking, while she worked her hips, gasping and panting as she drove him toward the edge. Moving a hand between their hot, heated bodies, he found her tender cleft, still swollen and waiting for his touch.

She increased her pace as he matched her rhythm, thrusting inside, while teasing her sensitive nub.

"Bill, I'm—almost—" She screamed out, and he lifted his hips and drove in hard, climaxing powerfully into her hot core as she convulsed around him.

Bill pulled her close and held her as her body, slick with sex, shuddered. He held her there, his penis still deep within her, while she collapsed against him, her soft blond curls tickling his cheek and her luscious lips nuzzling his neck.

True, he'd never been with a woman like this before. Never been so bold, so wild, so intense. Then again, he'd never been with Lettie.

$\mathcal{C}$HAPTER 9

Can I buy you a drink?"

Amy often came to Cowboys, the Atlanta bar known for fast-paced line dancing and bull rider wanna-bes, to dance away the stresses of work. She never came looking for a man specifically, rather someone who knew the latest steps, was willing to take a spin on the floor and would concede to Amy's adamant stance of returning home alone.

She wasn't like so many Atlanta women in their twenties who looked for heated action on the dance floor, then hoped for honest-to-goodness cowboys heating up their beds later on. Amy knew most of them were disappointed at night's end, anyway, because she'd swear 95 percent of the Stetsons in the room had never seen hide or hair of a horse.

But the six-foot-plus cowboy standing in front of her right now was in the other 5 percent. The real deal. Cowboy through and through, from the black Stetson on his gorgeous head to the just-as-black Ropers on his feet.

And, consequently, every female in the room eyed him like the last brownie at a fat person's convention.

Everyone but Amy, that is, who wished Landon Brooks would sidle up to someone else. He was way too tempting.

She knew because he tempted her daily.

"I asked if I could buy you a drink, Amy," Landon said, standing with his Wrangler-clad thighs and his give-me-a-shot smile.

Amy glanced at the two cellulars in her purse. The phones had kept her off the dance floor all night, though Brenda had said she'd sit out a dance and phone-sit if Amy wanted. Why couldn't one of them ring right now? And keep her from having to attempt small talk with Landon.

She glared at them, willing them to ring.

They didn't.

"I'm drinking Coke. I'm driving," she said, using as few words as necessary and hoping to dissuade him as she sipped at the straw in her half-empty glass.

"Another Coke on the rocks it is," he said, and motioned for the waitress.

Amy sighed as he sat down. The women at the surrounding tables turned their attention to the other men in the room, assuming this one had just been claimed.

A small stack of cocktail napkins sat in the center of Amy's table. If she had tape in her purse, she'd use one to write a "Still Available" notice and plaster it to Landon's broad back.

Why the devil didn't she keep tape in her purse?

She sucked on her straw until it made that obnoxious gurgling noise around the bottom of her empty cup and hoped the sound irritated the good-looking cowboy. In a minute, the band would resume playing and he wouldn't be able to hear her attempt to shoo him from the table.

He looked at her glass, winked as though she'd done something cute, then laughed.

Great. She'd managed to turn him on. Super.

Like Amy, Landon Brooks was a project lead for Adventurous Accessories. He wasn't on her team; he wasn't even in the sex toys section. He'd been hired for his nose, so to speak. According to Amy's boss, the company's president, Landon could pick a pheromone-emphasizing scent merely by inhaling. No tests required.

Amy, and every other Adventurous Accessories employee, had been impressed . . . and jealous. And, like every other female employee, she couldn't deny a little surge of pheromone-emphasizing *something* whenever Landon Brooks appeared.

Now was no exception.

The waitress arrived and he placed the order, asking for a couple of cherries to be included in the drink; then he turned back to Amy.

"You here with Brenda Henson? I saw her on the dance floor."

"Yeah. Brenda was in the mood for a little line dancing, and she knows I like the music here."

"Just the music?" he asked as the waitress brought the drink, and he withdrew one of the cherries by the stem. "Mind if I have one?"

"Why not? You ordered it," she answered, handing the waitress her empty glass.

"Yeah," he said, grinning as he popped it in his mouth. "I did."

The band returned to the stage and started an exaggerated version of "God Bless Texas," while Amy watched the only real Texan she knew skillfully maneuver the fruit in his mouth. She tapped her fingers on the table. "Well?"

His mouth stopped moving. "Well what?" he asked, easily forming the words in spite of the stem.

"I figure you're about to show me how you tied it in a knot. So, go ahead," she said, raising her voice above the music and trying her damnedest to act as though his tongue talents wouldn't impress her.

His smoky gray eyes drank her in, and he removed the stem.

"A double knot," he said, nodding his head and making his Stetson bob. Then he winked at her before turning his attention back to the dance floor. "So, do you like to . . ." he started to say, but stopped when Amy stood, left the table and flagged down the waitress.

He watched her return, then leaned across the table to be heard above the music, which had escalated to a low roar. "If you were hungry, you should've said something. I'll get you whatever you want."

"I took care of it."

"Do you always take care of yourself?" he continued, and a wicked grin claimed his face.

Amy fought the heat in her cheeks and hoped to hell he wasn't asking what she thought. Because she wasn't about to get into details with Landon Brooks about her orgasm-for-one ritual.

"I'm very self-sufficient," she said, jerking her head toward the approaching waitress.

Landon eyed the bowl the waitress placed on the

table, then started laughing. "Damn, you're competitive, aren't ya?" He stretched a long-fingered hand across the table and touched her wrist. "Listen, your toys are as good as my massage oils. Matter of fact, today's sales report had your orange stallion edging past my fuzzy navel. The stallion's ahead by a nose, so to speak."

"You're a riot," she said, trying her best not to look impressed by his wit.

He smiled. "We don't have to compete at everything, do we?"

"Not everything," Amy said, pulling a cherry from the bowl. "Just the things I'm better at. On your mark," she started as he grabbed a cherry, "get set."

"Go," he said, fighting a laugh as they both put cherries in their mouths and started a knot-tying battle any Boy Scout would envy.

By the time Brenda finished her line-dancing lesson, Amy and Landon had made their way to the very last pair of cherries, and were tied eight all.

"All right, lady, this is it," he said, fingering the last piece of fruit.

"This is what?" Amy asked.

"Winner takes all."

"Oh, this should be good," Brenda said, plopping in the third chair and fanning her flushed face. She withdrew a barrette from her purse and pulled up her straight black mane. "That's better," she said, picking up the drink menu and using it to fan her exposed neck. "Now, what exactly constitutes all?"

"If you lose, you owe me one dance tonight and one date this weekend," he said without batting an eye.

Amy smirked. He'd come up with that bet way too

fast. How long had it taken him to realize what he wanted?

"That sounds like two things to me," Brenda noted, holding up two fingers.

"So I'm greedy," Landon said, answering Brenda but eyeing Amy.

"And if I win?" Amy asked.

"You name it," he said. "And you can be greedy too, if you want."

Brenda gasped audibly, but Amy didn't flinch. "Fine. If I win, you never hit on me again. Never so much as flirt. Matter of fact, you only speak to me when absolutely necessary. At work. And never outside the office, like you've done tonight."

"An odd choice on your part, don't you think?" Landon asked, once again tipping that black cowboy hat. "So, if you win, you basically want me to leave you alone?"

"That's right."

"Reckon why that's so important to you?"

"Because you drive me crazy?" Amy supplied as Brenda snorted.

"Yeah," Landon said, seeming way too pleased with her response. "I think that's it." He twirled the cherry stem in his fingers. "So, are you ready?"

"Go!" Amy blurted, putting the cherry in her mouth and hoping she got a decent head start.

He was right, and he knew it. Something about Landon Brooks, cowboy, good ol' boy—and good-with-his-nose boy—drove her near out of her mind. And had driven her to a few orgasms too when she'd pictured his face while using her toys at home. Which ticked her off, since she couldn't control the image that always came first and foremost when she climaxed.

Landon Brooks, in nothing but a Stetson and boots.

Lord, she suspected he was good at everything.

Which meant she had to win this race. She didn't need a man—had never needed one—and Landon threw an industrial-sized wrench in her well-laid plan to steer clear of them. All of them. Especially the one smiling like a thief and holding his double-knotted cherry stem up for the world to see.

"Dang, you're good." Brenda breathily appraised him, her eyes practically glazing over, while Amy snarled.

Landon stood, held out a hand. "I believe you owe me a dance."

"I've got those phones to watch," she said, pointing to the cellulars sticking out of her purse, and wondering why they hadn't rung all night. Or why they couldn't start beeping out a happy tune now.

"I'll come get you if they ring," Brenda said, nudging Amy from her chair. Then she looked at Landon. "She promised her sister she'd catch her calls."

"On two phones?" Landon asked, his hand still outstretched.

"It's complicated," Brenda answered, then shrugged when Amy frowned at her. "Well, that's what you told me."

Amy took Landon's hand and ignored the tiny tingle it sent through her fingertips, over her wrist, up her heart and straight to her libido.

Super.

"You were holding out on me," she grumbled as he

led her on the dance floor and the band geared up for the next tune. "You could've beaten me every time, couldn't you?"

"Guilty as charged," he said. "So shoot me. You'd have never accepted the bet if I hadn't manipulated the situation a bit."

"Dang right, I wouldn't. Why'd you do it?"

"For a woman who creates bedroom toys for a living, you're amazing at misreading signs from the opposite sex."

"What are you talking about?" she asked, though she knew. He'd been putting out major I-want-you vibes ever since she'd been introduced to the cowboy with the phenomenal nose.

And she'd ignored them all.

Landon tipped one corner of his mouth in a crooked, sexy grin. "I've been trying to get to know you for two years, since the day you first stepped foot in the office. You're smart. You're funny. And you're complicated as hell."

"You're saying you like complications?" she asked, stepping onto the crowded dance floor.

"Live for 'em," he said. "And we're about to have a good one right now, together."

"How's that?" she asked, yelling over the beginning of her favorite Brooks & Dunn tune.

"You're gonna have to teach me how to boot scoot, or we'll damn get trampled out here."

While her eyes bulged and the music pulsed, he yanked her close. "So, show me how to scoot my boots, lady. And some day, I'll teach you how to do something new."

Amy's throat went dry. *That's* what she was afraid of.

She took a deep breath and decided he was right. They either had to start moving, or heed to the stampede.

"Left foot forward, pivot to the right," she said, demonstrating, while he followed, his laugh deep and rich.

"Left foot forward, pivot to the right," she repeated, completing her turn, and again, Landon Brooks, in black Ropers, black Stetson and cocky smile, did the same.

Lord, this wasn't going to be easy. "Now grapevine," she said.

"What?" he asked as the group started the move all around them, and Amy felt a little nervous.

"Here, watch me." She got directly in front of him and started crossing one foot over the other, then stilled when his hands slid around her waist.

"Sorry. This is going to take a little one-on-one." He pulled her to a small hardwood floor on one side of the dance area.

"This is for the instructors," she said, aware that they were on display for the entire bar.

"No one's teaching right now but you," he pointed out, then moved behind her. To Amy's dismay, he put his hands back on her waist, his thumbs pressing gently against her spine.

"What are you doing?" She jerked her head around and inadvertently swished his face with her ponytail.

"Peaches," he said, inhaling her shampoo. "Nice."

Her skin burned. "I asked what you're doing."

He grinned. "I figured it'd be easier to learn if I could feel you doing it. That's okay, isn't it?"

"What's okay?" she asked.

"Me. Feeling you. Doing it."

Amy's breathing hitched. She wanted to argue, but given she couldn't think straight enough to put words together, she simply nodded.

"Good," he said, and pulled her closer, while the bar watched, and Amy tried not to swoon.

Two hours later, she entered her apartment and wasn't surprised her sister hadn't returned from her date with Bill. "Good for you, Lettie," she whispered, dropping her purse on the table.

She withdrew both cell phones and moved to the couch to check for messages. Both had remained silent throughout the night, and she wasn't at all certain that was normal. She checked the call log once more. Sure enough, nothing had been received since this morning.

It made her a little nervous leaving the phones in Brenda's care while she danced with Landon, but Amy had never been one to shirk a bet, and she'd trusted Brenda to hustle the phones over pronto if anyone called.

Trust. A word she wasn't always comfortable with, and one that crept up continually when she recalled Landon Brooks pressed against her while they maneuvered through the "Boot Scootin' Boogie." That dance had never seemed so hot before. But with Landon, it'd been sweltering. Making her not at all comfortable with their little cherry-tying wager. It wasn't as if she didn't trust Landon to keep himself in order during a date.

She didn't trust herself. Particularly when dancing with him tonight had been so . . . fun.

Ever since she left Sheldon, she'd managed to stay away from men, from the temptations and the common need they fulfilled. A need she could conquer just as well with one of her toys and an ample supply of batteries. But she couldn't deny there was *something* about having a man touch her, the way Landon touched her tonight. And would probably try to touch her again on their date.

And to think, after leaving Sheldon, she'd have sworn the last guy to ever rock her steady boat would be a country boy. But Landon Brooks was as country as they came, and proud of it. Not from Sheldon, thank goodness, but from Texas. Where, supposedly, everything was bigger.

Amy wondered.

Her phone rang, and she jumped to answer it. Phone calls this late at night meant one thing. Bad news. She yanked the cordless from its cradle and punched the "talk" button.

"Hello? Lettie?"

A dial tone sounded through the line, and the ringing continued.

"Well, shoot," she said, hurrying toward the phones on the couch and quickly grabbing the red one. She flipped it over, noted the name of the fictitious hotel and answered. "The Palisades, this is Amy. Can I help you?"

"Amy? I thought your name was Colette," the elderly woman said from the other end. "We've been working with a Colette. This is Ellen Southersby, and I hired Colette Campbell to take my calls. I did dial the right number, didn't I?"

"Oh, hi," Amy said. "Yes, you called the right number. Actually, Colette isn't available tonight, so I'm taking care of her calls. I assumed she'd spoken with you about it."

The woman tsked into the receiver. "You know, she

did. I swear, I'd forget my head nowadays if it wasn't attached. But I suppose that happens as the years creep in, doesn't it? Sounds like you're a good ways from finding that out yourself." She laughed softly. "I do remember her telling me, though. You're her sister, right?"

"Yes," Amy said, genuinely enjoying the sound of an elderly voice. She'd never known her grandparents. But if she had known a grandmother, she suspected her voice would've sounded a lot like this woman's.

"I was calling to see if any of our kids tried getting hold of us tonight. We called them earlier with our cellular, so I didn't expect them to, and I felt certain you'd have let us know if they did, but I wanted to check, anyway. Walter says I'm silly to be so paranoid, but with us being"—she lowered her voice—"at this place and everything, I figure it doesn't hurt to be extra careful."

"Oh, that's fine. And no, they haven't called "

"It was okay to check in with you now, wasn't it?" the lady asked, evidently realizing the time. "Colette told me she was available twenty-four hours a day, but I didn't think to ask if that applied to you while you're filling in."

"Sure, it does, and I just got in myself, so it's totally fine."

"You just got in? Did you have a date?" the woman asked, not hiding her curiosity.

"No," Amy said, then added, "Well, not exactly, though I did end up dancing."

"What kind of dancing?"

"Line dancing. Country music." Amy leaned back, closed her eyes and relaxed on the couch.

"I've always wanted to try that," she said. "Maybe

Walter and I will give that a go next. We're finding our interests in—lots of things—are rather broad." Her voice held a hint of a giggle.

Amy's eyes snapped open. "You should try line dancing. You'd enjoy it, I'm sure."

"I bet we would," the lady said. "Matter of fact, I've found out this week that I enjoy lots of things. We both do. Isn't that right, honey?" she asked, and Amy heard the man's responding laugh through the receiver.

"You know, it's funny you mentioned that," Amy said, deciding the conversation topic had been opened up. And being a savvy businesswoman, she'd be crazy not to pursue it. "Because I could use a couple like you and your husband to help me. . . ."

*C*HAPTER 10

Pushing a cherry tomato around the bed of lettuce on her plate, Lettie couldn't muster up an appetite for lunch. Great sex, she realized, had that effect on her. How could she think about food when her mind and body kept focusing on Bill? And everything he did to her last night. Taking her there more times than she could count *and* finding that secret spot, which he'd hailed as her "treasure."

Fancy that, Bill Brannon, a pirate looking to pilfer. And coming up with gold.

Move over, Captain Jack Sparrow. Pirate Bill plundered her thoroughly and, thank her lucky stars, found the prize. Lettie had thought for certain she'd never catch her breath again after his first encounter with her G-spot. But she had. And then they'd gone at it again. And again. And again.

"You've hardly touched your salad," Cassie pointed out. Her long pink nails curved over the toasted bread of her turkey sandwich as she took a bite and eyed Lettie. Swallowing, she dabbed a paper napkin at the corner of her mouth to remove a stray drop of mayonnaise. Then she narrowed her eyes, dropped the napkin and held her palms up in surrender. "That's it. I can't stand it. Fess up, already. Was he that good? Or that bad?"

Lettie glanced around the small deli they frequented most afternoons for tasty sandwiches, crisp salads and juicy gossip. "Both."

"Well, it's about time someone got the job done right." Cassie relaxed her posture, grabbed her sandwich and took a man-size bite. She chewed gleefully, holding up a pink-tipped finger until she managed to swallow. "So? I'm waiting."

"For?"

One of Cassie's big blond curls dangled near her eye, and she blew it back into place before interrogating Lettie. "Details, girl. Start at the beginning. You went out for dinner and a show, right? What'd you eat? What'd you see? And then we'll get to the what'd-you-yell-when-you-finally-got-what-you-needed part."

Lettie bit her lower lip, looked at her friend from beneath her lashes, as though she were shy about the particulars.

As if.

At Cassie's bug-eyed response, Lettie laughed. "We never made it to the show. Or dinner, for that matter."

"Quit it," Cassie said, using her tongue to catch a sesame seed on her lower lip that was evidently stuck in her flaming red lipstick.

"I'm serious. Matter of fact, even though we drove to his house, we never made it out of the car." Lettie batted her eyes and smiled broadly. She'd attacked him in the driver's seat and ridden him like a first-rate stallion.

Which, by the way, he was. Then she'd wriggled and writhed until her vision blurred, her body exploded, and she'd come like there was no tomorrow.

Yep, that's the way it started, all right. Then they'd held each other until they were ready to give it another go, this time in the backseat. By the end of the night, they'd christened every inch of Bill's Camry, exterior included, since they'd ventured outside to cool off and ended up sprawled on top of his trunk. And, as she suspected, Bill Brannon had no reason at all to compensate.

"This is the guy you handed off to me, right? This one?" Cassie lifted a silver cell phone from her purse. "The contact for Integrated Solutions?"

Lettie nodded, staring at the phone and suddenly feeling sick.

A slim silver reminder of the lie.

She moved her fork around the bed of romaine as she pondered the implications of telling Bill the truth, as well as the implications of not telling him. They'd connected sexually last night, several times, but Lettie had felt a deeper connection too.

He'd touched her so tenderly, as though she were precious, a woman worthy of his full attention. A woman worthy of his love. Of course, he'd also thrown her down and got unbelievably kinky a time or two. But that didn't mean he was only interested in sex.

Or did it? He never said anything about it being more than two friends reconnecting. And did they *ever* reconnect. But—was that it? Did she want it to be?

"What's wrong?" Cassie asked between bites.

Lettie shrugged. "It's just sex."

"Great sex, you implied."

"Yeah." Which should make her happy, and it did. Still . . .

"But you want more with this guy?" She tapped the end of the phone.

Lettie stabbed a bite of salad and popped it in her mouth, made herself swallow. "It's ridiculous for me to want anything more. He thinks I'm in town for a week, that I'll be heading back to Tampa on Sunday and everything will be over and done."

She let her fork rest on the edge of the plate, but she tightened her grip on its handle. "I wasn't expecting anything beyond a bit of fun."

Did her words sound more truthful to Cass than to her own ears?

"Weren't you?" Cassie asked, snatching a square of cheese from Lettie's plate.

"I didn't think so."

Cass popped the cheese in her mouth, chewed and swallowed. "But now you're thinking you may want more than a little heated, and much-needed, mattress mambo?"

Lettie grinned at Cassie's never-ending stash of euphemisms for sex. "Who wouldn't?"

"Hey, don't rub it in. I'm jealous enough as it is. By the way, has anyone ever told you that food is a semi-adequate substitution for sex?" Cass picked up a whole pickle, held it to her mouth, then bit the end off with enthusiasm. "And that's how I feel about that."

Lettie laughed so hard she had tears, while most of the customers turned and gawked.

"Sorry," she managed, waving away their curious

stares. "We shouldn't be talking about this, Cass. I wasn't thinking."

"Oh no you don't. Just because my love life sucks doesn't mean I can't live vicariously through yours."

"You still haven't heard from Ken?" Lettie asked.

"Nope, and I don't want to," Cassie said, before sipping her soda. "The guy tried to use My Alibi. To cheat. On me," she continued, shaking her head at the irony. "Guess that's what I get for not telling him the truth about where I work."

"At least you found out before things got more serious," Lettie said, trying to point out the only positive in Cassie's recent breakup.

"Exactly. Who wants to end up with a liar?" Cassie asked, then continued to attack her pickle.

Lettie frowned. "No one, I'm sure."

"Well, damn," Cassie said. "I wasn't talking about you. Your situation is totally different."

"How?" Lettie asked. It sure sounded the same.

"You were doing your sister a favor—*and* doing your job. You didn't know your old high-school flame was going to be on the other end of the phone."

"He wasn't a flame; he was a friend. A good friend."

"If you'd told him about Erika before your date, do you think last night would've ended up differently?"

Lettie shrugged. She'd wondered the same thing all morning. "I don't know."

Cassie chomped another bite of pickle, chewed and swallowed. "The way I see it, there's only one thing you can do."

"Tell him the truth and hope Amy forgives me?"

"Yeah, you're going to have to tell him before it's all

said and done, but you can't tell him yet." Cassie poked her fork in the air with her words. "That's not what you need to do first, anyway. Hey, you gonna eat that other tomato?"

"Go ahead." Lettie pushed her plate toward Cass and watched her stab the round fruit and plunk it in her mouth. "Then what do I need to do before telling him the truth? And why should I wait?"

"You have to wait until Amy can get things settled with her friend," Cassie said matter-of-factly. "The last thing you want to do is let her think she can't trust you, right?"

Lettie's head ached. Of course, she didn't want to jeopardize her relationship with Amy, particularly in the trust arena. "Right."

"Tell Amy that when Erika gets back, she'll need to come clean with her uncle. Maybe offer to go with her to talk to him, you know, to soften the blow."

"Seems like it'd be more of a one-two punch," Lettie said, pressing her fingers against her throbbing temples. "He'd find out we both lied."

"He'd see you both made a mistake, but care about him enough to come clean," Cassie corrected.

Lettie had no doubt he'd forgive Erika; she was his niece. But would he forgive her for her part? And for hiding the truth once she learned he was Erika's uncle?

"Why shouldn't I tell him now?" Lettie asked. "After I talk to Amy."

"You want him, don't you?"

Like she could deny it. "Yeah, I do, but we're just getting to know each other again. I don't know if it's anything more than—"

"Uh-uh," Cassie said, waving a pink fingernail toward Lettie's nose. "The way I look at it, you've got a few more days to show him how things could be with the two of you, and Amy and Erika have a few days to figure out how to tell him the truth. Or how to deal with the fact that you're going to tell him. In the meantime, he'll see he can't live without you."

"But I'm still lying to him."

"With the intention of telling him the truth as soon as possible," Cassie added. She placed her empty plate on top of a red plastic carrier, then added Lettie's leftover salad. "I'll get this." Starting toward the trash, Cassie only managed a few steps before a phone in her purse began to ring.

Lettie held her breath and prayed it was Cassie's personal phone. Or one of her other clients.

Anyone but Bill.

Cass placed the tray on a table and, thank goodness, withdrew a bright blue phone.

Blue. Lettie couldn't think of a prettier color in the world. Of course, any color but silver would've been near perfect.

"National Engineering. This is Cassie. Can I help you?" Cassie held the phone away from her ear as the woman yelled through the receiver.

Rolling her eyes, she brought the phone back and answered, "Yes, ma'am, I'll be happy to give him the message. Would you like for me to have him return your—"

She shrugged, hit the "end" button.

"What happened?" Lettie asked.

"I've got Serial Seth," Cassie explained, quickly

punching in another number. "Evidently, he's been caught. Again."

Lettie laughed and watched Cassie call their most notorious client. "Serial Seth" wasn't a serial killer; he was a serial cheater, and he hired My Alibi as an accomplice to his crimes an average of three times per month.

"Seth, it's Cassie. You got a call from Tewanda."

Lettie shook her head. Seth was also known for the wild names of the women he dated, but Tewanda topped the list for most unique.

"Right. She said to tell you her friend Veronica saw you at Provino's last night, three hundred miles away from the conference you told her you were attending. Veronica also said you had your tongue miles down some bimbo's throat," Cassie said, then added, "Her words, Seth. Not mine. Or I should say, her scream, not mine. The woman was pissed."

Cassie nodded her head as Seth responded, then ended with an "Okay, so we've still got one out there, right? Got it. Fine."

Lettie grinned.

"You'd think he wouldn't need me for this assignment anymore, wouldn't you?" Cassie asked. She slid a pink-tipped finger in the top of her shirt to straighten her bra strap.

"But he does?"

"Oh yeah." Cassie finished fiddling with the strap, then continued her trek toward the trash can with the tray. "He gave *two* of them this alibi, believe it or not."

"You're kidding."

"Nope," Cassie said, returning to the table. "He's a real prize, that one."

"You ever seen him?"

"No, he books over the phone and pays with a credit card. But he's got a great voice. If the body matches, he's a looker. Then again, from what Tewanda said, if she ever sees him again, he won't be much to look at by the time she's done."

Lettie was about to ask what Tewanda said she'd do, but she was halted by another shrill ring, once again from Cassie's purse. To her dismay, this time Cass withdrew the silver phone. The phone she easily recognized, because she'd had it two days ago.

Frowning, Cassie punched the "send" button and started lying to Bill.

"Integrated Solutions, this is Cassie."

Bill gazed in admiration at the image on the screen. For two weeks, he'd been at a standstill on the Bentwood campaign, but after one night with Lettie, his brain overflowed with ideas. Damn good ideas, he'd say, eyeing the resulting product of her inspiration. The detail was still rough and required fine-tuning by the graphics department, but the concept was perfect.

A shiny black sedan sat front and center of a modest brick home at dusk on a summer night. With her hip nestled against the hood, a sexy blonde wearing a vibrant red dress lounged seductively. The long, smooth length of one leg was revealed by an intriguing slit to her thigh. She peered at the man, her man, keys in hand, walking toward the car. Electricity bristled off the pair, in their late twenties, the picture of youth and vitality.

They eyed each other with unabashed interest. Tempting. Desiring. Craving.

Bill turned his attention to the caption, hovering in the lower right corner: *Why Wait for a Midlife Crisis?*

He'd have the car altered to red, the dress to black, and that'd be that. Bentwood would love it. A new twist on an old idea, precisely what the man said he wanted in this campaign. And precisely what Lettie Campbell's inspiration had generated.

It'd been pure torture driving to work this morning, with the scent of their lovemaking lingering in his car. On his car. Hell, how long could he go before washing it?

Then again, they could wash it together. He imagined Lettie, her clothes sticking to every generous curve, every subtle indention. Suds sliding between them as they made certain no spots were missed.

They sure hadn't missed any spots last night.

Bill chuckled, low and deep in his throat. The scent would fade, but that didn't matter. He'd have it again. Tonight, in fact. And many nights after, if he had his way.

She'd been so responsive to his touch, her body on fire and ready for everything he offered. He leaned back in his chair and remembered finding that hidden spot. The way she'd come so hard, so intensely. She'd trembled all over. And screamed his name.

His name.

He'd always suspected there'd been a reason he hadn't given his heart over the past few years, and it didn't have to do with the teenager living in his home.

Although Erika's presence kept him from having an overly active sex life, he'd still managed. In fact, he'd experienced several intriguing females, many of whom wanted nothing more than to share his bed, his home and his life forever. But Bill had never been drawn to any of them. Now he realized why, with exact certainty.

He'd never had the one he wanted. The one he'd found, so many years ago, when she'd taken the small town of Sheldon by storm. And somewhere in the process, captured his friendship, and now was capturing his heart.

Last night, they'd confirmed what he'd always suspected. The two of them together were unsurpassed sexually. He was amazed his Camry hadn't burst into flames from the heat. But tonight, he needed to show her they could have more than exceptional sex. In fact, he planned to remind her that he was the friend she'd connected with so many years ago. To show her they could be everything to each other—friends . . . and lovers.

He'd made another reservation for dinner, bought tickets again for the show. Tonight—come hell or high water—he'd take her on a real date. No matter how much his dick begged to differ. Sure, he knew they'd end up hot and heated before the night was over, but first, he wanted to set her heart on fire.

Then he'd do the same everywhere else.

His envelope icon flashed, and his message box identified new mail from Alvin Bentwood. He'd only sent the rough draft an hour ago, which meant his client's response was either very good. Or very bad.

Bill opened the e-mail and grinned: *You nailed it. Go with it.—A.B.*

A man of few words, but the words he'd typed spoke magnitudes. Two 3-word sentences, and Bill was learning more and more how very much he appreciated the impact of three words.

Particularly when they were uttered from red-glossed, strawberry-flavored lips.

"Make me come."

"Do me here."

Yeah, his dick still pumped up the volume when he remembered her commands. But his true goal was to hear three new words from Lettie Campbell. Three words that, he suspected, she'd never said to a man before, but words he totally planned to hear.

She'd loved getting hot and sweaty in his car, but he'd seen her eyes, glistening in the moonlight after they'd made love. The complete trust, the unwavering admiration, the look of absolute awe—toward him. Then, when he'd walked her to the door, he'd seen more.

Lettie let her guard down, and he'd jumped at the opportunity to take advantage. She'd melted against him, losing herself in that intoxicating kiss. And then, as he walked away, he'd heard her sweet sigh of contentment.

Content and happy.

With him.

His phone pierced the silence of his office, and he brought his mind back to the here and now. Back to the ad on his screen, the one that effectively advertised the automobile, while blatantly advertising a night he'd never forget.

He took a deep breath, focused on the scope of the campaign, since Alvin Bentwood could very well be on the other end of that line. While at work, he had to stay centered on his current project—which, at the moment, meant centered on Bentwood Motors. After work, he'd stay focused on his life-long project.

Winning Lettie Campbell.

"Brannon," he answered.

"Hey, Uncle Bill. How are you?"

"Erika," he said, smiling. Not Bentwood, and he couldn't be more pleased. He'd missed her.

His eyes moved to two framed photos on his desk. One of him and Ginny at the beach, with bright blue water licking their ankles and their bare feet nestled firmly in the sand. She, the gorgeous black-haired teen beauty, and he, the grinning, admiring little brother. She looked so happy, so excited, so full of—life.

Sadness squeezed his heart, and he turned his attention to the other photograph. Erika, a near-exact image of the sister he had adored.

Erika was Ginny made over, with that long cascade of ebony silk falling down her back, the pixie face complete with dainty turned-up nose, and those dark eyes, like huge black marbles in the midst of a forest of lashes. Plus her gung-ho attitude, the determination to get exactly what she wanted, truly classified her as Ginny's heritage.

"The message service said you called. I'm afraid my cell phone doesn't pick up when I'm inside the conference area. Did you need something?"

"Just wanted to make sure everything was going okay. You learning plenty?" he asked. Damn, he was proud of her.

"Definitely. More than I had anticipated," she said, her excitement pulsing through every syllable.

"Wonderful. It's not easy for a young woman to find

her place in the world, but you're doing it, and I couldn't be more thrilled."

Silence echoed from the other end.

"Hey, I didn't mean to embarrass you. But this is the first time you've headed out on your own, and I'm really pleased. How many girls snag the first job they apply for right after high school? And you didn't bother going for slinging fast food. No, indeed. A computer job, from the get-go. Your mama would've loved this."

He looked back at his smiling sister in the photo. In truth, Ginny would've turned flips. She always wanted the best for Erika, better than what she'd had. Ginny left Sheldon with Roy Collins after graduating high school and returned pregnant five months later. Erika's father stuck around long enough to give his daughter a name, then promptly divorced Ginny and left town.

Naturally, Ginny had been afraid her little girl might inherit her not-so-wise genes when it came to the opposite sex. But Erika had been smart in her dating. She'd told Bill numerous times that she wanted to get through college first; then she'd think about finding Mr. Right.

Sure, she dated, but no one special. Not until this new fellow, whom Bill had yet to meet, had she even gone out with a guy more than a few times before moving on. She hadn't wanted to get too serious, too quick.

With the new fellow, she seemed somewhat serious, as far as Bill could tell. But the fact she left him here while she went to Tampa for her training session spoke volumes. Her education and work ethic still came first.

Thank God.

Bill wasn't ready to get into the whole you've-got-your-whole-life-ahead-of-you talk. He'd rather she experience life for a few years, then find the right guy and settle down. Without her uncle having to butt his nose into her business and immediately transforming from awesome uncle to weird-ass relative from hell.

A sharp exhalation hissed through the receiver.

"Erika? You okay?"

"I'm fine. How's your week going?"

Bill grinned. "I nailed the Bentwood Motors account." Thanks to Lettie.

"Awesome! That was a big one, wasn't it?"

"Biggest one this year," he said.

"How about anything else? Have you gone out or anything while I've been gone? You really should get out and have more fun, you know. You should meet *someone*," she said, and she let the last word hang, as though expecting him to say he had.

Funny, how his niece's intuition was always right on the money. The same way Ginny's had been. When it came to reading her brother's emotions, she'd always hit the nail on the head.

Ginny had known he'd fallen for Lettie way back when, had told him he should pursue her more aggressively. But being hesitant to ruin their friendship, he hadn't. Now, though, he was doing exactly what she'd requested, and he couldn't be more pleased with the results.

"Have you?" Erika asked. "Met someone?"

"As a matter of fact, I did run into an old friend from high school," he said, not wanting to tell too much too soon. Eventually, if all went well, he'd inform Erika that he ran into someone who was going to be much, much more than just an "old friend."

"Sounds great!"

He laughed. "How about you? Have you talked to your boyfriend from home while you've been down there? You said you really like this one—what's his name again?—Butch? I'm sure he's missing you."

Another surge of silence echoed through the phone.

"Erika?"

"I'm sorry, Uncle Bill. It's just that this connection"—she paused and he waited—"I'm losing my signal. I'll call you back another time. If you need me, call the message center. They're handling the calls for all conference attendees. Everything's fine here, though."

"Glad to hear you're . . ." he started, but the line went dead.

Bill put the receiver back in the cradle. He'd done a good job with Erika. There had been a short span of time right after she came to live with him where she'd leaned toward the rebellious side, trying her hand at partying and dabbling in alcohol.

She had been so certain her mama would beat the odds, defy what every doctor said was inevitable, even when Ginny had told her she wouldn't. Ginny had tried to prepare Erika, had told her to remember the good times they'd shared and had begged Erika, and Bill, to live life to the fullest.

At fifteen, Erika seemed to misunderstand her mother's wishes. Or perhaps her experimentations had been her mechanism for coping with her loss.

Bill didn't know. Losing Ginny was hard on both of them, but together they'd navigated the storm. In the end, Erika had come around, trusting him as not only her uncle, but also as her friend, a person who understood how she felt about losing Ginny.

Based on how she'd turned out so far, he'd say she was well on her way to becoming a successful, intriguing young woman. And as Ginny had instructed, he'd given Erika the letter Ginny had entrusted to him when Erika turned eighteen.

He hadn't been able to control the emotion, or the tears, when his niece took her mama's letter to her heart and held it there before retreating to her room to read Ginny's last message in private. It meant the world to Bill that he was able to give Erika another keepsake from her mother on the day she became an adult. And the letter obviously meant the world to Erika; she vowed to keep it with her always to remind her of what her mother wanted most.

She hadn't told Bill what the letter said, but he suspected he knew. Ginny wanted her daughter to find happiness.

So did Bill.

He pushed the frames together, so the two female images were side by side. They were so similar they could be twins, and Bill welcomed the similarities. Thanks to Erika, Ginny lived on. Bill's big sis would've been proud of her selection for Erika's guardian, seeing him handle a prone-to-be-rowdy teen.

Bill smiled. Now if he could convince Lettie Campbell to make the same choice, finding the same guy could handle a prone-to-be-rowdy adult.

$\mathscr{C}$HAPTER 11

Erika tied a thin strap of leather around the end of Butch's long braid. She'd been intrigued by a man with hair longer than hers; it'd been the subject of their first conversation when they met at a friend's party. Every girl there wanted to meet the "rough and rowdy biker dude," but he'd only had eyes for Erika.

She decided then and there that he was "the one." And she hadn't changed her mind, though the past couple of days hadn't left her nearly as enamored as she'd been before their trip. He was downright obnoxious when he drank and had no consideration whatsoever for her feelings when he had beer in his system. Unfortunately, the only time she'd seen him without a can in his hand was when they'd been in bed.

And even *that* had left much to be desired this week. Probably due to the beer.

But he loved her. He'd said so, several times. And she loved him too, when he was the intriguing guy she'd met in Atlanta, instead of the jerk he'd been on this trip.

Tonight, however, he'd only had one beer, and he was

getting dressed up in his black riding pants, boots and jacket. Surely, he planned to make up for his behavior the past two days.

Erika couldn't wait. Finally, the type of vacation she'd dreamed of, with a man who cared about her, a man who loved her.

"I've got plans tonight," he said, clasping his fingers together, then bending his hands to firmly crack his knuckles against his chest. "I'll probably be late getting back."

He stood, checked her handiwork in the mirror. "Nice job," he said, smiling at the neat braid.

Butch really did have a nice smile, accented by the handlebar mustache that tickled when they kissed.

While Erika fought the impulse to complain about his "plans," he leaned toward her and pushed his mouth to hers. The mustache didn't tickle this time; it scratched. And the kiss didn't do anything for her, at first. Then he deepened the gesture, moving his tongue inside and pulling her against his big, powerful frame.

Erika sighed. She didn't like that he had so many guy plans during biker week, but then again, he'd warned her that he'd have a lot of group functions, and that she'd occasionally be left on her own. At the time, she thought that'd be nice. She could stroll the beach, go shopping, do whatever else she chose to pursue on Tybee Island.

Right now, though, none of those things seemed appealing. Particularly since nearly half of the "gang" were female. And shapely in leather.

"Love ya." He broke the kiss, grabbed his helmet and headed out the door.

"Love you too," she said, but her words met a closed door. He hadn't waited for her response.

Erika quickly retrieved her mother's letter from the drawer.

I'll never regret chasing the dream, following true love. Don't you regret it either.

Did she regret it? No, she didn't. She wasn't going to be one of those jealous women who cringed every time her husband went out with the guys. And that's all Butch was doing. Spending time with the guys, which was a part of biker week. He'd said so.

She lifted the paper, held it to her face and inhaled deeply. Was it her imagination? Or did she truly smell a hint of her mother's flowery perfume on the page?

Her lower lip trembled. Would her mother approve of the dream she had chased?

Before she could ponder the answer, a banging knock sounded on her door.

"Butch?" she said hopefully. She quickly returned the letter to the drawer, then crossed the room.

Swinging the door open, she didn't meet Butch's burly gaze. Instead, she met eyes so light blue she could see through them, sandy blond hair and a wide white smile accented by tanned skin. She thought she recognized the guy; she'd seen him earlier, by the pool. "Can I help you?"

"I saw the biker group leave," he said, and his grin crooked up on one side, almost giving the appearance of shyness. He shrugged. "I noticed your boyfriend went along and thought you might be looking for something to do."

"You're asking me out?" Erika couldn't disguise her shock. Particularly when she thought about the difference in size of this lean, clean-cut college guy in his polo shirt and khakis and the big mountain of a man clad in leather that left her hotel room.

Did this guy not care for his teeth?

He laughed. "No, I'm not." Another shrug. "I've seen your boyfriend, and I do have some semblance of self-preservation."

Erika smiled. Cute and witty too. Not a bad combination. He'd make a nice date for a girl who hadn't already found her true love.

"But I did notice your boyfriend left, and I figured you might be interested in the party we're having by the pool."

"Who's we?" Erika asked, her curiosity piqued. She leaned around him to peer toward the pool area, where several guys were setting up band equipment on the raised deck.

"Mostly students from the University of Georgia. We decided to squeeze in another beach trip before the fall semester starts."

"I'm starting in the fall," she said, moving her gaze back to those eyes.

"You're going to UGA?" he asked, leaning against the door facing.

Erika took a tiny step back. "Georgia Tech," she clarified. "But I'm starting in the fall. It's my first year."

"Ahh, so we're rivals." He grinned brighter. "No matter, we'll still let ya come to the party."

"Gee, thanks." She shifted from one foot to the other.

"Don't mention it. So," he said, backing up, "you gonna stay in your room all night, or are you going to come down and have a little fun?"

"I guess you'll have to wait and see." She smiled, eased the door closed, but not before hearing his last words.

"Looking forward to it."

An hour later, Erika put on the new turquoise handkerchief top she'd bought that afternoon and a pair of khaki pants. She'd planned to wear the outfit for Butch, but it had the right look for a pool party, and she was curious about the college crowd. After all, she'd be part of that crowd soon.

Would Butch care if she went to an occasional party at Georgia Tech? Probably not, since he'd be attending his own biker things.

She pulled her hair up in a high ponytail, tied a turquoise scarf around the base, then appraised the look in the mirror.

Not bad. True, she looked rather young, compared to Butch and his leather pack, but for the college scene, she should blend. Or so she thought, until she made her way to the pool.

Thanks to an open bar, and several kegs by the beach, the majority of the partygoers were thoroughly smashed, and it was only ten o'clock. Disappointed, Erika steered clear of the pool, where several of the girls had jumped in and started a wet T-shirt contest. With the cheers of the guys on the side, and the intoxication of the females in the water, Erika had no doubt the shirts would be floating in the pool soon, or clogging the drain.

She sighed. So much for the college life. Partying wasn't her thing anymore. She'd been there and done that after her mother died—and thank God, she lived to tell about it. With no desire to go there again, she turned away from the crowd.

Deciding she wouldn't let the exquisite night go to waste, she slipped off her sandals and started down the wooden walkway toward the beach.

A full moon danced over the rippling water and showcased each perfect white-capped wave. Erika could think of nothing better than a long walk on the sand. Well, a long walk with the guy she loved would be better—but with Butch away at his biker thing, that wasn't an option.

She stepped off the wood and welcomed the feel of warm sand beneath her feet. The tiny grains tickled her heels and eased between her toes. She inhaled the salty air, closed her eyes and listened to the water splash against the shore.

"Nice, isn't it?"

Opening her eyes, Erika turned to see the sandy-haired guy who had invited her to the party.

"Very nice. And peaceful." She looked toward the pool, where, sure enough, shirts were flying.

"Hey, I want to apologize. I had no idea it was going to get out of control."

She raised a brow.

"Well, out of control this early," he corrected, and his smile beamed in the moonlight.

"That's okay. It gave me a reason to get out of the room and enjoy this gorgeous night."

"See, I knew all along you needed to get out of your room," he said, stuffing his hands in his pockets as he talked. The action pushed his shoulders forward, and reminded Erika of those guy models on her uncle's *Men's Health* magazines. She wondered if it made his abs ripple, the way it did those guys in the magazine.

Then she shook her head. She should *not* be wondering about this guy's abs. She was on a romantic vacation with Butch, wasn't she? Even if today hadn't been incredibly romantic.

"You going for a walk?" he asked.

"I was planning to."

He tilted his head and squinted through an overzealous ocean breeze. "Want company?"

Erika swallowed. Letting him come along would be nice, but probably wouldn't be wise. Not necessarily unsafe, since there were people everywhere along the beach, but definitely not smart for a girl who was in love with someone else.

"I'm Evan," he said. "Evan Carter." He extended his hand.

Erika laughed. Something about a handshake didn't quite fit the scenario of a guy asking to walk with her on the beach, but she took the offered hand and shook it firmly. "Erika Collins."

"Nice to meet you, Erika," he said, and once again, his grin took control of his face—and Erika's resistance. "So, are we going for a walk?"

Another laugh escaped, and she couldn't fathom a single reason why she shouldn't walk with him. What was the harm in walking, anyway? "Sure."

"All right then," he said, and he lowered to his knees in front of her.

Erika stared at him, then looked around to see if anyone was watching the odd display. Embarrassed, she whispered, "What are you doing?"

"Isn't it obvious? I'm proposing," he said, then laughed at her dropped jaw. "I'm going to fix your cuffs so your pants don't get wet."

Then he moved his fingertips beneath the hem and slowly folded the fabric until the cuff was even with her calf. And until Erika's heart attempted to beat right out of her chest.

How could the mere brush of his fingers against her ankle send that kind of tingle through her flesh? And how could she stand for him to do it to the other leg?

"Evan?" she asked as he turned his attention to cuff number two.

God help her.

"Yeah," he said, stopping the motion with his knuckles gently grazing her leg.

She swallowed. This was the same reaction any woman would have to a guy fixing her pants for the water. Wasn't it? "Nothing."

That tempting grin flashed again; then he finished turning the cuff and stood. "Now you're ready."

Oh yeah, she was ready. But she had to remind herself what for. A walk on the beach. That was it. Butch would be back in a little while. Then she'd meet up with him in the room to talk about how much they missed each other tonight and to set things straight between them again. That's what they would do.

And she'd be fine—as long as she remembered.

$\mathscr{C}$HAPTER 12

Amy slipped her heels off and wiggled her toes, then leaned back in her office chair. She'd had a heck of a day trying to determine the problems with Pinky. Closing her eyes, she concentrated on the product test results and tried to define the cause for the vibrator's dismal performance. Could Wallace have been right? Did some women actually require a man?

Her phone rang, and her eyes snapped open. She punched the speaker's button. "Amy Campbell."

"Can you talk for a second?" Erika asked.

Amy picked up the receiver. "Of course." She was more than willing to take a break from her thoughts to visit with her friend. Plus she was feeling antsy. Normally, she darted to and from her office all day participating in meetings and testing products. But today, she'd stayed holed up inside with the door closed. Not because she couldn't have benefited by visiting some of the other departments, but because she wasn't ready to face Landon Brooks after their heated exchange on the dance floor last night.

Could she see him, communicate with him, without showing how he affected her? Could she pull off the nonchalance after she'd had no less than three orgasms last night while calling out his name?

And if Pinky did that for her, why the heck didn't it have the same effect on the test group?

"Things aren't going so good," Erika said, pulling Amy away from her own game of cat and mouse with the Texan and back to the game Erika was playing with biker dude Butch.

"What happened?" she asked. "Wait a minute. Aren't you doing that all-day beach ride today?"

"We were supposed to, but he decided it was a man thing and went without me."

Ouch. "Oh," Amy said, for lack of a better word. If she spouted he was the scum of the earth, or a sleaze, she might regret it later when Erika decided to keep the guy, no matter what. Then, thinking better of her decision, Amy figured she had nothing to lose. He shouldn't hurt her friend.

"I'm coming to get you. I'll be there in a few hours." Tybee Island wasn't that far away. She could have Erika out of there before dark.

Erika laughed. "No, don't come. It's okay. I can handle him, and besides . . ."

"Besides what?"

"It feels kind of awkward admitting this, but—"

"Go on," Amy coaxed. "What happened? Tell me."

"I met another guy."

Amy sat forward in her chair. "There? When? How?"

Erika cleared her throat. "Butch has been kind of doing his own thing over the past day or so, you know, the biker stuff, so I had some time to hang out on my own."

"And?"

"Last night I went to a pool party. Or I started to go to a pool party, but it was a bit wild and reminded me too much of the time right after . . ."

"After you lost your mom?" Amy supplied, knowing Erika had gone through a rough time, a wild time, after her mother had died. Although Erika didn't talk about it much, she'd stated that if she never had another drop of alcohol again, that'd be completely fine.

"Yeah. So I ditched the party and decided to take a walk alone on the beach. The beach is breathtaking here, by the way, really incredible."

"And you met someone?" Amy asked, trying to bring her back to the subject.

"Yeah," Erika said dreamily.

Amy couldn't hold back a grin at her friend's tone. Erika had seemed happy about Butch, but she'd never sounded this . . . smitten. "Well? Tell me about him."

"His name is Evan. He asked if he could walk with me, and I let him. Actually, he was one of the college guys throwing the party, but he wasn't drinking. See, his dad is an alcoholic, so Evan doesn't touch it. He's afraid he might like it if he does."

"Sounds like you two had a pretty deep discussion during your walk."

"We did."

"And there's more," Amy deduced.

Erika exhaled. "He's nice."

"Nice?"

"Yeah," Erika admitted. "Strange, huh? I mean, I

don't like nice guys. Or I didn't think I liked nice guys. I never have before. But he was so sweet, and he seemed really interested in me. We ended up talking about everything, where I'm from, where he's from, his past, my past, going to college, you name it."

Amy focused on the biggest item in that list. "You talked to him about your past?" Erika hadn't talked to *any* guy about her past, particularly about the loss of her mother, or the difficult time she had after she died. If that was what she referred to, that said plenty about this "nice guy" she'd met on the beach.

"I couldn't believe it either, but he asked me if I wanted to go for a walk, and we did, and one thing led to another. . . ."

No way. "You slept with him?"

Erika laughed. "Are you kidding? I barely know him. But what I was trying to say is that one thing led to another, and I ended up telling him my life story. Now I feel, well, connected to him."

"What about Butch?" Amy asked. Merely a week ago, Erika swore Butch was her soul mate.

"I don't know. I mean, the thing with this other guy was more of a friendship kind of deal. Gotta admit, it caught me by surprise that I could talk to Evan about everything."

Amy drummed her fingers on the desk. "You can't talk to Butch?"

"We've never really gotten around to it," Erika admitted.

"Did you kiss him, the guy on the beach? Evan?"

Erika didn't answer.

"Erika?" Amy prodded. "Did you?"

"Yeah, we kissed."

"And?" Amy continued, suspecting it was no ordinary kiss, especially when she heard Erika's sigh through the line.

"And he's leaving tomorrow. So that's the end of it, I'm sure. Butch will get back from the beach run; then we'll work out this friction we've had the past couple of days, and everything will be fine."

"Will it?" Amy asked. Was Erika trying to convince Amy? Or herself?

"Sure. Anyway, I just wanted to talk to someone about last night."

"Right. And you don't want me to tell you to go ask this Evan guy to hold off leaving for a few days so you two can see what happens?"

"No. Definitely don't tell me to do that," Erika said.

"Sorry. I think you should figure this out. Look what happened to my sister and your uncle when they stuffed their feelings under a rug. Twelve long years of both of them being miserable."

"Hey, he hasn't been miserable raising me. I'll have you know I've kept his life plenty exciting. And they're making progress, aren't they?"

"I'll say. But this alibi thing . . . she's really torn up over knowing the truth about your training seminar." Amy swallowed. She'd already told Lettie she would convince Erika to tell him when she returned; unfortunately, she hadn't yet told her friend. "Have you thought about telling the truth to Bill?"

"No," Erika blurted. "No way. It'd kill him to know I lied."

Amy frowned at the phone. "Well, I've gotta tell

you—it's killing her to lie to him. Lettie really cares about Bill and wants to tell him the truth."

"But she won't, right? You said she promised you."

"She did," Amy said. "But she says she won't keep lying to him, and I believe her. What's more, I think she's right. If the two of them are going to have something long-term, she has to tell him the truth."

Erika groaned dramatically into the phone. "How long do I have before she tells him?"

"She said she'd wait until you come home."

"So, what should I do now?" Erika asked, her dread evident.

"You want to come on home and get it over with?"

"No. I'm not at all ready for that. I promised my mom I wouldn't hurt him, and I can't see any way that this won't hurt him. Man, this is *so not* the way I planned this week."

"Like you said, there's a reason all of this happened," Amy reminded. "Your uncle and Lettie are getting hooked up because of your trip, and you met Evan."

"I didn't say Butch wasn't my true love," Erika reminded. "Just that Evan is very . . . nice."

"Well, maybe you should take advantage of this chance to see how things stand with Evan. Go see the guy," Amy said. "Find out what's happening with him, so you can figure out if you really want to keep this thing going with Butch."

"You know what?" Erika asked.

"What?"

"You're right."

"I usually am," Amy said, laughing. "Now keep me posted on what's happening."

"Will do."

Amy disconnected and stared at the phone. Yeah, she was usually right when it came to other people's relationships. Her own, however, was another story.

Who was she kidding? She'd never had a "relationship." Sex, yeah, she'd tried it. Big deal. She got way more out of Pinky and the remainder of her never-ending stash of Adventurous Accessories products. But there was something to be said about the emotional involvement with a living, breathing partner. Granted, she didn't know what she'd say about it, necessarily, but there was *something* to be said.

She'd definitely felt emotionally charged last night, and Landon hadn't even kissed her. How would she handle their upcoming date? Or seeing him at the office, for that matter.

The hard rap on her door made her jump. She looked at the clock. Four forty-five. Fifteen minutes and she'd have made it scot-free without seeing Landon Brooks today. She'd be fine tomorrow, but everything was still too fresh today.

Still too hot.

Dare she hope it wouldn't be Landon on the other side of the door?

"Come in," she said, then relaxed in her chair when Wallace Baker entered.

Thank goodness it wasn't Landon.

But why hadn't it been? She'd totally expected the cowboy to visit her office today, to tease her about their dance last night and their upcoming date this weekend. However, she wasn't disappointed he hadn't shown.

Was she?

"I wanted to let you know the results are in for the second round of tests on the new product," Wallace said, extending a handful of papers toward Amy.

"And?"

"Same outcome. I'm afraid you're going to have to market it as an enhancement product for couples, rather than a singles deal."

"Super." She'd truly hoped the new tests would nullify the previous results. Amy hated changing the marketing strategy for her baby. The whole purpose of Pinky was to provide a surefire way of hitting the G-spot without a man. How the heck were all those women missing the bull's-eye? "How many did you test this time?"

"Fifty."

She shook her head in defeat. "All right. Thanks for letting me know."

"Sorry it wasn't the news you wanted, but it really isn't a bad thing. The product still works. It just works better if there is actual stimulation from a partner as well." He gave her an awkward grin, which pushed an extra batch of wrinkles into his right cheek. "Guess you could say *man*-ual stimulation helps."

"Right. Thanks again, Wallace," she said, ignoring the pun and dismissing him in as nice a way as she could muster, given her disappointment with his findings.

"I'll see you tomorrow then," he said, and left her office.

Amy dropped the graphs, charts and reports on her desk. No need to hope he'd missed a factor. Wallace Baker was notorious for including all pertinent details, which meant Pinky would be marketed as a couples product.

But she'd been using it solo. And she'd hit the mark. Every time. With thoughts of a cowboy in his Stetson on her mind, every time, unfortunately.

She looked at the clock. Five minutes past five. The day was over, and she hadn't seen one glimpse of the dancing cowboy.

Fine. She'd been hiding from him, hadn't she?

Dismayed at her disappointment, she propped her bare feet on her desk, leaned back in her chair and closed her eyes. So he hadn't stopped by her office to flirt. No problem. She hadn't wanted him to, anyway.

"That good of a day? Or that bad?"

Amy jerked upright, slamming her heels against the desk on their way to the floor. "Ouch."

Grimacing at her stinging feet, she straightened in her chair and faced Landon Brooks, standing dead center in her office. Had Wallace forgotten to close the door? And why hadn't she noticed? "I didn't hear you come in."

"I gathered." He stepped closer, and Amy waited for him to sit in one of the chairs facing her desk.

He didn't. Instead, he moved around the desk, propped a hip, clad in pleated black pants, against the edge and appraised her. "Wanna talk about it?"

"About what?" she asked, hoping her speeding pulse wasn't evident in her neck. Because she would swear it was beating harder than humanly possible. Heck, she could feel it in her ears.

"About whatever has you looking so flustered. Or is it me?"

If she were an honest woman, she'd tell him it was her newest product *and* him.

So she'd be half-honest.

"My most recent invention didn't pass the muster on the test subjects," she said as the rampant pulsing in her ears gradually slowed to a steady thud.

"How many tests?"

"This is the second go-around, with eighty subjects total, so far." Finally, her pulse was closer to normal. Thank God. But the fact that Landon Brooks was now closer than normal probably wouldn't help it stay that way.

One corner of his mouth tipped down. "Sorry. But you'll make it work."

She couldn't fight the small smile at hearing his confidence in her abilities. Yeah, she'd make it work. Unfortunately, she'd probably only get it to work for couples, and that hadn't been her goal. "You're right. I will."

He reached out, touched a finger to her chin and tilted her face toward his. "And I haven't factored at all into your frustration level? Because if not, I'm losing my touch."

Amy inhaled his scent. God, he smelled good. Her heart rate pumped up the volume again.

And then she had it.

"You were testing one on me!" she said, pulling away from his heated touch. "Weren't you? Which one was it? And how sneaky!"

He looked at her as though she'd lost her mind. "What are you talking about, Campbell?"

She gathered her wits, which wasn't easy with the all-encompassing male crowding her space, with his starched white shirt, formfitting black pants, end-of-the-day-tousled blond waves framing a to-die-for face. "You were wearing one of your scents last night, emitting all those charged pheromones, and I simply couldn't resist. That's the reason I dreamed about you all night, isn't it? *That's* the reason I couldn't stop thinking about you today. It isn't you; it's the smell! Go on, admit it."

She had him, and she felt a surge of triumph in that knowledge.

Until he smiled.

Oh. No. What did I just say? That she'd dreamed of him last night? That she'd thought of him all day? And from the look on his luscious face, he had no doubts what kind of thoughts she'd been having.

No matter. They didn't count. She'd have them for any ol' Joe wearing that pheromone tosser. So he need not look so damn cocky.

"Oh no you don't," she said, pointing a finger at him.

"What?" Landon asked, holding up his hands in defense. "I haven't said a word."

"No, but you're looking like you won some sort of Mr. Macho contest or something. The fact that I've been thinking about you, a little bit, doesn't mean anything, since it was scent-induced. So you get that idea right out of your head, Brooks."

"If I recall, you said you'd dreamed about me all night and thought about me all day," he said, not looking upset at all by the way he was making her skin flush. "I'd say that's more than a little bit, wouldn't you?"

She shrugged, straightened the papers on the right side of her desk and ignored the hunky cowboy on the left. "Doesn't matter. Like I said, it was scent-induced. So I'm a normal female, just like all of the test subjects who swoon over your products. Yeah, the smells make them want to have a few orgasms, big deal. It's the fragrance doing the trick, not the man."

"So did you?"

"Did I what?" she asked, moving the graphs to the top of the stack. Not that she needed them there, but she sure as heck needed to keep her eyes averted from Landon Brooks.

"Have a few orgasms?" he completed.

She jerked her gaze toward the door and was thankful to see it closed. Sort of. True, she didn't want her coworkers walking by and hearing *this* conversation. But she also didn't want to be trapped in her office with Landon Brooks while having *this* conversation.

"I don't see anything work-related in this discussion," she said, turning her attention back to the gray-eyed, way-too-confident male.

"It could be," he said.

"How's that?"

"If I were charting whether the scents were effective enough to bring a woman to masturbate, then it'd definitely be a work-related topic."

"Are you charting that?" she asked.

Say no. Say no.

"Not at the present time," he admitted.

Hallelujah.

"Then there's no reason for me to answer your question."

His smile broadened, if possible. "Well, in truth, your answer wouldn't help."

She blinked. "Why not?"

He leaned down, close. Way too close. Then he placed a long finger on her temple and slowly eased it along her jaw to her chin. As he'd done moments before, he tilted her gaze to his. "Because, Amy, last night . . ." Landon paused and moved even closer.

"Yeah?" she managed.

"I wasn't wearing *any* of the Adventurous Accessories products."

Another heavy, and disbelieving, blink. *Oh. No.* "You weren't?"

He shook his head. "No, and today, I'm not either." His words fanned her lips.

She swallowed. "You . . . aren't?"

"No. So adding the facts that you dreamed of me last night"—he edged even closer, God help her—"and thought of me all day," he said, then leaned in and nipped her mouth, while her panties went completely wet. "Wouldn't help my findings."

He brought his hand behind her neck, slid it beneath the cascade of hair and pulled her forward. Then he ran his tongue across her lower lip. "Tell me something, Amy."

"What?" she whispered.

"In your dreams, did we kiss?"

She nodded.

"Show me."

Have mercy. She'd fought him, fought this exact type of situation, for as long as she could remember. Surrendering to the pull of a man. Surrendering to the pull of her libido. To something other than a battery-operated toy.

"Only if you want to," he added, his words tempting her, bringing her so close to something that she'd been certain she never wanted. And he wasn't forcing her into it, which made it harder to admit . . . that she wanted it.

Right here. Right now.

He was so close already, all she had to do was lean forward a little, and she was there. Touching his lips. Touching Landon Brooks. Her mouth met his with a hunger for more. A hunger to mate, to linger, to devour. And she did.

She ran her hands over his face while she slipped her tongue between his lips and explored the mesmerizing, intoxicating taste of Landon Brooks. And, Amy admitted, a taste wasn't nearly enough.

Standing from her chair, she pressed her body to his and clawed her fingernails down his back as she pressed her core against the bulge in his pants. He felt so hard, so massive, so . . . right.

She wanted him. Now.

"Landon," she whispered as another loud knock penetrated the heated gasps, moans and pants within her office.

Amy's eyes flew to the door. How could she have forgotten where she was? "Ohmigod."

He laughed, then smoothed her hair from her face. "You look fine, Ms. Campbell. Slip on your shoes and you'll be as professional as always. Only you and I know about the tiger hiding beneath your business clothes." He gave her another soft kiss, then backed away from her desk. "But this weekend, if you'll let me, I'd love to help you set that tiger free." He moved to the door, placed his hand on the knob. "Without the aid of scents," he added, and Amy's world tilted off-kilter.

"Right," she whispered, smoothing the front of her top.

Her pants were wrinkled beyond measure, but she wouldn't worry about that now. It was the end of the day, after all. And she'd just experienced a heat more potent than any reprimands she might receive if her boss was on the other side of that door. Which he probably was. Most Adventurous Accessories employees hit the exit running—promptly at five o'clock—primarily because they knew that was when Vernon Miller liked to have his heart-to-heart meetings. These encounters generally lasted above and beyond an hour.

Landon opened the door, and a hint of Vernon's trademark houndstooth hat peeked from the other side. He was a good four inches shorter than Landon and practically hidden by the cowboy in the doorway, but it was definitely her boss in the Texan's shadow.

"Well, hello, Brooks," Vernon said upon entering. "I didn't interrupt a meeting, did I? Because I can talk to you about these figures later, if I need to, Campbell," he said, holding a copy of Wallace's findings.

"We were discussing Ms. Campbell's newest product," Landon said, "and I was trying to see if there was anything I could do to help her improve upon it."

"Excellent," Vernon said. "You know how much it pleases me when my departments work together."

"Yes," Landon said, stealing a glance back at Amy and winking. "I do."

$\mathcal{C}$HAPTER 13

Lettie swiftly moved the charcoal over the page in an effort to correctly capture the image.

"Are you trying to tell him something?" Amy asked, peering over her shoulder to view the latest sketch.

Amy would know by the intensity of the markings on the paper that Lettie had something on her mind. For as long as she could remember, Lettie had handled frustration by closing off the rest of the world and concentrating on her dream.

Sure, the dream had varied as years progressed, but it had always centered around her designs. When those creative juices started flowing from her head to her hand to the page, she felt release. Not an orgasmic kind of thing, but a powerful freeing of anxiety, nonetheless.

As a little girl, she'd tapped in on this personal method of healing when her mother had purchased used Hasbro fashion plates from the Sheldon five-and-dime. Some of the thin plastic panels were missing, but there were enough to convert Lettie's spark of imagination to a flame. With the help of that toy, she'd mixed and matched tops and pants, blouses and skirts, combining the plates to produce amazing wardrobe sketches. Creating her own masterpieces, totally befitting a runway model, in a six-year-old's opinion.

Wanda Campbell hadn't had a tremendous amount of motherly instincts, but every now and then, she'd come through with flying colors. That trip to the five-and-dime was undoubtedly one of those times.

"Tell who something?" She didn't look up, her attention too in tune with her idea to allow her vision to wander. The gown was white satin with tiny spaghetti straps at the shoulders and a beaded bodice befitting a bride, as did the train flowing from the plunging back. The cut was sleek and sexy, yet the beaded detail and intriguing train undeniably sweet.

Innocent. Virginal. Pure.

Exactly what she was going for.

"It's incredible," Amy said as Lettie finished the last stroke of charcoal on the page.

Examining the finished product, Lettie placed the pad on the kitchen table. "Yeah, it is." And it had taken the edge off her anxiety, if only for a while. Until Bill Brannon knocked on their door, she suspected.

"I asked you a question, by the way," Amy reminded.

Lettie's brow furrowed. "What question?"

"Are you trying to tell him something?"

Lettie placed a square of wax paper over the design, then closed the pad. "I'm not showing it to him. Besides, this isn't a wedding gown."

"If you say so."

Lettie didn't get to respond before a knock sounded at

the door and her pulse skittered. "Is the dress too much?" she whispered.

"It's perfect. You should wear green more often; it brings out your eyes. So, do you want me to get the door, or do you want to?" Amy had begged her to have Bill pick her up at the apartment, since she was dying to see the two of them together; this time, Lettie had conceded. Heck, if Amy accidentally let something slip about Lettie's actual place of employment, it really wouldn't matter. She was going to tell him the truth, anyway. Soon. As soon as Erika came home.

"I will," Lettie said, her heart racing as she crossed the room.

Opening the door, she was bombarded by a flash of color. Bright, vivid pink.

"Oh my," she gasped.

Extending a crystal vase with a dozen—make that two dozen—pink roses, Bill smiled. And every ounce of Lettie's apprehension dissipated.

"You look amazing," he said.

"Thanks." She held the vase and stood there a moment, tattooing this image—the way he looked, the words he said—on her mind forever. Here was something she could hold on to and revisit every now and then.

Amy coughed from her perch at the kitchen table.

Lettie blinked, grinned, then turned toward her sister. "Bill, you remember Amy, don't you?"

He entered the apartment, and Lettie noted the sharp black suit, making him look every bit the dashing businessman and setting off his dark features, jet-black hair, dark brows, intense eyes.

Lord, how she wanted this man.

"Of course, I remember you, Amy. Though I must say, in my mind you were still twelve."

"Gee, thanks." Amy stood, ignored his outstretched hand and hugged him. With the impromptu action, her ponytail whacked him smartly in the face.

Bill flinched, then laughed. "I didn't mean that negatively. I can't believe how you've grown up."

Lettie placed the vase on the table and admired the exquisite arrangement. "Bill, these really are gorgeous."

"I'll say," Amy agreed, leaning over to inhale one of the blooms. "We always loved roses, didn't we, Lettie? Remember snitching some out of Mr. Feazell's garden?"

"How could I forget? He said he was going to have us arrested." Lettie fingered one of the blooms.

Bill chuckled. "Arrested? Old Man Feazell? You're kidding."

"Nope," Amy said, shrugging. "He was sure enough mad, but we were young and didn't know any better."

"Guess he figured if we had the fear of incarceration in us, we'd stay out of his rose garden," Lettie said. She could still see the weathered man in his overalls shaking his fist at them in warning.

"Worked, didn't it?" Amy said, inhaling another bloom. "We never went back." She straightened from the table. "Oh, and speaking of not coming back, I won't be coming back here tonight, Lettie. Did I tell you that already?"

"No, you didn't," Lettie said, cocking a suspicious brow at her conniving sister.

"Brenda asked me to hit Cowboys with her again tonight. We'll be out pretty late, and since the place is close to her apartment and our office, I figured it'd be easier for me to stay there."

"Did you?" Lettie didn't buy a word of it, and from the knowing look on Bill's luscious face, he didn't either.

"Yep," Amy said, unaffected by their stares. "Just wanted to let you know so you wouldn't worry. Guess you'll have the place to yourself. And I'll bring those things by your office tomorrow morning."

"Things?" Lettie asked.

"Yeah," Amy said, pointing toward her purse, where two slim phones protruded from the side pocket.

Lettie swallowed. How could she have forgotten about her clients? Or about the fact that Amy was, once again, taking her calls? "Are you sure that's not a problem?"

Amy grinned, turned toward Bill. "Will you take her out and help her have some fun? And try to convince her that her little sister has grown up and actually enjoys helping her out, for a change."

"Will do," Bill said, wrapping an arm around Lettie, while Amy grinned triumphantly.

"Good," Amy said, stepping forward and motioning them to the door. "Then you guys should head out."

"Yeah, we should," Lettie agreed.

"Our reservations are for seven," Bill said, grinning at Amy as though thanking her for her considerate departure plans.

"All right." Lettie moved toward her sister and hugged her tightly. "You're too much," she whispered as Amy giggled.

"By the way, if you need to use any of my things

tonight," Amy said, pulling away from Lettie's embrace, "feel free. My apartment is your apartment, you know."

Lettie bit her inner cheek to keep from laughing. She knew exactly which "things" Amy referred to, the bulging bag of sex toys in her little sister's bedroom. She also caught the apartment jab.

My apartment is your apartment.

Amy was *so* gonna pay for this.

"Y'all have fun," Amy called as they headed out the door.

They entered the elevator, and the old contraption steadily worked its way toward the first floor.

"You do look amazing," Bill said.

"I'd have to say the same for you." He looked every inch the *GQ* guy in the suit, like a man who knew what he wanted and went for it. A man in control. She wondered if what he wanted, for longer than a week, was her.

Putting an arm around her waist, he led her from the building to his car, then opened her door.

It felt incredible to be pampered by Bill, and Lettie decided to enjoy the feeling for the short time she had it. In a few days, Erika would be back, and she'd risk ending all of this when he learned the truth. But for now, Lettie would cherish every moment.

She took a deep breath and gathered her composure as he closed her door and walked around the car. If she eventually lost him because of the truth, so be it. But she wouldn't—couldn't—live the rest of her life knowing she wasn't honest to Bill.

"I love the roses," she said as he climbed inside.

"It isn't the first time, you know." He leaned across the seat and fingered a blond tendril dangling in front of her ear. His fingernail grazed her cheek and sent an arrow of eagerness to her core.

She'd worn her hair up to match the formal appearance of the green cocktail dress she'd borrowed from Amy. At the time, she had no idea Bill would don a suit, but it didn't surprise her they were in sync on appearance. They'd certainly had quite a few in-sync performances last night. Why wouldn't a couple so together in their sexuality be as in tune to each other in every other way?

"Isn't the first time?" she questioned, straightening the fabric of her skirt as he started toward the interstate.

"That I've given you roses."

"You mean the rose from the MARTA station?" That rose was currently in a crystal bud vase by her bed, where she could see it easily and think of Bill.

He shook his head. "Not that one. Roses. Plural. This isn't the first time I've given you roses, Lettie."

Her hands stilled against the soft green fabric as she processed the implication of his words. She'd received roses four times in her life, and all four times had been in the Sheldon High School gym during the Valentine's Day assembly.

As a fund-raiser, members of the Student Government Association sold roses every February for the traditional program. On Valentine's Day, the entire student body gathered in the gym as the flowers were distributed. Students could purchase roses in one of three colors, red, white or pink.

Red indicated love. White equaled friendship. And pink meant, "I'd like to get to know you better."

Each Valentine's Day, the students waited with bated

breath as the names were called to see who received the coveted roses.

The red flowers generally prompted an "ahhh" from the crowd, then whispers about who was going out with whom. The white flowers usually prompted a hug from the classmate or classmates who'd made the purchase for their friend.

But the pink roses gained the most response from the crowd. Those were the ones typically received from secret admirers. Consequently, those were the ones that generated the most stir in the noise level of the gym.

During her freshman, sophomore and junior years, Lettie had received a dozen red roses from whoever she happened to be dating at the time. She'd known they were coming every year, since secrets were a rarity in Sheldon's gossip-prone halls.

So the roses from those first three years weren't the ones that caught her unaware. It was the assembly of her senior year that threw her off-guard.

She'd decided she would leave Sheldon as soon as she graduated, start her new life in a bigger city and hopefully pave the way for Amy to move in with her when she graduated. Because of those plans, Lettie had decided a steady boyfriend was something she didn't need and had stayed away from serious relationships during her senior year.

So, of course, at that Valentine's assembly, she'd expected for the first time in her years at Sheldon High that her name would remain uncalled. However, after the last name appeared to have been announced, Mindi Kirkland, the SGA president, stopped the students from gathering their things with the announcement that she'd forgotten to distribute one student's flowers.

Lettie, like every other student, sat back down and waited to hear the last name called.

"Lettie Campbell. Twelve pink roses," Mindi proclaimed, her voice throwing an extra punch in the announcement.

A lower classman distributed the flowers, pale pink, wrapped in green tissue paper and tied with a red ribbon. The card wasn't signed, as most of the SGA-purchased flowers weren't, but it read, *I really do want to get to know you better.*

"Do you know who sent them?" Lettie asked Mindi after the assembly.

"Not a clue. It was a last-minute order, evidently, and no one seems to know who paid for them."

Then Bill made his way toward her and examined the flowers. "Any idea who sent them?"

"None at all," she answered.

"Maybe if you think about it, you'll figure it out," he said, grinning.

Lettie had seen his statement as coming from her best friend. Now she saw it as more.

"*You* sent those roses on Valentine's Day." It wasn't a question, but she wanted to hear him affirm the truth.

"I wanted to get to know you better," he said.

"But you knew me better than anyone," she countered. "I talked to you about everything."

Bill had sent those flowers?

"Why didn't you tell me?" she asked.

"I'd planned to on graduation night. But we never made it that far."

The spot below each ear pinched and burned, and tears spilled free. "I never considered—never dreamed—that it was you." She hadn't even tried to find out who sent the roses, hadn't wanted to know. A relationship at that point would have complicated her plans to leave, and she wouldn't stand for anything holding her back. But she also hadn't imagined those flowers were from Bill.

He pulled into a parking spot at an Italian restaurant, one she recognized due to its label as "Atlanta's Hottest." Then he shut off the car and turned in the seat. "Come here." He brought one hand behind her neck and slowly eased her toward him, then softly kissed her tears away. "I didn't mean to make you cry."

"If I had known before graduation night, we could have, well, we might have . . ."

He smiled, and the tender gesture slid over her skin like warm butter.

"So we'll make up for the time we lost." Then he grinned even brighter.

She wanted to point out how hard it would be to make up twelve years in a span of three days, since he thought she'd return to Tampa then, but she didn't want to ruin the moment.

Lifting her hand to his lips, he kissed her knuckles softly. She splayed her fingers as his thumb teased her palm. Then his tongue slowly probed the sensitive indention between each finger. The thrill of his thorough exploration pulsed through her with every flick, every lick.

By the time he finished, her panties were drenched,

the car temperature had risen at least ten degrees, and Lettie's personal thermostat was off the chart.

"I believe if we continue, we'll have a repeat performance of last night in the restaurant's parking lot, which, I believe, would be ample cause for arrest."

She laughed, kissed him softly. "You're right. Besides, I'm hungry."

"I could tell," he said, winking.

"For food, I mean."

"Right, that too."

They exited the car and he held an arm around her as they entered the restaurant. Then he announced their arrival to the maître d'. In minutes, they were seated, and Lettie couldn't imagine anything better than an elegant dinner with Bill Brannon by her side. She didn't think anything could dampen her spirits. And nothing did, until their meal had nearly ended, the last glass of wine had been served . . . and Bill reminded her of the charade.

"I talked to Erika today. Everything's going great. She says she's learning plenty from Integrated Solutions. Your company must do an awesome job with the training program."

Sucker punched. And she hadn't even seen it coming.

"You know, you still haven't told me what you're doing for them in Atlanta," he continued. "Seems like if they were going to offer a training session here, she could've taken that one, instead of going to Tampa. The company that hired her is here. You'd think they'd have trained her locally and saved the expense."

Lettie focused on what she'd learned about Erika's employment over the past week. Bill's niece actually had been hired as a computer operator at a reputable company in Atlanta, so My Alibi concocted a faux training organization to get her ready for the job. In fact, her new position wouldn't begin for another week. It had been a perfect setup for cheating, Lettie recalled.

She swallowed, gained her bearings. "I believe they wanted to provide a beach locale to make it more appealing to their new employees."

It would've been so easy to tell him the truth now, but she'd promised Amy she'd let Erika tell him personally.

He scanned the menu. "Makes sense, I guess, but I was still surprised they were willing to do it, since she's only there for the summer."

Erika hadn't covered that when she booked her alibi for the week. Why would any company splurge for training in Florida if she was only employed for the summer? And why wouldn't Bill question it more?

Simple. Because he trusted Lettie to tell the truth.

Her stomach pitched in a slow roll.

"Are you okay?" he asked, probably noticing how her face now resembled the hue of her dress.

"Rest room?" she mumbled.

He pointed toward a hallway in the rear of the restaurant, and Lettie made a beeline for the door.

An attendant waited inside with bottles of perfume, makeup fresheners, fragrant soaps and hand towels. Lettie waved her away and moved to a pedestal sink, splashed water on her face and groaned at the mascara making a jagged path down her cheeks.

"Man troubles?" the attendant asked, handing her a towel.

Lettie breathed in deeply, looked in the mirror and hiccuped. Loudly. Not very ladylike at all, particularly for a place like this, but the woman merely shook her head and reached for the palettes of makeup.

"Let me help you." She gently guided Lettie to a red velvet settee and patted at her damp face with a tissue.

"Men," the woman mumbled, taking a makeup wedge and applying a dab of foundation to the trails created by Lettie's tears. "Can't live with them—"

"Can't shoot 'em," Lettie completed, remembering Wanda Campbell's favorite saying.

The elderly woman grinned, pushing rosy cheeks toward her eyes. "I was going to say you can't live without them, but shooting works too, I suppose."

"Problem is, I don't want to shoot this one. I want to love him."

"Need to talk?" The woman moved to Lettie's eyes and started reapplying mascara.

"I lied to him. I'm still lying to him," Lettie said, and the completeness of her honesty stung.

The woman nodded knowingly and handed Lettie a small mirror to review the final product, which, in fact, looked really well-done.

"Does he love you?" the sweet lady questioned.

"I don't know." Lettie shook her head and shrugged, then tipped the woman generously.

She cupped Lettie's chin and brought her crinkled face close. "Sweetheart, if you wanna know, ask. Indeed, you'd be a fool not to. And tell him the truth."

"Tell him—"

"The truth. And don't hold back. Tell him the rest too."

"The rest?" Lettie asked.

"Don't you think if you're wondering about love, then he may be wondering too?"

Was he?

And if he was, then what?

$\mathscr{C}$HAPTER 14

Having influential friends had its advantages, as Bill learned tonight, when he located their seats at the Fox. His campaign advertising the theater's ongoing restoration project, promoting the Fox as the only theater in the nation with a full-time restoration department, purportedly boosted season ticket sales by 25 percent. As a thank-you, the project coordinator offered the best seats in the house, along with a private reception room, whenever Bill had the need for a special occasion.

Yesterday, he'd called Zack Power, the coordinator, and reserved both the tickets and the room for his first date with Lettie. Then he'd promptly called this morning to apologize for not showing, explaining he'd been with the woman of his dreams and they'd inadvertently lost track of time while becoming reacquainted.

Honesty ended up paying off, since Zack had a soft spot for romance. He didn't hesitate in offering the tickets and the room again tonight. This time, Bill would take full advantage of both and give Lettie a date she'd remember forever, hopefully as much as the hot-and-heated one they'd had last night.

But for different reasons.

Last night, he'd made sure she felt sexually desired and wanted—as if she'd ever have reason to doubt. Hell, Lettie never entered a room that all heads, male and female, didn't turn to watch.

But tonight's goal would be more difficult to accomplish, since tonight he wanted to make certain she felt cared for emotionally. He wanted to remind her that he was more than a man with whom she'd had hot-and-heated sex. He was also her friend.

So he'd shown up for this date equipped with every weapon in his arsenal for wooing Lettie Campbell. Pink roses, a fancy restaurant, a Broadway production and their own private haven, where they could celebrate at the end of the night. And during his carefully planned itinerary, they'd talk, hold hands and get to know each other again, without sex navigating the conversation.

If everything went as planned.

Unfortunately, something had happened at the restaurant that changed her mood, and Bill was clueless as to what. But whatever had caused her retreat, it had carried over throughout the performance. She'd been extremely quiet, and although she hadn't balked when he held her hand or draped an arm around her, she hadn't melted into him either.

"Did you enjoy the show?" he asked as the curtain went down the final time. He'd seen the performance before, the Broadway production of *Hairspray*, but he'd never seen it with Lettie. Bill suspected he could repeat plenty of things with her, and they would seem brand-new. More intriguing, unique, because of sharing the moment with the woman he adored.

"Yes," she answered, using no more words than necessary.

What had happened?

"She reminds me of you," he said, pointing to the character's photo on the front of his Playbill.

"Tracy?"

He nodded.

"You see me as overweight with big hair?" she asked, and thank goodness her teasing tone had returned. Finally.

Bill grinned. "No. But I do see you as standing out, and refusing to let your uniqueness stop you from getting what you want."

Lettie's slender neck pulsed as she swallowed. Her eyes widened, and the tiny golden rays pulsing from the pupils sparkled in a sea of forest green. "Bill?"

"Yeah."

"I want you."

Three words. Again. And, like every time before, just as potent.

He'd planned to try to keep his libido under control and woo her, at least until he took her home. But there was no way in hell he'd ever deny Lettie Campbell what she wanted. Particularly when what she wanted was him.

He reached forward and claimed her mouth.

Ignoring the people shifting around them and attempting to find passage out of the crowded theater, Bill kissed her as though they were the only two people in the room. And, thanks to his friend's generous offer, they would be soon.

Raising his mouth from hers, he grinned. "Come on," he said, taking her hand and leading her away from their seats.

Her smile broadened in approval. "There's nowhere for us to go." She indicated the congested crowd at each exit.

"Trust me."

She blinked, and her smile said everything he needed to know, but her words also packed a powerful punch. "I do."

Two words this time, but he hoped to hear her say them again. One day.

"Come on." He clasped her fingers with his and headed out a side door.

Zack had provided simple directions for finding their private room, and Bill had no trouble locating the Landmarks Lounge within the theater. When the project coordinator told him the name of the suite, Bill had wondered whether it'd be elegant enough to impress Lettie Campbell. Upon entering, Bill's uncertainties vanished.

"Where did you get that?" she asked, staring at the gold key Zack provided. Then she stepped inside, and her mouth fell open. "Wow."

Zack had described the Landmarks as providing "1929 movie-palace allure." Bill had to concur. It was elegant to the extreme, and everything he'd hoped for. He'd included an article about the lounge in his campaign, but even the pictures Zack had provided didn't do it justice.

Moroccan tiled floors and walls gleamed in the flick-ering light of pewter candles. Gold-leaf detailing sparkled from all walls and fixtures. Exquisite mosaics abounded in all directions. Tasteful floral arrangements, with tropical flowers in vibrant hues and tantalizing scents, were placed sporadically around the marbled tables and in the recessed walls. The furniture, consisting of stately love seats and chairs, had been covered in solid black velvet.

Bill closed the door and locked it behind him. Privacy provided. Elegance provided.

Standing frozen, she took it all in, her arms held slightly out at her sides, as though maintaining her balance. He couldn't recall ever seeing her hair pinned up before. He would've guessed it wasn't possible because of her trendy short cut, but she had her waves piled high, with wisps escaping here and there adding to the appeal.

The green dress balanced on the very edge of her shoulders, plunging in a dramatic V in the front and back, and showcased smooth, silky flesh. Her skirt was longer tonight, reaching below the knees. On a normal woman, a woman without an eternity of legs, it would've probably stopped above the ankles. But not on Lettie Campbell, whose legs went on for days.

The high heels, a perfect match to the hue of her dress, had sexy straps lacing her slim ankles. He'd been surprised to see she'd worn stockings tonight and wondered if they stopped at her thighs.

So much for wooing her.

He wanted her again. Wanted in her again. To feel her slick, wet heat engulf him, drive him to a maddening frenzy of sexual desire and fulfillment. Hell, how would he ever convince her he wanted more than sex when he could take his pulse with his dick?

As if reading his mind, she turned, her eyes a deeper green, heavy lidded and filled with desire. "Bill?"

"Yeah."

"You got this for me? For us?"

Now wasn't the time to get into particulars, such as, he didn't pay a thin dime for the privilege of the room. Besides, he *had* worked his ass off on the Fox campaign; so in a way, he'd paid for it, hadn't he? Damn, he was getting good at being bad.

"Yeah," he said, without so much as a flinch.

"And this?" Lettie asked, moving toward a chilled bottle of champagne and a tray of hors d'oeuvres. She turned and looked at him, and her eyes were even more ablaze, fiery with undiluted lust.

God, she thought he'd sprung for all of this. And hell, he couldn't tell her different.

"No," he said, crossing the room and placing both hands on her shoulders. The silky fabric tingled against his palms, as did her skin. From the moment he'd picked her up and noticed the sexy straps balancing provocatively, holding up that double V, he'd visualized exactly what he wanted to do with this dress.

Ready to bring that vision to life, he pushed the straps down to her elbows, trapping her arms at her side, while her breasts were completely bare. For him.

"It isn't for us, Lettie. It's for you. Everything here, me included, is all for you."

He cupped her breasts and palmed their fullness, then massaged the swells, pushed up by the bunched fabric. Lowering his mouth to a pebbled nipple, he sucked it thoroughly, while his thumb and forefinger rolled the other. Then he swapped sides and repeated the process while Lettie squirmed, her arms straining against the binding of her sleeves.

"I can't wait."

Another combination of three words that made his dick want to dance. Pump. Thrust.

He pushed on the sleeves, and her dress hit the floor in a soft *whoosh*. The air in his lungs left his body with the exact same sound.

"Damn." It was the only word that came to mind. He'd never seen anyone, anything, as erotic as the image before him. Lettie stood before him in emerald thong panties, a matching garter belt, thigh-high stockings and strappy heels. Nipples still excited from his touch protruded, evidently straining to have his lips on them again.

"I thought you'd like it," she said.

Bill didn't respond. Verbally. His cock responded aplenty.

"Do you? Like it?" she asked, a hint of nervousness, even shyness, in her tone.

Salivate. Yeah, that's what he needed to do right about now. His tongue lolled about his mouth until finding the ability to help form words. "I like it."

She reached up and removed a pin from her hair, then another, and another, dropping them to the floor, one by one. They *pinged* softly against the marble as her short blond waves toppled toward her face and neck. Then, after the last pin fell, she closed her eyes and ran her fingertips through her curls, massaging as she went, and pushing those delectable breasts out a little farther in the process. "Mmmm, that feels better."

It was more than he could take.

Her eyes fluttered open as he lifted her from the floor.

Bill wasn't certain how they crossed the room, but they had, with Lettie's long, lithe legs wrapped around his waist and her wet, hot center pressed against his groin.

He set her on the marble bar, then unfastened his pants. "You want me?" he asked, freeing his aching cock. In less time than he thought possible, he sheathed his length with a condom and pushed it against her wet center.

She spread her legs wide and arched into him. "I want you."

"Then you'll have me." He didn't take time to remove her panties. His need was beyond waiting and, from the hunger in her eyes, Lettie's was too. He shoved the damp fabric aside and plunged inside, pumping into her core while she convulsed around him, flexing and grabbing him with every stroke. He'd barely touched her clit when she began to shake and tremble, then screamed his name.

Bill pushed to the hilt, deep within her, while her slick walls engulfed him, consumed him, claimed him.

With her body still quivering from the aftershocks of multiple climaxes, Lettie turned the key in the lock and opened her apartment door. She hesitated before speaking and wondered whether the next move, one she'd been thinking about all night, would be the right one.

Should she ask him to spend the night before Erika returned? Before he learned the truth about her job?

Would he stick around once he knew she'd lied?

She bit her lip. God, she wanted to be honest with him. More than anything, she did. Well, almost more than anything. And therein was the problem. There was something she wanted more than being truthful to Bill Brannon.

She wanted Bill Brannon. With or without the truth. Any way she could have him. So much that her chest ached at the thought of losing him.

"Do you want to stay?" she whispered, timidly turning her head to view his response.

"You know I do."

Lettie smiled, pushed the door open and led him inside. It was past three A.M., so she should've been exhausted. She should have, but she wasn't. Her body was alive, exhilarated at having Bill for an entire night, in her apartment, in her bed.

"Are you thirsty?" she asked, feeling as though she should go through the motions of guest etiquette, before she stripped him to that glorious birthday suit and took him straight to bed.

"No."

"Hungry?" she asked.

"For food? No."

Downright devilish, the look he had now. And determined. As though he knew exactly what he was hungry for, and exactly how willing she was to supply.

Lettie scanned her apartment. Did any of the items appear too personal, too in sync with her tastes to seem as though this were Amy's place? Not really. Besides, she and her sister had similar preferences. And the photographs on display would be natural fixtures in either her place or her sister's.

Nothing should cue him in on their co-residence. When she told him the truth, she'd tell him about her living arrangements as well. God, she hoped he'd return after he heard the fact, instead of her never-ending reserve of fiction.

"Which room do you use when you're here?" he asked, nodding toward the bedroom doors on opposite sides of the living area.

"That one's mine," she said, pointing toward the left. "I even decorated it and keep a stash of clothing here. For whenever I visit." *Liar, liar, and yep, pants on fire.*

"I assume you visit often?"

Please change the subject to something that doesn't involve a bald-faced lie, Lettie silently pleaded.

"As often as the job sends me this way," she answered, which was a half-truth, right? She did come home from her job. To this address. Each day. Okay, that was pushing it, but she had no choice, or she'd lose him. Correction, *might* lose him. She didn't know for certain, and she sure wasn't chancing it.

Not tonight.

Besides, she'd promised Amy she would let Erika return and have a chance to smooth things over with Bill.

He drew her close, nuzzled her neck, then pushed one green strap past her shoulder. "Are you ready for bed, Lettie?"

A shiver shimmied down her spine. Unfortunately, it wasn't due to sexual desire; it was something different entirely. Fear. And it caught her so off-guard, she didn't have a chance to stop her mouth from echoing her mind's whispered warning.

"Is this only sex?" she blurted, then slapped a palm to her lips as though she could push the words back in. Then his hand stilled on her arm, and she knew she never could.

Breaking their connection, he stepped back, his jaw flexed and his mouth set in a straight, rigid line.

"Sorry," she whispered. And she was. Truly.

He took one hand to his forehead and massaged his temples, then ran his palm down his face, pausing for a moment when he reached his mouth. His chocolate eyes studied her and his head shook slightly.

An arrow of intense regret pierced her heart. She turned from those beautiful eyes, walked to the couch and plopped down, her skirt fanning around her like flower petals. She glanced at the rose-filled vase.

"It isn't the first time I've given you roses."

"I don't know what's wrong with me," she said. "I swear I don't. But I can't do it. It seemed wonderful, having a week of phenomenal sex with the most incredible guy in the world, but I don't think I'm cut out for it anymore. Or at least not with you. At the end of the week, it'll be time for me to go back, and it'll be over. I'm getting too attached, Bill. And when it ends, it'll kill me. In all honesty, the more I'm with you now, the more it'll hurt. I—I guess I'm wanting more than sex."

She expected him to remind her she'd known from the beginning what this was. A week of fun while she "visited" Atlanta. Old friends connecting again, and in the process, fulfilling their basic physical needs.

Nothing more, nothing less.

What she hadn't expected was Bill Brannon, crossing the room to kneel in front of her, taking her hands in his and saying the words she longed to hear.

"I want more too, Lettie. And I want it with you."

Her lips trembled, eyes watered. What exactly was he saying? "You're sure?"

"I know we have a lot to discuss. The distance factor, your job, my job, what we would be willing to do to make this thing work. But I'm willing to work on those things if you are. Tonight, I'd planned to try to show you, tell you, how special you still are to me. But I botched it by letting the date move back to sex again. Honestly, Lettie, I've wanted you for so long, cared about you for so long, I couldn't resist if I tried."

A warm tear trickled down her cheek. "I've wanted you too."

"Tomorrow, let's spend the entire night together, at my place. I'll cook, we'll talk, learn about each other again, beyond the way we can set sheets aflame."

She smiled, and the movement pushed a few more tears over the edge. "We haven't actually made it to any sheets yet," she reminded.

His laugh was low and easy. "Tell you what. Let's change that tonight."

Lettie tilted her head, wondering if he'd changed his mind about moving beyond sex.

"Not what you think," he clarified. "Let me sleep with you, hold you while you dream."

"Nothing more?" she asked, not completely certain that was what she wanted, but intrigued by the thought of spending an entire night merely sleeping in his arms.

"Unless you change your mind. Then, of course, I'm happy to oblige."

Bill watched the first golden rays of morning spill into Lettie's bedroom. The light moved along the sheets, emphasizing a long leg she'd uncovered during the night and playing with the highlights in her hair. He leaned up on an elbow and watched her sleep. She was beautiful, and she was his.

Finally.

She snuggled against him, creating a perfect fit. A perfect bond.

"I guess I'm wanting more than sex."

More than three words this time, but they'd packed a wallop. Hell, he'd nearly blown it. By trying to prove he could be more than a friend, he'd led her to conclude that he only wanted her body. And she had decided she needed more.

Thank God.

Tonight, he'd make every effort humanly possible to pay attention to her heart. Now that he knew that's what she wanted as well, he believed he could pull it off. And then, when she saw he was smitten by the whole package—the friend he'd known for years and the lover he was still getting to know—they could move forward. To more heated nights *and* more commitment.

Lettie twisted in the sheet, scooted against him and mumbled something incoherent.

His dick, in typical sleeping-next-to-a-naked-woman mode, translated her murmur as an invitation and pushed against her leg.

Fluttering her eyes open, she gave him a slow, sleepy smile. "I thought you said we were just going to sleep."

"I did, and I meant it."

Her leg moved against his hard cock. "Then what's this?"

He smiled, shrugged. "A wish?"

She laughed, snuggled closer and moved a hand between them to curl around his length. "Mighty big wish."

"Lettie," he said, warning. "I really want to prove it isn't just sex."

With a look of pure seduction, she pulled her hand to the end of his erection, swirled a finger around the tip. Then she brought it to her mouth and licked the moisture away. "I know, but . . ."

"But?" he asked, his voice tense under the strain of his need.

"But I really need to come." She stretched in the bed and the sheet skittered below her pink-tipped breasts. "I mean, I can take care of it myself, in the shower, but—"

"Not while I'm here, you won't." He rolled over, spotted the single pink rose with its surplus of soft petals. "Perfect," he said, withdrawing the flower from the vase. Then he leaned toward the floor and withdrew a handkerchief from his pants pocket.

"What are you doing?" she asked, her voice still sleep-sexy.

"I'm doing what any man worth his salt would do in this situation."

"Which is?" she asked, raising up on her elbows and staring at the items in his hands.

"I'm going to make you come."

"Just me? You're not going to?" she asked, looking extremely skeptical.

"No, I'm not. Until you see I want more than my own gratification from this relationship," he said, tying the handkerchief around her head, "I'm not going to indulge. But, you do realize, I don't expect it to take long for you to see my intentions are good."

She smiled and settled back on the pillow with the blindfold in place. "In other words, I shouldn't wait too long to figure it out."

"Hell, I hope not."

Her laugh teased his senses, made him smile and almost—almost—made him forget his straining dick. No doubt, the drive back home to get dressed for work would be hell. And his own morning shower would be frigid.

"I—"

Bill waited. One word, but he'd known where it was heading. She was nearly there, nearly ready to say what he longed to hear. But she'd stopped.

"Yes?" he asked.

"I . . . can't wait."

"Neither can I," he admitted, though what he waited for went well beyond the climax she was about to experience.

Well beyond.

Grabbing the top edge of the sheet, he slid it slowly down her body, making certain to touch every curve, every indention, every nuance making up the perfection of Lettie Campbell.

She shivered when it hit the floor and moved her hands to her stomach.

"Are you cold?" he asked.

"A little."

"Then I'll make sure to get you good and warm." He moved up the bed.

"I'm counting on it." Her hands fisted, then slowly opened again.

Bill watched them, practically shaking on her flat abdomen, and he knew what they longed to do. Placing the rose on the side of the bed, he took her hands in his and slid them upward, until her fingertips touched her nipples. "Go ahead."

She bit her lip. "I want *you* to touch me. I've always had to help things along. This time, I want it to be you. Just you."

He'd misread the signal, and he couldn't be more pleased. No one else had been able to get her there without her help?

Good to know. Because not only would he get her there on his own, but he wouldn't lay one finger on her until she climaxed. As long as Lettie's body was indeed as responsive as he believed. He'd felt her responsiveness, knew how strong her sensuality was. With the blindfold increasing her awareness of every touch, he had no doubt he'd get the job done.

And get it done right.

"Okay." Taking her wrists, he slid her hands away and placed them at her side. "Hold on to the sheet, and whatever you do, don't move your hands. I don't need your help to get you exactly where you need to be."

A slight smile played with her lips as she gripped the sheet in her fists.

Bill held the rose directly above her face, waited until he saw her inhale its sweet scent.

"I love roses," she whispered.

"I know." He lowered the soft petals to her forehead, eased them across the top of the blindfold.

She sucked air through her teeth as the flower crossed one cheek, skimmed the bridge of her nose, then moved to the other cheek. Bill twirled the stem as he passed over her mouth, letting each opened petal tease her lips.

"I'll do that again," he promised as her hands tightened their grip on the sheet. "But lower."

Nodding, Lettie licked her lips as the petals continued down her slender neck, then to one ear, teasing the sensitive shell before venturing to the other side to do the same.

Her breath came in short, urgent gasps, and her breasts urged upward with each inhalation.

Bill slid the rose to one breast, covering her areola completely with the full bloom. It was beautiful, the full breast, rising and falling beneath a cascade of pink petals.

He shifted on the bed and totally believed his dick was ready to explode on its own accord. Gritting his teeth, he battled his worthiest opponent and, amazingly, kept from climbing on top of her and letting his dominant extremity have its way.

"Bill?" she panted as the rose settled on the opposite breast.

"Yeah."

"Have. To. Come."

Not one to disobey a direct order, particularly when it came from Lettie, he trailed the petals down her quivering stomach, watching her abdomen dip inward as he passed.

"Spread your legs."

She moaned, an urgent sound from deep in her throat, and spread those perfect long limbs. Opened her delicate center like the petals currently caressing her thigh.

He inhaled the intimate scent of her essence, sweet and alluring.

"Please." She inched her legs even wider and tipped her hips in palpable invitation.

Bill brought the head of the rose to her wet opening, twirled the stem and watched the petals moisten.

Her fingers opened, then grabbed tighter to the sheet. "I'm—close."

He continued to twirl the petals, teasing her sensitive folds, then easing it toward her swollen pink bud. "Tell me what you feel."

She thrashed her head back and forth on the pillow, her blond waves tousling around the white handkerchief. "I can't."

Bill watched her try to hold back on her impending climax. She was fighting it, trying to make the moment last.

"Do you want me to tell you?" he asked, more than eager to help intensify the sensation by talking her through the culmination.

"Yes," she said, her hips pumping against the petals now, her core dripping, so very close to bursting free.

This would be the toughest thing he'd ever done, no doubt. Talking her through what would possibly be her strongest climax ever—without touching her physically. Without giving into his needs.

Sweat beaded on his brow, above his lip, but he swallowed through it. Taking a deep breath, he proceeded to drive the woman he loved—and he did love her—over the edge.

"You feel soft, velvet petals, dampened from your sweet juices, teasing your most intimate flesh," he said, taking the rose from her clit and sliding it along her labia. He put pressure on the stem when he reached her vulva, allowing the petals to graze inside; then he turned the stem.

She inhaled, then held her breath through the sweet invasion.

"Now the petals are teasing you, coming inside, but not nearly enough to reach that burning spot, the one you let me find, the one that sends your body soaring. You want to be touched there so badly, it hurts. And yet, the petals continue to twirl, teasing and edging you closer. Closer, but not nearly close enough."

She licked her lips, moved her head again from one side to the other.

"But there's another spot, isn't there, Lettie? One that will get you there. And one that's totally open, completely visible to me while I look at you. Every part of you. Beautiful and hot and wet. You are hot. And wet. Aren't you, Lettie?"

She nodded, capturing her lower lip with her teeth.

"Now you're waiting, because you know I won't let you down. And you feel the petals easing their way back to that spot, the one you know will take you where you want to go. The rose is there now, and you feel it. Every damp petal." He flicked the head of the flower over her clit, slowly, then quicker, then faster still. "It's pulling at your core—that mad, pulsing rush, that urge to set it free and let everything go. Spiraling from your most intimate center, pushing outward, screaming for release."

And as the rose petals continued to flick and twirl and tease, Lettie did exactly that. Her scream echoed through the room as her body convulsed and her release drenched the sheets.

CHAPTER 15

I thought that kind of thing only happened in romance novels or B-grade movies—" Cassie said, her eyes popping at Lettie's confession.

"Excuse me," Amy interrupted, "but any kind of morning orgasm qualifies as an A-plus movie in my book. I mean, really, Lettie? He got you off with a *flower*?"

Lettie was seriously rethinking her decision to invite Amy to join them for their daily lunch gossip. Particularly since her sister had more than her share of cheerleader spirit left over from high school, and her voice carried pretty dang far. But Amy had voluntarily manned Lettie's phones last night, and had willingly offered to return them at lunch. Now Lettie realized Amy wasn't here solely to return the phones. She wanted the scoop.

"Wait a minute," Lettie said. "Can you repeat that, please? I think someone at Turner Field actually didn't hear you."

Amy casually removed her jacket and hung it on the chair. Then she popped a chip in her mouth and grinned, thoroughly pleased with every customer's attention zeroed in on her sister. She gave a little one-arm shrug, and the tiny straps of her layered tank tops, one lime green and the other fuchsia, slipped off her shoulder. With a flick of a finger, she tugged them back in place.

Even in a black pantsuit, Amy still pulled off the sexual presence associated with a sex toy designer. "You should be proud, sis. Shouting from the rooftops, even. Heck, Jeff never pulled it off with his own equipment, did he? And Bill did it with a flower?" Marveling, she tossed two more chips. "Heck, I may have to come up with a petal-tipped vibrator."

"I'd buy it," Cass chimed in, almost before the words left Amy's mouth.

Lettie grinned.

"All right, tell us the rest, already," Cass urged.

"What rest?" Amy asked.

"Details, of course. She can't tell us he got her off with a flower and leave it at that."

Amy laughed. "I should have lunch with you guys more often." Then she eyed her sister. "Cassie's right. So spill."

Lettie took a deep breath and prepared to divulge, but the ringing in her purse halted her attempt. "Why do they always call during lunch?" she asked, withdrawing the leopard-spotted phone.

She glanced at the back of her newest client's cellular, then answered. "Villa at the Cove, this is Colette. Can I help you?" She listened to the woman's request. "Certainly. If you hold on, I'll be happy to check his room." She pressed the "mute" button, then looked at Amy and

Cass. "What kind of guy tells her he's going to a day spa for his alibi?"

"He chose it?" Cass asked.

"Yeah, he said she'd believe that. Guess he gets into pampering," Lettie said as Amy snickered.

Lettie pressed the "mute" button again. "I'm sorry, Ms. Lowell, but Mr. Silverstone isn't in his room right now. I'll be happy to take a message, or I can leave your name and number for him to return your call." She wrote the name and number on a notepad, then said good-bye to the woman, while Amy choked on a chip.

Cassie immediately started beating her on the back, then yanked one of Amy's thin arms straight up in the air, until Lettie was certain she'd pull the thing out of its socket.

"Take it easy there, Cass," Lettie warned. "That arm's connected, you know."

Amy's coughing subsided, and she wiped the resulting tears from her cheek. "You aren't supposed to hit me if I'm coughing," she said, glaring at Cass. "It's when someone is choked and *not* coughing that you hit them."

Cassie shrugged. "So maybe I just wanted to hit someone." She laughed, and Amy forced a grin.

"Are you okay?" Lettie asked. "Really?"

"Yeah," Amy said, reaching for her glass, then sipping her Coke until her eyes cleared. "Did you say Ms. Lowell? And Mr. Silverstone?"

Lettie nodded. "You know them?"

"Slay Silverstone? And Emerald Lowell?" Amy asked, patting her throat as she swallowed thickly.

"Yeah," Lettie said, raising her brows at Cassie. "Friends of yours?"

"Not necessarily friends, but they work for me."

"They work at Adventurous Accessories?" Lettie asked. "He didn't put his place of employment on the form."

"Product testers," Amy enlightened.

"Oooh, you don't say," Cassie said, leaning forward in her chair. A thick blond curl flipped toward her eye, and she quickly stuffed it behind her ear. "Exactly what products do they test?"

"Mostly mine," Amy said. "In particular, the vibrators."

Lettie's eyes bulged. "Wait a minute. Is he the one you were telling me about?"

"Yeah," Amy said, then giggled. "And I don't really know why he'd need an alibi for Emerald. They're very honest about the fact they merely enjoy sex. There's no commitment involved, or so they say."

"Well, from what he said when he hired me," Lettie informed, "there's no commitment on *his* side. However, the woman is fairly obsessed, so he wanted a break. He's not even really cheating on her, just staying at a hotel in town to have a little peace."

"Emerald? A stalker?" Amy said, then added, "You know, I could see that. Especially since she knows first-hand about his equipment."

"What about his equipment?" Cass asked, making a great deal of headway through her bag of chips. Her red-glossed lips worked double time, and she munched loudly while she waited.

"Let me tell her," Lettie urged, eager to see Cassie's reaction to this.

Amy laughed out loud. "Go ahead."

"He's not just a tester," Lettie said, grinning broadly. "He's a model."

This time, Cassie choked, but quickly regained composure by beating her ample chest, barely contained by a skimpy leopard-print tank. "I know. I shouldn't have hit myself, but it worked." She quickly popped another chip. "He's a model?"

"Oh yeah, for their *biggest* seller," Lettie said.

"Really?" Cassie asked, her eyes growing even wider.

Amy nodded. "Afraid so, but that isn't the most interesting part."

"Go ahead," Lettie said, not wanting to steal all of Amy's fun. "You can tell her the rest."

"Well?" Cassie urged. She wiggled pink-tipped fingers in a gimme-gimme gesture.

Amy leaned forward and lowered her voice to a whisper. "One of our newer products had to be altered, because when he really heated it up, it melted."

Cassie grabbed Lettie's purse, dug inside, then withdrew the animal-print phone. "Look, the phone matches my outfit; it was meant to be." She looked pointedly at Lettie. "Sorry, girl, but he's mine. You've got your man already, and I could use a little . . . What was his name again?" she glanced at the back of the phone—"Some Slay Silverstone in my life."

Lettie grinned. "Fine. But you're taking more than your share of clients this week. You sure you want another?"

"Hello, woman," Cassie said, pulling the phone into her cleavage. "This is a man with a model penis and a hot cock, to boot. I not only want him. I need him."

All three cackled with laughter as Cassie continued

clutching the spotted phone against her heart. "Come on, Slay baby, call me."

"Actually, you need to call him and give him the message, don't you?" Lettie asked.

"Ooh, I suppose I do. And if you two don't mind, I think I'll do this one in private." She took the phone, left the table and hurried outside, her spiked heels clicking madly on the tile floor.

"Okay. Tell me about everything with Bill," Amy said.

"Not without Cassie. She'll make me repeat it, anyway."

"All right, then while we're waiting, maybe I should tell you about Landon."

"Landon? As in, the cowboy who drives you crazy at work?" Lettie asked, a little surprised. She'd detected Amy's infatuation, even if her sister hadn't admitted the fact.

"Yeah," Amy said, her green eyes glittering. "And the one who plans to drive me crazy this weekend."

"What happened to the toys-are-good-enough thing you had going?"

Amy shrugged. "Beats the heck out of me, but right now, the main toy I want to play with wears a Stetson and Ropers."

Lettie grabbed Amy's hand and squeezed. "Tell. Me. Now."

"There's not a whole lot to tell yet," Amy admitted. "I mean, two nights ago, I went to Cowboys with Brenda and ran into Landon. We ended up in a heated dance lesson—"

"You took a dance lesson?" Lettie asked, knowing

Amy was a natural on the dance floor, particularly when it involved country line dancing.

"He wanted me to teach him to boot scoot, but that was after we had a cherry-stem-tying contest."

Lettie slapped a hand to her mouth, then slid it to her neck. "You're pretty good with a cherry stem."

"He's better," Amy said, practically beaming.

"Is he now?" Lettie couldn't contain her smirk. Had Amy finally met a guy who could make her reconsider her "don't need a man" theory?

"He won."

"Which means he won—what exactly?" Lettie asked.

"A dance and a date," Amy said, grabbing the macadamia nut cookie she'd purchased and taking a big bite, in spite of the fact she hadn't started her sandwich.

"So you danced that night," Lettie supplied.

"Oh yeah, and then we heated up my office the next day."

"Really? Care to explain?" Lettie couldn't remember the last time Amy had looked so intrigued. It was a good look on her sister.

"Nope," Amy said, munching and grinning.

"Nothing?" Lettie asked, in a mock pout. "For someone who wants to hear about what happened with Bill, you sure don't act like it."

"Oh, okay," Amy conceded. "Well, let's see. I guess it'd be safe to say I now know that everything really is bigger in Texas."

Lettie slapped her hand on the table and ignored the resulting sting in her palm. "You know?"

Amy leaned forward, dropping her voice to a light whisper. "I felt it up close and personal yesterday, through a barrier of clothing. But this weekend, I could verify the assumption."

"Will wonders ever cease? Amy Campbell, the girl who swore she'd never need a man, actually wants one."

"Trust me, I'm still adjusting to it too."

Lettie laughed. "Did you see him last night? You went to Cowboys with Brenda again, didn't you?"

"We went back, but he didn't show."

"Disappointed?" Lettie asked.

"Not really. I'm thinking it'd be nice for our next bit of time together to occur somewhere other than a bar."

"Any idea where he's taking you?"

"He said dinner and a movie."

"And sex?" Lettie added.

"He didn't say, but I'm sure counting on it."

Lettie scooted her chair toward her sister's and leaned toward her ear. "It's been awhile, hasn't it? I mean, have you been with anyone since Cam?"

Cameron Brown had been Amy's only high-school fling, or at least the only one Lettie knew of. And although Amy had never provided a lot of detail about the relationship, Lettie had gathered the boy worked hard to get what he wanted, then promptly dropped her cold.

"I haven't been with anyone else. Ever," Amy confirmed. "And truthfully, I hadn't planned to. But Landon makes me want to rethink that decision."

"Good for you," Lettie said, and she meant it. Amy deserved to have fun with something that didn't require batteries. A bona fide cowboy was probably just the ticket to show her what she'd been missing.

"All right," Cass said, returning to the table. "Slay

was glad we handled his female problem so eloquently. He really has a wonderful personality, doesn't he?"

"As if that's why you talked to him so long," Lettie accused.

"Can I help it if I want to meet the guy who melts vibrators?"

"Are you going to? Meet him?" Amy asked.

Cass grinned. "Well, I didn't ask him out. Yet. We're still getting to know each other."

"But you're going to?" Lettie asked, somewhat surprised at Cassie's forwardness. True, she'd always been one to take the bull by the horns, but she'd never gone after a client.

"No," Cassie answered. "However, if I handle this right, he's gonna hit on me." She broke off part of Amy's cookie and tossed it in her mouth. "And if I'm lucky, that hit'll be a grand slam with a big bat."

"You're something else, Cass," Amy said, shaking her head, then turned her attention back to her sister. "Okay, Lettie. Now tell us about the rest of your time with Bill."

"Yeah," Cassie added, snapping her fingers. "Tell."

"We didn't exactly start the date with a rose orgasm," Lettie admitted.

"Damn, it's even got a name," Cass said, smirking while she chewed. "Then how do you start a date that ends with a flower petal screamer?"

"Lord, sis, I never thought I'd see you this—"

"This what?" Lettie asked.

"Satisfied," Amy said.

Oh yeah. She'd been satisfied, all right. Even more because Bill hadn't. He'd tended her every need, completely, giving her body more pleasure than she'd ever

known without intercourse, yet never allowing himself
the same fulfillment. Because he'd wanted to show her
she meant more to him than his own gratification. And
proving to her that he was still the selfless, considerate
friend she'd known for years. Bill gave her a glimpse of
the kind of man she could give herself to, completely, for
life. A friend and lover, and a man she could trust with
her body and her heart.

"Are you gonna tell us, or do we have to swipe your
lunch?" Amy asked, plucking her fork through a tomato
garnish on her sister's plate, then adding it to her chicken
salad sandwich. "You went out to eat, then to the Fox,
right?"

"Yeah." The word escaped on a dreamy breath.

"And then?" Cass nudged.

"He had the best seats in the house and one of the private reception rooms reserved for after the show." Lettie's smile burst free, taking complete control of her
face.

"You did it in the Fox?" Amy asked loudly. Very.
Loudly. And once again, she drew every customer's attention with her animated tone.

Lettie cleared her throat, blushing at her own excitement. "Amazing, Amy, how you can take something totally romantic and make it sound completely trashy." But
she grinned, and her younger sister grinned right back.
Who'd have thought the two Campbell girls would find
two men that made their hearts flutter, in the same week?

"Nope. I'm not going to feel sorry for you today, Lettie. Nice try, though. I give you an A for effort. But anyone who starts her day with a rose between her legs isn't
going to get an ounce of sympathy from me," Amy said.

Cass choked on her sandwich, waving pink nails fiercely in front of her face as she fought to regain control. Finally, she lifted her glass and sipped her tea. "Okay, you two. You've got to warn me before you start this sisterly banter, especially when it's orgasm humor. I can't remember the last time I got choked, and now it's happened twice in one meal. Lord help me, I've gotta stop hanging with you two."

An elderly woman at the next table shifted in her chair, while the white-haired gentleman across from her grinned like a thief.

"Anyway," Lettie continued, "he had a private room reserved and we"—she cleared her throat again—"took advantage."

"I'll say you did," Amy agreed. "How many times did you, you know, hit maximum advantage?"

"More than I could count."

"Damn." Cass shook her head, sending fat blond curls bobbing, but continued eating. "Then again, I bet I could hit maximum advantage a few times with Slay, if the rest of him matches his voice. Talk about sexy." She looked at Amy. "It does, doesn't it? I mean, the guy is incredible, isn't he?"

Amy nodded and giggled. "Right off a *Playgirl* cover, Cass. But I want to hear the rest of this. Okay, Lettie, then what?"

"Then he brought me home."

"And you asked him to stay," Cass completed.

"Yeah, but—"

"But what?" Amy put her sandwich back on the plate and pushed it forward, obviously letting Lettie know she had her undivided attention. She didn't plan to miss a single word describing what came next.

"I stopped him."

"Get out!" Cass exclaimed. "Why on earth would you do that?"

Lettie lowered her voice to a whisper, trying to keep from embarrassing the couple at the next table, and herself, any more than Amy had already managed. "I told him I didn't want just sex."

"No friggin' way," Cass said, and unlike Amy, she continued plowing through her sandwich. She took a big bite and swallowed, partially. "What'd he say?"

"He said he didn't either."

Amy's face split in a cheek-to-cheek grin. "Told ya."

"He said he wants more. With me. The friendship—"

"And the sex," Amy completed.

"Get. Out," Cass said between bites.

"Really," Lettie said.

"And then you had great sex, woke up in the morning and got a dose of rose petal," Cass concluded.

Lettie ran a finger down the side of her glass. "Not exactly."

"Okay, then what happened?" Amy asked, clasping her hands beneath her chin like a little girl listening to the teacher at story time. "Tell us."

"Then he said he wanted to prove he wanted more. Actually, he asked if I would spend tonight with him at his place."

At Cassie's uplifted brow, Lettie added, "Not for sex, but for quality time together. A get-to-know-each-other night."

"How did *that* progress to a rose between your thighs this morning?" Cassie asked.

"He wanted to sleep with me. *Sleep*. Said he wanted to hold me while I dreamed."

Cassie sighed.

Amy sighed.

And the woman at the next table . . . sighed.

The elderly fellow with her, however, yelled for his check.

Lettie, Cassie and Amy held their giggles best they could as the man ushered his wife out of the deli, presumably so they could go home and take advantage of that sigh.

After they'd gone, Cassie turned her attention back to the subject at hand. "All right. How'd you get to the flower?"

"When we woke up and he was pressed against me," Lettie started.

"Naked, of course," Cassie supplied.

"Yeah. I told him I needed . . ."

"What?" Cass asked.

But Amy cackled with delight and clapped her hands together. "You told him about your morning ritual, didn't you?"

"I don't do it every morning," Lettie proclaimed, but Amy simply shook her head. Heck, she'd never been embarrassed about anything sexually, but something about discussing her need for an orgasm to start her day—while at the tiny lunch diner—made her ill at ease.

"Put it this way, you know how most people need their cup of coffee?" Amy asked, and Cass nodded. "Well, when she bought the apartment, she brought her very own showerhead, and she utilizes its pulsating action every morning." She redirected her gaze to Lettie. "Okay, you told him you needed your fix for the day, right?"

"Yeah," Lettie said as her cheeks blazed and her companions grinned. "But he didn't want me taking care of things myself, *and* he'd promised we wouldn't have sex."

"So he got you off with a rose. Gotta give the guy major points for resourcefulness," Cass said, pulling her lips into one of those half-smile, half-frown things, while Amy snorted.

"Lettie, did you tell him about your job yet?" Cassie asked. "Is that why I haven't heard from him today? Or Erika, for that matter. Does he know you live in Atlanta?"

Cassie had a knack for finding the hole in things. This time, unfortunately, proved no exception.

"She's going to tell him as soon as Erika gets back," Amy said. "Right, Lettie?"

"Yeah." Lettie chewed her lower lip. "I told you I'd let her explain first, and I will. But—"

"But what?" Amy asked.

"I've lied to him, and not a little lie either. What if he can't forgive me? I've never lied to Bill before. Matter of fact, he was the only guy in Sheldon that I could always talk to, always tell the truth. We were so close then, and we still are, even more now that we've taken things to the next level." She frowned. "I'm afraid that because of our friendship, the lie will hurt even more."

"He said he wants more than sex with you, right?"

Cass asked. "He's wanting a relationship, and no relationship is perfect, Lettie."

Lettie nodded, but a frisson of nervousness made her shiver. Then a shrill ring echoed from her purse.

Glad to have a diversion from her thoughts of lying to Bill, she picked up the red phone. "The Palisades, this is Colette. Can I help you?"

"Colette, this is Ellen Southersby."

"Hello, Mrs. Southersby. Your son called this morning, and I left the message on your voice mail in the room. Did you get it?"

"Yes, dear, and I returned his call. Thank you for letting me know."

"No problem. That's part of my job. Is there anything else you needed?"

"Actually, there is," Ellen said.

"All right. What can I help you with?" Lettie asked.

"It's more what your sister can help me with, dear. You wouldn't by chance be planning to see her today, would you?"

"Amy?" Lettie asked, casting a curious gaze toward the brunette at her table, who had taken a sudden interest in her sandwich.

"Yes, dear. I need to ask her some questions about the products she sent. Would you be able to give me her number, or would you ask her to call me whenever it's convenient?"

"Products?" Lettie questioned, while Amy looked out the window and started whistling a Brooks & Dunn tune.

"Yes, dear. I'm quite intrigued with them, but I wasn't quite sure whether to use the Passion Parties Revelation or the Romanta Therapy Sensual Warming lubricant with the Super Deluxe Smitten. Would you happen to know?"

Lettie's face burned. "No, I'm afraid I'm not sure which lubricant you use with that, but Amy's right here. I'll let you ask her."

"Oh, good dear, because I'm also not sure what size batteries to put in the Pulsing Orbiter."

"I'm sure Amy can help you with that, Mrs. Southersby. Hold on." She extended the phone to her sister, then whispered, "I can't believe you did this."

Unfazed, Amy whispered right back, "They'll love it." Then she grabbed the phone as Cass did a poor job of disguising her laughter.

"This isn't funny," Lettie said. "She's wanting to use them as product testers."

"Sounds like a good plan to me," Cassie said, while Amy described batteries, lubricants and O-time.

"O-time?" Cassie asked Lettie.

"Evidently, she keeps a chart of which products produce the longest-lasting orgasms."

"How much does she charge for that chart? And the products? What do they usually run?"

Lettie shook her head in disbelief. "I'm sure she'll be happy to tell you."

"Good. By the way, what's a Smitten?"

"It's a rubbery kind of glove thing that massages all over, but it has little nubs on it," Lettie explained, then modified, "Actually, it has little nubs on one side, and longer nubs on the other."

"Sounds like you could've described Amy's products for them," Cassie said, grinning.

"Only the ones for singles," Lettie mumbled. "But hopefully, that'll change soon."

"I'll say." Cassie took another bite of pickle as Amy continued answering the older lady's questions. "So, have you ever, you know, used Slay's product?"

"No," Lettie answered quickly.

"Why not?"

"Do you want me to be honest?" Lettie asked.

"Of course."

"Fine. It's because the darn thing is too big. I mean, that's gotta hurt."

"Oh Lord, I hope he calls back." Cassie picked up the leopard phone and ran a pink nail down its length as Amy finally disconnected. And had the nerve to smile.

"Everything going well at Love Beach?" Lettie asked, sending an accusing stare at her sis.

"All right. I confess. I'm guilty, but she really did want to try the products." She handed the phone back to Lettie.

"And have they tried them out?" Cassie asked.

"Some of them, but they're saving the best ones for tonight."

"Should I let you man their phone again tonight?" Lettie asked.

"Probably so, in case they need any questions answered regarding technique."

"Right," Lettie said, trying not to smile, but failing miserably. "Well, here. And next time, before you start pawning your products off on my clients, ask."

"Got it," Amy said, placing the phone beside her tray on the table. Then she turned her attention toward another shrill ring, this time coming from Cassie's purse.

Lettie looked at Amy, then Cassie.

Cassie swallowed her last bite and glared at her purse. "Probably not important."

Lettie lifted the purse, blazoned with a glittery photo of Elvis, and peered inside, where the fluorescent blue face on the silver phone gleamed. Her throat closed in, chest constricted.

This was not happening.

But even as her brain argued the reality, she lifted the phone and handed it to her friend. "Answer it."

Cass nodded, shooting a wary look at Amy as she clicked the "talk" button. "Integrated Solutions."

Lettie held her breath, lifted her water glass and guided it shakily to her lips. More lies to Bill.

"Yes, Mr. Brannon," Cass said, dropping her eyes to the table, "I'll give Ms. Collins the message and ask her to return your call."

She bit her lower lip. "Yes, I know Colette."

Amy shrugged, while Lettie placed her glass back on the table with a bit too much gusto, causing the water to slosh over the side. What was Bill asking?

"Yes, she is in Atlanta this week," Cassie said, lifting her palm toward Lettie in a calm-down-I'm-taking-care-of-things motion.

Nevertheless, Lettie's heartbeat tripled instantly. Was he going to find out the truth now? This soon? She swallowed hard, closed her eyes, and saw pink rose petals scattered in the wind, floating away, while she reached frantically to capture just one. And came up empty handed.

"Integrated Solutions doesn't have a phone number listed for Atlanta. We work directly with our clients there, so Colette would be reachable at the client's number. Hold on, let me see if I have that number handy."

The rose petals swirled together like a mini tornado, bolting away from Lettie at breakneck speed. Her eyes popped open. This was *not* happening.

But Cassie continued speaking calmly, without a care in the world that Lettie's perfect week with Bill appeared to be ending right here and now.

"I'm afraid I can't find the number to the business at this moment," Cassie continued. "I'm sorry. We aren't allowed to give out the cell numbers of our employees; however, if you have her email address, you can reach her that way." She paused, smiled, then added, "I'm sure she'll get right back to you then. She's probably in a meeting with our client."

Amy placed her hand on top of Lettie's, which was grasping the edge of the table in a white-knuckled grip. "She's taking care of it," Amy whispered.

Then Cassie snapped the phone closed, smiled triumphantly, and echoed, "I took care of it."

"What did he say?" Lettie asked.

"He simply wanted to know if I could tell him how he could get in touch with Colette Campbell, so I told him how. No big deal. Oh, he's already sent you two emails, by the way, so you might want to get back to the office and check your Integrated Solutions email addy. Sounds important."

"Cassie, I owe you," Lettie said, standing from the table.

"Hey, get your sister here to hook me up with the hottie that melts the vibrators, and we'll call it even."

$\mathscr{C}$HAPTER 16

Lettie stepped off the MARTA train and scanned the busy station, particularly the big concrete pillar where Bill had been leaning so casually two days ago. But the man who sent her pulse into overdrive was nowhere to be seen.

She opened her pink clutch purse and withdrew the printout of his email, scanned the text.

Let's spend some time together. Will 3:00 work for you? If you can get away from work this afternoon, meet me here.

An address followed, and Lettie had immediately recognized that it was on the same street as his office and Jitters. But the last line of his email made her think she wouldn't be visiting his office, or sharing a cup of coffee.

P.S. I hope you're dressed comfortably.

Grinning, she tucked the paper back in her clutch, then glanced down at her outfit. She'd dressed for work after he left this morning, so Bill had no idea just how comfortably she had dressed. Or how sexy. Or how pink.

The shiny pink slip dress wasn't her typical attire for My Alibi, but she'd felt overly sensual after the orgasm this morning and had wanted to wear something indicative of the way her day had started. Something to remind her of Bill. Although the dress was ultra-comfortable, she was fairly certain this wasn't the type of "comfortable" he'd implied.

Lettie smiled. There weren't too many things she couldn't do in a dress, even one as sexy as this. Although the black and pink pumps could prove an obstacle. She sighed. So, she'd take them off. No problem. Nothing was going to stop her from having fun with Bill.

A frisson of anxious anticipation skittered through her as she walked down the busy street toward the address on the paper. She couldn't wait to see him, and was thrilled that she wouldn't have to wait until tonight.

Her heels clicked rhythmically against the sidewalk as she passed Jitters, then continued beyond his office. Lettie remembered walking this same path with Bill two days ago, then she laughed.

The rec center. That's where he was taking her! Undoubtedly, Bill had decided the two of them could use a little play in their day. What did he have in mind? As if she didn't know. The memory of those big black ropes arcing through the air sent another shiver through her flesh.

What fun!

She continued happily down the street and anticipated finding Bill beside Regina and the other little girls at the recreation center. True, it'd been quite a while since she'd jumped double-Dutch, and she'd never jumped in a dress before, but Lettie had no doubt she could pull it off.

Excited, she checked the numbers on the next building and was shocked to see she had passed the address Bill had provided. Disappointment flickered through her. The recreation center was another block away.

She turned around and swallowed past the regret. So they weren't playing with a bunch of kids this afternoon. She'd still be with Bill, and that's what she really wanted. Sighing, she backtracked, until she located the correct address.

A shoe store?

Thinking she'd misread the numbers, she withdrew the paper once more and double-checked. This was definitely the address. She opened the door, and a blast of frigid air made her gasp. But the heat in the dark eyes waiting inside warmed her to her core.

"I was beginning to think you weren't coming," Bill said, standing beside a big display of Keds.

"You didn't get my email saying I'd be here?" she asked, moving toward him and trying her best to act mature and civilized, when all she wanted to do was jump in his arms and kiss those gorgeous lips.

He smiled, and Lettie gave up the act. She laughed, hurried toward him and hugged him. He'd foregone a jacket, and his starched shirt emphasized the muscled man beneath. Lettie turned her head toward his neck, nuzzled him playfully, then fingered his tie. "I haven't been able to stop thinking about this morning," she admitted.

Bill kissed her softly, then indicated the pink dress. "I gathered that from the outfit."

Leave it to Bill to remember Lettie's clothing choices typically matched her mood. "You like the dress?" she asked, stepping back to offer him a better view.

"Oh yeah," he admitted. "And while it may not be the most appropriate clothing for what I have in mind, it will definitely make things interesting." His eyes all but smoldered.

"What do you have in mind?" she asked, eyeing the large shoe display.

"I'll show you. But first, I need to know your shoe size. Six?" He held up a pair of white tennis shoes.

She grinned. "Seven."

"I was close," he said, turning toward the cashier. "We'll take a pair of these in a seven."

"Yes," Lettie said, moving beside him while he paid for the shoes, "You were close."

They left the store and started down the street. "Do you know where we're going?" he asked.

"I have an idea."

"You up for a little double Dutch, Lettie?"

"I can hardly wait."

Within ten minutes, they entered the rec center playground and found the chanting group of girls in the same shady spot as they'd been two days ago.

"Hey, Mr. Brannon," Regina called, running over to greet them. She wore a pink and yellow shorts set, and her braids were christened with matching pink and yellow beads. Smiling broadly at Bill, she winked, then turned her attention to Lettie. "Mr. Brannon told us you were coming to jump today."

Lettie cast an accusing eye at the gorgeous, grinning man. "Pretty sure of yourself, aren't ya?"

He noted her pink dress and gave her a heated look that immediately brought thoughts of this morning's orgasm to mind. "Let's just say I didn't think you'd turn me down."

Lettie was suddenly very aware of her nipples pressing against her lacy bra. "I guess you were right," she said, barely controlling the desire in her tone. They were standing in the middle of a playground, after all.

"I guess I was."

"You are jumping then, right?" Regina asked, thankfully clueless to the sexual tension zinging between the two adults.

"Yes," Lettie said, taking her attention from Bill to the adorable girl. "I'll jump."

"Then come on," Regina said, grabbing Lettie's hand and tugging her across the yard. "She's jumping!" Regina yelled to her friends, who all applauded, while Lettie sat on a bench and swapped shoes.

Bill had never seen a whole lot of appeal in the look many Atlanta businesswomen adorned while heading to and from the office. Tennis shoes just didn't fit with the power suits, in his opinion. However, he reasoned that wearing those high heels while pounding the concrete would be a burden most women wouldn't want to bear, so he understood why they donned tennis shoes during the lengthy treks to work, then slipped into their business shoes upon arrival.

But looking at Lettie, her sexy little pink dress clinging to her curves and the cute white Keds on her feet, Bill changed his tune. He really liked this look.

"Well," she said, standing from the bench and striking a pose, "What do you think of my outfit?"

He raised his brows and nodded in approval. "No complaints here."

She giggled, then moved toward the girls, who already had two big black ropes circling through the air. "Okay, here I come!" she yelled, then bounded between the loops and started jumping.

The girls surrounding the ropes cheered wildly as Lettie quickly started the fancy footwork she'd learned at Sheldon so many years ago. Bill laughed. He may have taught her the basics of double Dutch behind that stage curtain, but Lettie had perfected her technique aplenty since that first time.

Evidently, she still remembered the most popular chants for the activity too. While her Keds punched the asphalt, she squealed, "Hey, do you know this one?" Then she continued, "Apple sticks—make me sick— make my heart beat two-forty-six . . ."

Bill sat on the bench and watched, mesmerized by the girl he'd adored so many years ago merged with the woman who was currently taking his breath away, and making his own heart beat two-forty-six. Her blond curls bounced madly and her smile was absolutely contagious, as he could attest by all of the grins on the little girls' faces. And on his own.

Then Lettie, her feet still moving to the beat, stopped chanting with the tiny group and looked at Bill. Her body may have been bouncing madly, but her eyes were locked on his and holding him captive. The look she gave him was one of sincere gratitude. Was she thankful he'd brought her here? Yeah, she was. And more. He swallowed. Obviously, he'd done more for Lettie today than he'd realized, until now. She'd broken free of that settled professional persona and had worn the sassy pink dress that was currently moving up and down on her thighs and providing sporadic glimpses of white lace underneath. And she'd broken free of being the controlled adult and let the fun-loving girl of the past enjoy a spontaneous game of double-Dutch.

She'd opened up today, for him.

As if knowing his thoughts, she mouthed a silent "thank you" mid-jump.

Bill grinned, tipped his head in acknowledgment, then turned toward a shrill ringing echoing from her pink purse.

The ropes tangled as Lettie darted toward the noise. "I'll get it!" she said, her eyes wide with panic.

Bill sighed. At least he gave her a few moments away from work commitments. Undoubtedly, this was her client on the line, and she'd have to return to work. "Here," he said, handing her the purse.

Still panting from her jump, Lettie reached for the pink bag. Her fingertips touched his hand, lingered there for a moment before sliding the purse away. She visibly swallowed. "I really enjoyed this," she whispered, her eyes glistening as though she were on the verge of tears.

"I did too," he said, while the ringing continued. "I guess you need to get that."

"I guess I do."

CHAPTER 17

LBROOKS: Can't wait till weekend. Want to go out before that?

*A*my looked at the flashing interoffice message on her computer monitor. She'd rarely seen a use for the chat feature Vernon had wanted for his employees. Now, however, her opinion changed. Landon couldn't wait until the weekend?

She grinned. Last night, she'd been thinking the same thing when she'd headed to Cowboys again, hoping to see the good-looking Texan on the dance floor. When it hadn't happened, she'd been more disappointed than she cared to admit. Then today, she'd gone through all the motions at work, ventured to other departments, had her meetings and had silently prayed for some sort of interaction with Landon Brooks in the process.

It hadn't happened.

And again, she'd been disappointed.

Had he felt the same thing? This odd sensation in the pit of your stomach like you wanted something to happen—couldn't wait for it to happen—but had to wait, anyway.

She read the screen again: *Can't wait till weekend.*

ACAMPBELL: When?
LBROOKS: Now.

She looked down at her black pantsuit and colorful tanks beneath. If she'd known he wanted to go out, she'd have definitely brought a change of clothes.

ACAMPBELL: After work?
LBROOKS: No. Now. Vernon is always telling us to take an afternoon or two for research. Let's research.

Amy laughed out loud. Lord, he was one feisty cowboy. And he was right. Their boss did encourage project leads to research. In fact, Vernon Miller told them in no uncertain terms that they were to go out and investigate the intricacies of physical interaction between couples.

Which was exactly what she and Landon planned to do.

ACAMPBELL: Where do you want to go?
LBROOKS: It's a surprise. Are you ready?
ACAMPBELL: As ready as I'll ever be.
LBROOKS: On my way.

And within five minutes, the tall Texan she'd thought about nonstop all day stood in her office wearing his black Stetson, black shirt, black jeans and, naturally, black Ropers. He looked every bit the dark and brooding, rough and ready, willing and able, cowboy.

"You wore that to work?" she asked, not used to seeing him in anything but business clothes at the office.

"Let's just say I'd hoped you would say yes."

"Am I dressed okay?" She indicated the suit. It wasn't overly fancy, but it didn't fit the casual but sexy look he had going. "Because we could go by my place, and I could change, if you want."

"No time," he said. "I don't want to miss a minute. And I've got it covered."

"Have you got reservations somewhere?" she asked, her curiosity spiking.

"Not exactly." He crossed her office and kissed her softly, while Amy's heart beat out a jittery, happy tune. Then he took her hand. "You ready?"

"I guess so. What do you mean you've got it covered?"

"Trust me," he said, leading her out.

"I am. Haven't you noticed?" she asked as they moved down the hall.

"Yeah, and I like it. I have a question, though." He opened the side door of Adventurous Accessories and led her toward his truck, a big black Dodge Ram Dually. It suited him, particularly while he wore his cowboy duds and looked like he was ready to take on the toughest bull—or anxious female.

"What's the question?" she asked, staring up at the intimidating truck.

"Have you ever changed clothes in a vehicle?" he asked, opening her door, while Amy wondered how the heck to climb in.

"I've changed in the car before. Why?"

"Because I bought you something to wear." Then, to Amy's amazement, he lifted her from the ground and slid her up his body until her behind hit the seat.

She tingled . . . everywhere.

"You bought me something?" Amy liked surprises. From everything Landon had said and done so far, she was finding out this cowboy was full of them. Turning, she saw a green tank and black shorts folded on the backseat.

Landon climbed in on his side. "It'll be more comfortable, considering where we're going."

"You're in jeans," she pointed out.

He shrugged, grinning. "Jeans will work for me."

"They won't work for me?"

"Okay. I confess. I've been thinking about seeing those long legs uncovered for quite a while."

She looked down at her black heels. "But my shoes . . ."

"Sandals, size six." He nodded his Stetson toward the backseat. "They're under the shorts."

"How'd you know my sizes?" Amy asked, reaching through the open console area to check the tags.

"Your sister."

"Lettie?" she asked, once again surprised. "How did you get her number?"

"It wasn't that difficult. You have her info listed as backup contact in the executive roster. I called her a couple of hours ago. I'm afraid I may have interrupted something at her work. She seemed very uncomfortable when she answered the phone, but when I told her who I was and what I wanted, she didn't seem to mind helping."

Amy laughed. "I'm sure she didn't. Then I'm supposed to climb back there and change, right?"

"Unless you want to change in the front seat." He tilted his head as if questioning his suggestion. "Or if you'd rather, you can head back into the office and change in one of the rest rooms. I'm just anxious to get where we're going."

"And you like the thought of me getting naked in your truck," she completed.

His smile provided his answer.

"I trust you won't peek," she said.

"I don't remember promising that," he said, and raised sexy sandy brows.

"No, you didn't."

He'd see all of her before the night ended, if this date went the way she thought it would. So, why not tease him a little now? He asked for it, anyway, didn't he?

She crawled through the opening to the backseat as he backed up, then headed out of the parking lot. Removing her jacket, she shimmied out of her colorful tanks. She'd worn a strapless red bra, but now she debated. . . .

"All right. I have a question," she said, tossing the two tanks on the other side of the backseat and silently praising the tinted windows. She could torture the secretive cowboy, and the only one who'd see would be him.

"Shoot," he said, stopping at a red light.

"I can't figure this shirt out. It has one of those shelf liners, so I guess it's up to you."

"What's up to me?" he asked, his gray eyes connecting with hers in the rearview mirror.

"Bra or no bra?"

Take that, cowboy.

His throat bobbed as he swallowed, but then, as she was quickly learning was his custom, Landon Brooks surprised her again.

Ignoring that the light could change at any moment, he turned in the seat. Looking at her, then letting his gaze fall to her chest, he specifically studied the two swells of flesh plumped over the cups of her strapless bra. "No bra," he said, then continued watching.

Amy's skin prickled beneath his stare, but she wasn't about to back down. She loved a challenge, and the look he gave her said he'd just issued one. Big time.

Without taking time to second-guess her response, she curved one arm behind her back and undid the clasp, then let the red satin material fall to her lap.

His gray eyes smoldered and the slow shake of his head provided a genuine display of appreciation. "Woman, you'll be the death of me."

"I'm counting on it." The cars behind them honked their disapproval. "I think the light changed," she said, not making an effort to cover the nipples currently reaching for the cowboy in the front seat.

"Right," he said, twisting in the seat. "You realize you're going to pay for this later."

"Pay for what?" she asked, pulling the green tank over her head.

"For this rise in my Levi's."

"Funny," she said, wriggling out of her pants and sliding into the shorts. "I could've sworn you wore Wranglers."

He laughed, and it rippled over her skin, ending directly between her legs.

She slipped her feet into the sandals, then crawled back to the front of the truck.

"Do you like them?" he asked, taking his eyes from the road to survey his choices in clothing.

"They're perfect."

"Good." He reached a hand to her bare thigh and caressed it slowly, while her insides jumped, and the phone in her purse rang.

"Oh Lord, I nearly forgot," she said, scrambling to pull her purse from the front floorboard. "I've got to take this."

He shook his head, but kept smiling. "Just so you know, you probably won't be able to hear your cell phone ringing where we're going."

She swallowed. *Whoops*. What would she do about that? She'd promised to field the Southersby calls for Lettie.

Punching the "talk" button on the red phone, she answered, "The Palisades, this is Amy. Can I help you?"

Landon stopped at another traffic light, then turned and gawked at her greeting. Amy held up a finger and mouthed that she'd explain later.

"I need to leave a message for Walter and Ellen Southersby," the man said.

"Certainly," Amy answered, grabbing a tiny spiral notebook and a purple Adventurous Accessories pen from her purse. "Go ahead."

"This is their son, Harold Southersby. Just tell them Sylvie's play was changed to tomorrow night. And tell them I don't want them cutting their trip short because of it, but I knew Mother'd hit the roof if I didn't let her know about it." He chuckled. "She hates missing anything her grandkids do, but tell her Sylvie will have three more performances, and she shouldn't worry about missing one." He paused. "You know, that may be too much for you to cover. Wanna just have her call me?"

"I'll tell her to call you," Amy said, "but I got the message and will give it to her as well. Is there anything else I can help you with?"

"No, that's it."

"Then have a good day, Mr. Southersby."

"You too," he said, and disconnected.

She turned to Landon. "I need to make a call."

"And then you're going to explain, right?" he asked.

"I'll try."

She dialed Love Beach and entered the extension to Walter and Ellen Southersby's room.

"Hello," Ellen answered.

"Mrs. Southersby? Hi, it's Amy with My Alibi," she said as Landon's brows shot up a notch.

"Oh, hello, dear, we're absolutely loving these products, and I've recorded all the information you asked for," she said.

"Really?" Amy asked. "You liked them?"

"Yes. In fact, we wanted to try a few more, so we ordered some additional things. Not many, since you'd provided practically everything we needed, but we did purchase a few bottles of the edible massage oils."

"Which flavors?" Amy asked.

"Chocolate and strawberry. I've got to tell you, they're absolutely heavenly."

"Well, it just so happens I'm with the project lead for

that department, and I'll be happy to let him know," Amy said, grinning at the confusion evident on Landon's fine-chiseled face.

"Oh yes, dear. Please do that. So, have you heard from one of our children? I'm assuming that's why you called, and we simply haven't had time to contact them today. Today was exploration therapy."

"Exploration therapy?"

"Exploring erogenous zones. I never realized my body had so many, or Walter's, for that matter. Behind the knees. Who would have thought soft kisses behind the knees could make you . . . Well, let's just say I've been pleasantly surprised by everything I learned throughout the day's lessons."

Amy grinned. "Sounds neat. And actually, I did hear from one of your children. Harold."

"Really? He doesn't usually call. Is everything okay?" she asked, concern etching her tender voice.

"He seems fine, but he wanted to let you know Sylvie's performance has been moved to tomorrow night." Amy went on to relay the remainder of Harold's message and the fact he didn't want their trip cut short because of his daughter's performance night being altered.

However, Ellen Southersby would have no part of it. "Nonsense. That's opening night, dear," she said, then evidently put her hand over the receiver while she called to her husband to begin packing. Amy heard the muffled words and waited for Ellen to return. It was nice to hear the woman's quick affirmation of priorities. Yes, the older couple was still pursuing their sexual aspirations, but not at the cost of their grandchildren.

"Amy?"

"Yes, ma'am?"

"We're going to head on home tonight. I'll need to order roses for my granddaughter, and I want to go see her tomorrow to help her get ready for the show. She has the lead in the school play, you know."

"How old is she?" Amy asked. She may have only "met" Ellen Southersby this week, but she'd grown fond of the lady.

"Eight. But don't let her age fool you. Our little Sylvie has talent. Wouldn't be surprised if we don't see that girl on Broadway later on."

"Sounds great," Amy said, enjoying the enthusiasm in the older woman's words.

"So I suppose you won't have to field our calls anymore," Ellen said. "I'll let Harold know we're on our way and that our cellular will now catch a signal. But I truly appreciate everything you and your sister have done this week to help make our trip a success."

"No problem at all," Amy answered.

"And Amy?"

"Yes, ma'am?"

"I'd love to do that product-testing thing you talked about, if you still need testers in our age bracket. You can send them to the address on our My Alibi form, if you want."

"I'm always looking for product testers," Amy said.

"Fine, dear. And, one more thing."

"What's that?"

"If you don't mind, can you send them in something discreet? A brown unmarked box, or something along that line? I can't imagine what Mr. Wilkins, my postman, would think if he saw something labeled with your company's name arriving at our house."

Amy laughed out loud. "I totally understand."

"Good, dear. Well, we're going to pack now, and you don't have to worry with the remainder of our My Alibi week. We'll be heading on home to see our Sylvie."

"That sounds great. I'll talk to you soon."

"You too, dear," Ellen Southersby said, then disconnected.

Amy turned off the phone and plunked it back in her purse. At least she wouldn't have to worry about fielding calls tonight while she and Landon went wherever he'd planned. "Okay," she said, turning her attention back toward the handsome male in the driver's seat. "All taken care of."

"Were you talking to someone about my products?" he asked.

"As a matter of fact, I was," she said, then barreled into a lengthy explanation of Lettie's employer, Mr. and Mrs. Southersby, and Amy's part in making their week at Love Beach a bit more fun.

Landon listened with interest. "Incredible," he said when she finished.

"What? My Alibi? You haven't heard of the company before?"

"No," he admitted, "but I meant that a couple their age would be so completely in tune with each other physically and emotionally. Still looking to fulfill each other's needs, to explore everything sensually."

"I thought the same thing."

"I'm going to be like that," he said, and nodded his head for emphasis.

"Yeah, I bet you will," she said, and knew it was true. Landon was extremely sensual and extremely sexual, very much in tune with the opposite sex. And, Amy realized, as her body continued to respond to every word, every look, every touch, from Landon Brooks, so was she. "Landon?"

"Yeah."

"Where are we going?"

"Right here." He turned the truck into a large parking lot.

Amy swung around in the seat, then laughed out loud at the blinking lights, colorful flags soaring and red-and-white-striped roofs dotting the tiny buildings surrounding the perimeter of the complex. "Really?"

"You remember that staff meeting when Brenda introduced the cotton-candy-flavored massage oil?" he asked.

"Yeah, I remember."

"She said it reminded her of fun and carefree times, of having fun at the fair," Landon continued.

"Right," Amy said, her throat closing in at his memory, and at his thoughtfulness.

"Then you said you'd never been to a fair, that they didn't have them in the small town where you grew up. Plus you'd never made it to a big city to attend one either, right? You joked about it, like you were poking fun at where you came from, but to me, you seemed a bit bothered. Although you still approved the cotton candy oil," he added, smiling.

"I did. And it's one of our best-sellers."

"True, which is why it's about time you experienced the inspiration for that oil." He parked the truck merely feet away from the sign identifying the Fulton County Fair.

Amy waited for him to turn off the engine, then crawled across the seat and kissed him thoroughly. She cupped his jaw, a bit prickly from his five o'clock shadow, and ran her tongue inside his luscious mouth to explore the deliciousness of Landon Brooks. And, consequently, felt the rise he'd indicated in his Wranglers. "You weren't kidding, were you?" she asked, pulling away and nodding toward the jean-clad bulge.

"Heck, I'm controlling it now."

"Really?" *Dang, what's it like when it isn't controlled?* "You sure you don't want to, you know, do anything first?"

He chuckled deeply. Throatily. And the sound made her nipples salute within the thin tank top.

Landon noticed. "You better watch that," he said, and ran a fingertip over one protruding point. "Or we'll never make it out of the truck."

"Do you want to make it out?" she asked, her tone as seductive as possible.

"What I really want to do is peel that shirt off, latch onto this," he said, pinching a nipple, "and drive you completely over the edge."

"Okay by me."

He shook his head. "But I'm trying to do something special for you here." He pointed to the Ferris wheel in the distance. "Ride the rides, eat some candy, watch the fireworks. Then later, we can make some fireworks of our own."

"I've never been on a Ferris wheel," she admitted.

"Then let's go." He opened his door and climbed

down, then reached for Amy and helped her to the ground, once again sliding her down the front of his body and nipping her lips when their mouths met.

Her knees wobbled when she finally reached the ground.

"But later, I do want to see those fireworks," she said. "All of them."

"Done."

CHAPTER 18

Landon purchased park wristbands, allowing them to ride everything they wanted, as many times as they wanted. Or, rather, as many times as she wanted, since this was her dream. Her green eyes were absolutely alight with excitement, and he was thrilled to be the one providing her with the fun.

For the past two years, he'd tried to get to know the secretive, sexy female. She'd mesmerized him in staff meetings, with her knowledge of sex and her admitted lack of desire for sexual partners.

"You don't need a partner to orgasm," she'd said on numerous occasions, "and our job is to make sure we can provide the products necessary to make that possible."

Each time, Landon had countered by informing her that the products could also be used to enhance a couple's bedroom repertoire. And each time, Vernon Miller had agreed with both of them. He wanted products for singles and for couples—and between Landon, Amy and the additional project leads at Adventurous Accessories, they had all bases covered.

But he'd often wondered if the intriguing brunette had ever given the opposite sex a try. And if she had, had some guy bruised her heart? Had he caused her distrust toward men in general that Landon witnessed at every staff meeting?

That was what Landon had guessed, throughout his two years attempting to learn more about Amy Campbell.

While they ate caramel apples and watched a guy on stilts perform, Amy told him about her sister and the way she'd reconnected with her friend from the past. Amy seemed totally transfixed by the story of their friendship rekindled and the new relationship.

Her love for her sister touched his heart, as did her description of the love Lettie had found with Bill. Did Amy realize that by describing the perfection in Lettie's relationship, she had described what she desired too? As in, someone who could be totally trusted, someone who could be your best friend, and lover.

And did she know Landon was interested in helping her experience all the feelings she'd described?

"He'd felt more than friendship all along," Landon surmised, listening to the key points in the story and learning more about Amy with every fact.

"Yes," she said, moving to the next carnival booth. "Isn't that incredible? But she was a little slower figuring out what the two of them could have, beyond friendship."

"What about you?" Landon asked, handing the booth attendant five dollars and grabbing the first of three baseballs, then flinging it toward a stack of cans.

They fell with a loud crash.

"Wow," Amy said, watching the man put the cans back in place. She took a bite of her caramel apple, moaned her approval and asked, "What about me?"

"Are you also slow at figuring it out?" he asked, taking down the second batch of cans. He turned to face her as the fellow resituated the stack once more.

"Figuring what out? You mean, love?"

He smiled. Had she never said the word in reference to herself? She looked as though it practically choked her on its way out. "Yeah, love."

The corners of her full mouth tipped down for a brief second, but Landon noticed.

"Never had it," she admitted, then laughed through the awkward moment. "How'd we get on that?"

"You started it," he reminded, "by talking about Lettie."

"I guess I did," she said as the third pyramid of cans hit the ground. The booth attendant asked Landon to pick his prize.

"What'll it be?" he asked, pointing to the huge animals on display.

"I always wanted a Chihuahua," she said, noting the three-foot-tall stuffed dog.

"That one," Landon said, then accepted the big-eared toy from the man. "So, if you did find it, someday, do you think you'd be slow figuring it out?"

"Love?" she repeated, and he laughed out loud at the odd croak the word formed on her lips. Was she that terrified of the emotion?

"Yeah, Amy," he said. "Love."

"There's no way to know," she said. Then, as Landon

took her hand and headed toward the next section of rides, he heard her whisper, "Yet."

He fought the urge to give her a cat-that-caught-the-canary smile. He was making progress. True, they were just getting started in this relationship, and he had no idea where it'd head over time. Still, he wanted to know she was open to it leading everywhere. And now, he believed, she was.

Excellent.

Amy stopped walking. Her attention had moved to the House of Mirrors, where a father and daughter made their way through, laughing and poking fun at each other as they bumped into the walls.

Landon watched her examine the pair, her brow furrowing slightly when they exited the transparent building and high-fived their victory. Amy's slender throat pulsed with a thick swallow.

"You okay?" he asked.

She nodded, quickly regaining her composure. "Yeah, just thinking about giving that a try."

He knew there was more, much more, to the emotion he'd seen on her face, but he also knew she didn't want to discuss it further. No problem. He'd waited two years to know the real Amy Campbell. She was starting to get used to trusting him, to trusting any male, so he wouldn't push her. Not now. Not ever. "I'm game if you are."

She smiled, a beautiful, full grin that had caught his attention the first time they'd been introduced. Amy Campbell didn't merely smile with her mouth; her entire face gleamed with enthusiasm, with life. And given the sadness that he'd seen a moment ago, he reveled in helping to produce that image. "Let's go."

They got in line and waited their turn. When they finally reached the top of the stairs leading to the display, Landon asked the attendant to watch their pet. Then he pointed to the stuffed Chihuahua.

The guy laughed, placed the big dog beside him and gave them the go-ahead to begin.

"Wait," Amy said, putting her palm against his chest. "Ladies first."

"I figured we'd go together."

"Nope."

He shook his head. "You're wanting to race?"

"Definitely."

"You realize you could hurt yourself if you walk into one of those glass walls," he warned.

"I'll risk it."

"Dang, lady, are you this competitive at everything?"

"Guess it comes from those cheerleading competitions in high school. Or maybe it was track."

Or maybe it's the fact that she didn't want to accept help from a man. Didn't want to admit that she might need him, want him.

But Landon wanted her to realize he wasn't that kind of guy. He'd never hold the fact that she desired his help, or that she desired him period, over her, as something to toy with her feelings, play with her emotions.

"All right," he said. "Ladies first. I'll turn around so I won't see which way you head."

"Fine."

He listened to her giggle echo against the glass as she entered the maze; then he heard her yell, "Okay, you can come in now!"

Landon moved forward, but the entrance was low and

promptly knocked his Stetson off his head. He turned to pick it up.

"You'll never catch me that way, slowpoke," Amy called. Her cute figure was distorted by the mirrors and glass walls, but she still looked breathtakingly gorgeous.

Landon grabbed his hat and laughed, then headed into the maze.

In less than four minutes, he exited on the other side.

He turned and saw Amy, her hands in front of her as she struggled to find her way through.

"All right, smarty," she said, frowning at him through the wall panels. "How'd you do it?"

Landon laughed. "Can I go in and get her?" he asked the attendant.

"Sure thing, bud."

He moved inside, following the exact route he'd taken before. When he neared her, he slowed his pace, waited until he found the opening leading down the path she'd taken, then held out his hand. "Come on, Miss Independent. This way."

"I would've found it eventually," she said, but smiled when she grabbed his hand and followed him quickly through the maze.

"Thanks," Landon said to the man as he handed them their stuffed dog.

"No problem."

"All right, how'd you do it?" she asked, eyeing him suspiciously as they headed toward the Ferris wheel.

"An old trick I learned as a kid, the first time I went to the fair and tried to tackle the House of Mirrors."

"I'm listening."

"I ran in and promptly barreled into the first wall.

Here's the evidence," he said, pushing back the hair on his forehead to reveal a tiny scar.

"Ow!"

"Yeah, but I wouldn't quit, even though my mother stood outside the place begging me to stop. I kept banging into wall after wall, until finally the man running the booth came in to help."

"Stubborn, huh?"

"When I want something, I can be."

She tilted her head as though trying to read more into his answer, which was fine by Landon. He meant more by it, and she might as well understand he didn't give up easily. At anything.

"So then what?" she asked.

"He came in and told me how to get out; then I simply walked through."

"How do you get out?"

"Right hand, right wall."

She stopped walking. "What?"

"You keep your right hand on the right wall. Never venture toward the center and never make a left turn. As long as you keep heading in the right direction, you'll never go wrong."

"Really?"

"Yeah."

She turned around and marched back toward the House of Mirrors.

"What are you doing?" Landon asked, though he knew.

"Going to beat ya."

"Why doesn't this surprise me?" He followed her

through the line and back up the steps, handed off the dog to the guy at the door, then let her enter first.

Within three minutes, Amy had exited the display and was doing a celebratory dance on the exit platform when he walked out.

"Happy now?" he asked.

"Incredibly."

They continued through the park and once again let the attendant dog-sit while they rode the Ferris wheel and took their turn rising to the top of the park as the metal structure circled through the air.

"Look, there's your truck," Amy said, pointing toward the parking lot and the big black Dually parked near the gate. "It almost looks spotlighted under the entrance sign."

"Yeah, it does."

"It seemed to get dark fast," she said, noting the charcoal sky.

"That's why I wanted to come early. Actually, the fair closes in a half hour."

"Oh," she said, disappointment in the single word. "Man, I wanted to ride that too." She pointed toward the Wheelie, a round apparatus that circled horizontally on the ground, then extended vertically and continued its rapid spin.

"We've got time," he said, pleased with her announcement. He'd planned on steering her toward that ride at the end of the night, anyway; he had his own plans for the Wheelie.

They climbed out of the Ferris wheel, grabbed the stuffed Chihuahua and jogged across the park to get in line for the ride.

"This looks like fun," Amy said.

"My thoughts exactly."

Within minutes, they boarded a tiny metal box built for two.

"Holy cow, it's smaller than I thought," Amy said, taking Landon's hat while he climbed in. There was no way his Stetson would fit inside the confines of the car. "Where do you want me to put this?" she asked, holding up his hat.

"I'll put it with your dog, if you want," the fellow running the ride said.

"Thanks." Amy handed him the hat and the dog, then climbed in to sit in front of Landon.

He pulled the top hatch down and waited while the attendant ran around the cars and checked to make sure they were all locked in.

"Last ride for the night," Amy said. "But I'll bet it'll be a good one."

"It will," he promised as the engine on the structure whirred to life and they started circling.

The wind produced from their rapid swirl whipped through the slits at the top of the car and caused Amy's ponytail to slap his face.

Amy squealed her excitement, but her squeal halted immediately when Landon's hand ventured up her thigh.

She turned her head. "Landon?" Her voice was near silent, due to their fellow passengers' screams, but he heard.

His thumb moved within the loose leg of her shorts, ventured into her panties and focused on her clit. "Yeah," he breathed into her ear while she arched in the seat. He nipped her lobe. "Tell me not to stop," he said, circling the tender area and sliding his fingers down her heated folds. "Tell me you want to come."

"I . . . do."

The cars circled faster, wind whipped harder as he worked his thumb over her tender cleft and she gasped. He increased the friction, circling her as quickly as the cars on the ride circled into the sky, while Amy bucked beneath him.

"I'm about to," she said, her hips lifting off the seat to press harder against his hand.

He slipped two fingers inside, then groaned at the tightness of her, gripping his fingers like a fist. "Hell, Amy, you're incredible."

"Have to . . . scream," she said, and he could feel her holding back on the emotion her body yearned to set free.

"Let it go," he said. "Come on, Amy. Let me be a part of it this time. Don't wait. Don't go home and do it alone. Let me get you there. Everyone's screaming. Go ahead, set it free. Let me feel you let go."

And she did. Powerfully, violently, completely.

*C*HAPTER 19

Erika picked up another black seashell and placed it in her mesh bag, then continued walking down the beach, kicking the water as she progressed and wanting to drown in her misery.

Butch and the biker babe. He'd promised nothing had happened.

Yeah, right.

Because what she'd seen merely moments ago let her know something had happened. Or if it hadn't happened before, it was sure happening now.

What made her look through the window before opening the door to their room? Had she heard them? She didn't think so, but for whatever reason, she'd sneaked a peek through the crack in the curtains, like some high-school kid spying on her boyfriend. She saw Butch, naked and writhing on top of the biker babe. The big rebel flag tattooed on his back waved at Erika as he thrust in and out of the squealing female.

Erika's chest clenched, lunch threatened to make a rapid exit.

"Stop it," she warned her stomach. "He's not worth it." And that was the truest statement she'd made all week. Who had she been trying to fool? She'd pretended she was all grown up and had found the man of her dreams from the get-go, had honestly thought she'd tamed a wild man.

"Hmph," she said, picking up another black shell. At least half of that was true. Butch was wild, all right. But he hadn't moved one centimeter toward taming the beast. And right now, she could care less—about taming him, loving him or staying with him another day.

Which really ticked her off, given all her clothing was currently tucked away in a dresser merely feet away from the naked biker duo.

She laughed out loud. "Naked biker duo" sounded like cheesy cartoon characters.

Picking up another black shell, she stepped into the surf, rinsed it off, then watched as the ridges captured the afternoon sunlight.

How long until Butch got done banging leather lady? And how could Erika get her things out without causing a scene? Moreover, where the heck would she stay until it was time to go home? And since she'd ridden over on Butch's motorcycle, how the heck would she get home?

She sniffed, breathed in the salty air. Dang, this was a bad day, regardless of the white sand, turquoise waves and golden sunshine. Proof that you can't judge a book by its cover.

"I thought you only liked the white ones."

Erika turned, not believing she hadn't dreamed the voice. "Evan?"

He walked toward her, his bare feet leaving prints in

the sand and his Georgia Bulldogs T-shirt pulling across an impressive set of pecs. Funny, she hadn't noticed before how muscled he was.

"I thought you left already."

She had asked at the front desk, but there wasn't a room registered in his name. She hadn't known the name of the friend he was staying with, but even so, the guy said the "college group" had left. *That* had begun her bad day. Butch and the biker babe merely added insult to injury. But now things were definitely looking up.

"I was supposed to. But the guy I rode with met a girl and wanted to spend some time with her before we head out. We're leaving in a couple of hours."

Erika had ventured out into the water to rinse off her latest shell, and he stepped in after her. At the same moment, a large wave burst toward the shore and smacked both of them.

Erika blinked through the salty splash on her face. Then, realizing she'd dropped her bag of shells, she turned to chase them as they drifted with the waves.

"Hang on, I've got it," he said, reaching out and snagging the bag. Then he looked up at her with blue eyes the exact color of the waves around their feet.

"Thanks." She took the bag, pausing when her fingertips brushed his.

"No problem." He looked at the shells within the mesh. "But I thought you told me you only collect the white ones."

Erika shrugged. That was true when they'd spotted the pearly ones in the moonlight. But today had called for black. Until now.

"I was having a rough day."

"The biker guy?" Evan asked, jerking a thumb back toward the hotel, where Butch was undoubtedly still seeking satisfaction from the woman in their bed.

"Yeah."

"Mind if I'm honest with you?" he asked.

"Not at all."

A salty breeze ruffled her hair, and he tenderly pushed a strand from her face, tucked it behind her ear. His fingers were wet and sandy from capturing her bag, and the odd sensation of them against her heated skin sent a frisson of anxiety to her chest.

"You don't seem like the biker babe type."

She laughed. "You already know my type?"

"No," he said, squinting in the sun and making those blue eyes even more potent within the sea of brown lashes. "But I'm figuring it out. Matter of fact," he started, then grinned.

"What?"

"I'd like to figure out more right now, if you're willing to spend a couple of hours with me until I have to catch my ride."

She looked back at the hotel and thought about the mistake she'd made believing she could tame Butch. Believing she could love Butch. And perhaps the biggest mistake of all—believing he was her true love. "I think I'd like that."

Amy waited while Landon opened the door to his apartment. She'd practically attacked him in the truck and had actually asked him to pull over so they could complete what he'd started on the Wheelie, but he'd insisted their first time wouldn't be in a vehicle.

Which was fine. She guessed. But she hadn't wanted to wait.

However, now that the locks clicked open on the door to his apartment and she entered the realm of Landon Brooks, she felt queasy.

"Landon?"

"Yeah?" he asked, wrapping an arm around her, pulling her close and kissing her ear.

"I'm afraid."

His entire body tensed. "You're afraid? Amy, if you don't want to," he said, shaking his head, "then we won't. I won't push you into doing something you don't want to do. But I thought this was what you wanted."

She looked up to see his eyes, but they were hidden in the shadow of his hat. So she brought her hands to his face, then eased them to the brim, tilting it back so she could watch his reaction to her words.

"That isn't it," she said. "I'm afraid I'm not as experienced as you, and . . . you might be disappointed."

His smile warmed her heart. "Oh, honey, you won't disappoint me. And you're a sex authority, in any case, or Vernon Miller wouldn't have hired you."

"There's a reason I'm always promoting the toys for singles," she informed, and held her breath while she waited for his response.

"Yeah, I figured that," he admitted. "And I don't know exactly what your experience has been in the past." He held up a hand, then added, "I don't need to know. But I do know that whoever you were with that didn't bring pleasure to both parties involved should be shot."

She smiled. "Go on. Tell me how you really feel."

"Tell you what, why don't we relax a bit before things get overly heated. I want to make sure you're doing what you want to do, okay? And if you're not ready, I'll drive you home. But be prepared, I will expect a good-night kiss at the door."

"Deal," she said, her nerves settling. "So, what do you want to do?"

"I've got an idea. Sit down, and I'll fix us something to drink." He indicated the sofa.

"I don't drink," she said. "Never have. I like going to bars, but I always drive, and I always drink Coke. I just go because of the dancing."

"Good to know. But that's not the kind of drink I meant. Sit down and relax," he directed. "And trust me." He took off his hat and placed it on her head. "There. Looks better on you than me, anyhow."

"I sincerely doubt that," she said, then winked at the cowboy heading toward his kitchen.

Within minutes, Landon Brooks returned, holding a tall parfait glass in each hand, and sat beside her on the couch.

"Sundaes?" Amy asked, eyeing the cherries on top of whipped cream.

"Coke floats," he corrected, and handed her one.

"Oh wow, I haven't had one of these since I left Sheldon. They sold them at the five-and-dime."

"Let me guess. They had the old soda fountain fixed up with a long counter, tall bar stools and plenty of cold treats."

"Pretty much." She licked the top off the whipped cream, then withdrew the tall spoon he'd placed inside the glass and licked the sweetness off the metal.

Landon's gray eyes smoldered as he watched her tongue on the spoon. His throat pulsed thickly as he swallowed, then spoke. "We had one too," he said, "in Beaumont."

"I love Coke floats." She removed the spoon and tilted the glass to drink the liquid from beneath the floating ice cream.

The whipped topping met her mouth and gave her a foamy mustache. She pulled the glass from her lips and, laughing, prepared to wipe the white substance away.

"Oh no," Landon said, catching her hand. "I love whipped cream." Then he leaned close and licked the confection from above her mouth.

Amy's breath lodged in her throat.

"Delicious." His eyes were even more intense, even more seductive.

"Landon?"

"Yeah?"

"I think I've had enough Coke float."

"What would you like next?" His face displayed a hint of hope, and she answered it with the truth.

"You."

Taking her glass, he placed it on the table beside his. "Perfect." Then he put her hand in his and led her to the bedroom.

Amy watched him turn on the light, then dim it to a pale romantic glow. Her nerves were racing, but she didn't want to stop. She wanted this. To be with a man. Completely. To be with Landon Brooks. Completely.

"Are you okay with this?" he asked, standing behind her and wrapping his arms around her body, warming her with his touch. His hands cupped her breasts, and her nipples burned for more.

"Yes."

His bed was like his truck, big and impressive. The thick wooden posts and massive carved headboard reminded Amy of something worthy of Paul Bunyan. But totally suitable for Landon Brooks. He was everything male and everything powerful. Everything she'd been scared of . . . until tonight.

True, she was still fearful of being hurt, of being used and discarded the way her mother had been. And the way she'd been with Cameron. But there was also that tinge of hope, just beneath the surface, that hinted at something more. Perhaps something more with Landon.

He picked her up and placed her reverently in the center of the bed.

"You're still sure?" he asked, slowly unbuttoning his shirt. Amy watched as the sprinkle of hair she'd viewed at the top of his chest formed a slender path to the top of his jeans. His chest was broad, with dark flat disks centering each side. His stomach was washboard solid. His hand moved to his belt, but stopped while he awaited her answer.

"I'm sure."

His boots thudded as he pulled them off and dropped them to the floor, then socks, pants and his black briefs. The thickness of his erection, the length of it as it seemed to grow even more beneath her gaze, made her breathing catch.

"Amy," he said, climbing on the bed.

"Yes?"

"I want you."

"I know. I want you too."

"But I don't want to hurt you," he added.

"I . . . don't know if it will hurt or not, but . . ." She paused, wondering how much to say; then she decided if she was going to trust him, she was going to trust him completely. "I've only been with one person," she admitted. "And it's been three years."

"Did you like it then? With him?"

"No."

"Did you come?"

Amy hesitated, then answered. "No."

He ran a finger down her cheek, brought it to her trembling lip. "I promise you," he said, "this time you will."

She smiled. "I believe you."

"Good." He brought one hand beneath her shirt, moved it to cup her breast, then gently kneaded the firm mound. "Do you like that?"

"Yeah."

"I want you to tell me if anything hurts. And I want you to tell me what you like, okay?"

"All right." She had assumed a guy asking what you want him to do—what you like or don't like—would be a turnoff. It wasn't. At all. It was sweet . . . and empowering.

"I'm assuming you know what to do with the toys to get you where you need to go, right?" he asked, moving his hand slowly toward the other breast as Amy's belly quivered.

"Yes."

"So tell me what you do," he said; Amy closed her

eyes and thought about all the times she'd had orgasms in her bed while thinking of him.

Dare she tell him now?

"I don't know if I can," she whispered.

"Can have an orgasm with me, or can tell me how you have them on your own?" he asked, now moving her tank top up her belly and pulling it over her head.

Amy lifted up from the bed as he removed her top, but left her eyes closed.

"Amy?"

"Yeah."

"Open your eyes."

She did, and the heat in his eyes nearly scorched her. "I'm not used to someone seeing me when I come," she said honestly.

"Has anyone ever seen you?" he asked, one finger traipsing down her belly and playing with the clasp on her shorts.

"Did you see my face in the Wheelie?"

He laughed. "No, I didn't."

"Then no, no one has seen me."

Another deep rumbling laugh made her pulse skitter. "Good. I'll be the first. But I want you to watch too. I want you to see how excited I get when I see you come."

"Don't you want inside me?" Sure, she hadn't originally wanted a man, but now that she'd changed her mind, she didn't want anything less than complete fulfillment.

"Yes. After we've taken care of you. If you're used to those toys, it may take a bit of effort, and I'm totally willing to oblige."

She swallowed. It did take her a while with the toys,

but she liked that prolonged length of time before she came. Would it take her longer with a real man, since she spent so much time playing with her toys? And why hadn't she considered that before?

Easy. She hadn't expected to be with a real man.

But she was now. A hot cowboy who was hell-bent on giving her pleasure tonight.

What if she couldn't get there without a toy?

She nearly laughed. Well, of course, she could. She'd certainly got there in the Wheelie, and screamed like the world had ended, to boot. But that was in an exciting locale, with wind racing and the ride soaring. What if she needed something extra to push her over the edge?

Would Landon be terribly disappointed if she couldn't get there with him?

"Landon?"

"Yeah?" he asked, tugging her shorts down her legs. "Damn, you've got a lot of leg here, lady."

"Thanks, I guess. Um, Landon?" How could she ask him? And how could she not?

"Yeah?"

"What if I can't orgasm without a toy?" She squinted and braced for his reply.

He actually laughed. "Amy, what do you think you did at the park?"

"I meant without all the excitement and stuff. What if I can't get there in a regular bed?" Not that this bed was regular. Heck, there wasn't anything about Landon Brooks that could be considered regular. The beyond-regular rod between his legs was another prime example.

Could she handle all that?

"Oh, I'm not worried about it," he said, sliding her red

satin panties along the same path her shorts had followed.

"You're not?" she asked as he hummed in approval at her intimate flesh before him.

"No, honey, I'm not."

She raised her head and watched him move his hands up her inner thighs, push her legs apart and look at her womanhood. It made her feel awkward, being on display for him. Did he like what he saw? Because that hum sure sounded like he did, but couldn't he say something to let her know for sure? And what would he say?

"I want to taste you," he whispered, moving up the bed.

Well, yeah, he could say that.

She gasped as his tongue licked her clit. "Oh wow."

"Yeah," he agreed, "Wow."

His hands massaged her legs, then her hips, then crept up to tease her nipples. While he thoroughly explored her intimate flesh, Amy fought for control.

Who had she been kidding? Not be able to come? With this kind of action happening between her legs?

"Landon," she warned.

"Mmmm-hmmm."

"I'm going to. I'm almost there."

Another sound of agreement echoed through the room.

"But I want you in me when I do," she said, and she meant it. She wanted to come *with* him, and if he didn't stop what he was doing, she wouldn't make it. "Please!"

He smiled broadly as he raised up, then moved his body up the bed. Reaching to the nightstand, he slid the top drawer open and withdrew a foil packet. Within seconds, thank goodness, he'd sheathed his long, hard length.

"Now," Amy ordered.

"Aren't you afraid you might not be able to come without a toy?" he asked, and pressed the head of his penis against her burning core.

"I'm going to come without you if you don't get inside me right now," she said, her entire body on fire. "Now, Landon!"

"Anything the lady wants," he said, plunging inside, then sucking in his breath. "Oh, Amy, you're so tight." He stopped his motion. "Are you sure I'm not hurting—"

She bucked her hips to pull him in deeper. "Don't you dare stop," she said. "I'm so close. Please . . . don't stop."

He grabbed her hips and matched his rhythm to hers, pushing in deep, pulling out, going in farther, pulling out. In and out, in and out, until her world exploded and Landon growled through his release.

Amy Campbell finally understood the meaning of complete.

$\mathcal{C}$HAPTER 20

Erika shakily wiped tears from her eyes as she waited in the emergency room lobby. She'd never liked hospitals, didn't care for doctors. But right now she was glad Savannah Memorial had been as close as it was to Tybee Island. And she prayed the doctors on staff were as good as what the nurses had claimed.

Not that any of them had come out and told her anything at all about Evan's condition.

God, how did this happen?

She stuffed her hand in her pocket, fingered her mother's letter. She'd chased the dream and ended up with a nightmare. A nightmare named Butch.

"Oh, Mama, help me." Standing, she walked back to the information desk. "Can you tell me anything about Evan Carter? Please?"

"He's with the doctor now," the nurse said. "And his family should be here shortly."

Erika sobbed her thanks.

She moved back to the chair and slumped down, wishing she could go back and see for herself how Evan was doing. The "family only" rule kept her in the waiting area, however.

A kiss. That's what set Butch off. A harmless kiss?

Erika closed her eyes and replayed her afternoon. She and Evan, collecting seashells and enjoying each other's company on the beach. The way he looked when she turned toward him, his blue eyes sparkling in the sun. And the way he'd smiled when she asked him if she could kiss him. She'd run the back of her fingers down his jaw, smooth yet strong, and very different from Butch's. Then she leaned forward, touched her lips to his. . . .

She felt Butch's huge hand claw her shoulder, then jerk her painfully, away from Evan. "You little slut," he'd growled.

Erika cried, remembering his fist firing through the air toward her face. And Evan, shoving her from Butch's grasp and taking the blow. He'd have been more prepared to defend himself, had he not been so concerned for Erika. Amazingly, he kept Butch off her, and even more incredibly, he managed to get in a few hits of his own. But without a doubt, Butch had fighting dirty on his side. Sand in Evan's face. Fingers in Evan's gorgeous blue eyes.

Finally, thankfully, the beachgoers decided to stop watching and start helping. It'd taken six men to pull the two guys apart. Thank God Butch left. And thank God one of the men offered to drive them to the hospital in Savannah.

Erica moaned, and more tears dripped. How could she have thought Butch was her soul mate? Her head pounded so hard she could feel the throbbing in her neck. She'd messed up, big time, and she needed help. Help for Evan. And help for her.

She dialed Amy's number, then waited while the phone rang once, twice.

"You've reached Amy Campbell at Adventurous Accessories. Either you've called after hours, or I'm away from my desk. Please leave a message, and I'll return your call as soon as possible."

Erika tried her friend's cell. No response. She frowned. Cried. This was too much. She didn't want to deal with it alone. She couldn't.

Swallowing her pride, she dialed the one person who'd always been there. The person who loved her, cared for her, even through those rough times after her mama died.

Pushing her other hand in her pocket, she held on to her mother's letter for strength. God help her if Uncle Bill couldn't forgive her. And God help her if he refused to come.

Bill cut the top off a thick bell pepper and rinsed it in the sink, letting the seeds fall in the disposal. He sliced it in long strips, noting they were the exact hue of Lettie's dress from last night. Grinning, he added them to the other vegetables sautéing on the stove.

Her confession last night had stunned him, shocked him.

"I guess I'm wanting more than sex."

In other words, she wanted exactly what he'd prepared to offer all along. The emotional friendship they'd started years ago, and the intense physical bonding they'd started this week.

Yeah, he could still be bad with her, when he was so inclined. She'd sure enjoyed his rowdy persona the past two nights. But that wasn't what she needed to fall in love. She wanted the guy she'd known way back when, the one who'd bought her those pink roses and who'd always wanted to know her even better. The guy who'd spent the afternoon enjoying her company and who had reminded her how much fun they could have together with that impromptu game of double Dutch.

Inhaling the spicy peppers and onions, he added the chicken strips. Then he checked on the rice.

A regular domestic king, he thought with a smirk. But then again, he was more of a servant tonight, paying homage to his queen. And that thought, oddly enough, seemed more appealing than ruling his universe.

Tonight, they'd discuss the past, present and, most important, the future. Their future. Together. There were issues they hadn't even touched on, but issues they needed to discuss, nonetheless.

Was she happy living in Tampa? Or would she be interested in moving back to Georgia? Specifically, Atlanta. Exactly how fixed was her job location with Integrated Solutions? Since the company obviously had clients in Atlanta, could she keep her job and simply transfer here? Did she even want to?

What was her career goal? How could he help her make it happen?

And what about marriage? At thirty, Bill certainly had it at the forefront of his thoughts. He looked forward to the whole T-ball-dad kind of thing, particularly if Lettie was the T-ball mom.

Anticipation pumped through him. What would she

look like, Lettie Campbell—correction, Lettie Brannon—with her typically flat stomach swollen with his child?

And what would that child look like?

God, he'd never considered marriage and kids with any of the women he dated in the past. But with Lettie, it seemed natural. Logical, even. They belonged together. And nothing about their relationship resembled short-term status.

His phone rang, and he put the lid over the stir-fry, turning down the heat. He'd given Lettie fairly easy directions, though not all that detailed, since he figured she'd remember the way to his house after Tuesday night. But her mind wasn't exactly on the journey when he'd driven her here. Or when he'd taken her home, for that matter, since she was still recovering from an amazing bout of multiple climaxes in and on his car.

Chuckling, he snagged the receiver. "You lost?"

"Uncle Bill?" Her voice broke on the second syllable.

"Erika? Are you okay?"

"Yeah. Well"—she sniffed—"no. No, I'm not." A loud sob wailed through the receiver. "Oh God, Uncle Bill, I'm so sorry."

"What is it? Tell me."

"I shouldn't have lied to you. And now, he's—we're—at the hospital." She sucked in air and sobbed again.

Bill's fist clenched the receiver. He'd seen Erika cry before, had even held her when she'd suffered through those typical midteen crises, but he'd never heard her sound like this.

His stomach knotted. What had happened? And if

anyone had laid a hand on her, on his sweet niece, the girl who'd been the center of his life for the past three years . . .

"What hospital? Are you hurt? What happened, honey? Tell me where you are. I'll be on the next flight to Tampa. Don't worry, I'll take care of you."

This time, she wailed miserably, then finally gained enough control to speak. "I'm not the one that's hurt. It's Evan."

"Evan? Who's Evan? One of your coworkers?"

Another piercing cry blasted his ear. "No. No. He's a friend." She sniffed loudly. "I . . . need you, Uncle Bill," she cried. "I've done something terrible, and Evan got hurt. It's all my fault."

"Erika. Tell me what happened," he said, his words clipped and commanding as he barely controlled his frustration. "Where are you? What hospital? I'll be there as soon as possible."

"I'm . . . oh God, I'm not in Tampa. I'm so sorry. I'm in Savannah." She sobbed loudly. "Memorial Hospital in Savannah. I can't explain now, but I really want you here. I need you. He's hurt, and I'm so alone." Another aching wail penetrated the line.

Bill's head pounded as he processed the flurry of information she'd spouted. Thank God she wasn't hurt. But her friend was hurt *and* Erika was alone. Why? And why was she in Savannah?

Although he wanted all of his questions answered, the thing that mattered most was getting to his niece. Quickly. "Savannah Memorial, right?"

She sniffed. "Yeah, and I swear I'll explain when you get here but . . . oh God, I messed up."

"I'm on my way. Stay there, and call my cell if anything changes."

"I will. And, Uncle Bill, I'm so sorry."

He said good-bye, then hung up the phone. Hell. What had happened? Why was she in Savannah?

Bill slapped his pockets. Where were his damn keys? He moved to the bedroom and scanned the dresser.

Nothing.

Storming through the room, he stopped at the bathroom door and checked the marble counter. Again, no sign of his keys.

Taking a deep breath, he focused on when he'd come home from work. He'd taken everything out of the fridge to start dinner; then he'd gone to the bedroom to change clothes, laid his keys on the . . .

He jerked his head toward the nightstand, where the keys were perched on top of a thick novel. He snatched the keys, while questions without answers shot like bullets to his brain.

Why was Erika in Savannah?

Why hadn't she called to tell him that she'd changed cities?

Who the hell was Evan?

Why was he in the hospital?

And why wasn't she where she was supposed to be?

His head pounded so loudly he nearly didn't hear the doorbell. Crossing through the house, he flung open the door, but couldn't muster a smile. Even for Lettie.

"Hi," she said, a boxed cheesecake in her hands and a grin on her face. Then she looked at him. "Are you okay?"

"No, I'm not."

"Is something burning?"

"Aw, hell." He turned, but she rushed past, placing the cheesecake and her purse on the counter, then moving to the stove. She shifted pots and pans, grabbed a wooden spoon and started damage control.

Normally, he'd have commented on her appearance, which, as usual, was perfect. A sleeveless white top and fitted black pants with heels. She looked very chic, very date-ready. But tonight, the date wasn't happening.

He had to make sure Erika was okay before he could concentrate on anything else. Even when anything else included Lettie.

"I'm sorry. I've got to cancel for tonight. Erika needs me, and I've got to head to Savannah."

She dropped the wooden spoon in the pot and turned. "Savannah?"

"Yeah. I've gotta leave now." He moved closer, put his hands on her arms. "Actually, you can help me. She may need a female to talk to, and I may need you too. Will you come?"

She blinked, her mouth opening in a silent O.

"Can you do that for me?" he asked.

"What happened?" Her face drained of color, and it touched his heart that she was so concerned for his niece.

"She said she isn't hurt, but I need to see her to make sure. She was really upset when she called."

"Wait." She sounded almost tearful and, again, Bill was touched beyond words.

"I can't wait. She needs me."

"It's my fault. I should've told you," she said, visibly shaking.

Bill took in Lettie's tear-filled eyes, her frown. "What are you talking about?"

"It's my fault," Lettie repeated, shaking her head. "I'm so sorry, Bill. I should have told you. I knew I should have, but I couldn't. I . . . was afraid. You said she isn't hurt, right?"

"Told me what, Lettie? What do you know about this?" he asked, the throbbing in his head getting stronger.

Her head moved back and forth, body teetered. "She never was in Tampa."

What the hell? "So she went to another training facility. She should've told me, but that doesn't matter now. We'll talk about that later. What matters—"

"I was going to tell you when she came back. I swear. I would have told you earlier, but—"

"Told me what?"

"My company. I don't work for Integrated Solutions, and I don't live in Tampa."

He leaned forward, gripped the counter on either side of her and stared into green eyes that looked completely terrified. *Why? What does she know?* "Lettie, what are you saying?"

"Tybee Island. That's where she went with her boyfriend. She wasn't at a training seminar. I work for a place called My Alibi, and she hired us. Hired me."

"You better explain. Quickly." He reined in his emotions, for the time being.

"We supply alibis to people when they want to get away with . . . well, when they don't want someone to know where they are. Erika hired us, hired me specifically. I had no idea she had anything to do with you. If I'd known, I'd have never taken her as a client."

"She lied? To me? And you did too." His eyes narrowed, jaw hardened, world tilted. "Why?"

"I shouldn't have. I know that. And that's why I put my notice in today. I didn't want to lie to you, to anyone, again. I never meant to hurt you," she said, her tone frantic as she stepped toward him, and a surplus of tears fell freely from those traitorous green-gold eyes.

Emotion overpowered him. He stepped back, looking at a woman he thought he knew. "Don't."

"I'm sorry," she whimpered. "Please, Bill. I made a mistake, a horrible mistake, but I'm sorry. And I"—she swallowed—"I don't want to lose you. I couldn't bear it."

"I'm going to find her," he said through clenched teeth. "You can see your way out."

Her tear-dampened eyes widened. "What are you going to do?"

It was more than he could take. He'd nearly come undone listening to Erika's sobs. Now the woman he thought he knew, thought he loved, had lied to him. Repeatedly. And wanted to know what he was going to do about the result?

"I'm going to find her, and help her." He slammed his fist against the counter. "Damn it, Lettie. Why didn't you tell me?"

"I don't know," she whispered.

He glared at her. He didn't have time to discuss this now, and he wasn't at all certain he wanted to discuss it ever. "God help you if anything, anything at all, has happened to her."

CHAPTER 21

Lettie's nose twitched when Amy, carrying two plates, entered the breakfast nook.

"How much weight have you lost?" Amy asked, placing the plates filled with beef tips, mashed potatoes and gravy on the table, then sliding one to butt up against Lettie's sketchpad.

Though Lettie knew the food smelled wonderful, at the moment, it turned her stomach. She continued working on her newest gown.

"I asked you a question," Amy said, plopping down and taking a bite of potatoes.

"I don't know. I haven't had a chance to get on the scale."

"Haven't had a chance? You've been moping around here with your nose in that book for two weeks." Amy reached out, grabbed one side of the bulky pad and yanked it away.

Lettie glared at the long line of charcoal slashing the page. "Did you have to do that?"

"Evidently, I did." She closed the book as Lettie

gasped, grabbed a square of wax paper and quickly thumbed through the pad's pages to locate her current drawing. Then she slid the wax in place to keep the image from smudging, despite the gray streak ripping down the page like a determined bolt of lightning trying to strike . . . her.

Great. Nothing like a vivid image to put things in perspective.

"Eat," Amy said.

Lettie vehemently decided not to answer, but her stomach growled like a dog at a postman's leg.

"See? You're hungry. Eat," Amy commanded, then took a bite of meat.

Lettie narrowed her eyes at her sister, but she couldn't deny her body's craving, so she spooned a bite of potatoes. Garlic and butter, salt and pepper, teased her deprived palate and she moaned.

Amy grinned. "Thank God."

"I've never been able to turn down your cooking."

"For someone who can't, you've done a heck of a job faking it the past two weeks."

"I've eaten enough to get by," Lettie said, taking another bite. She knew the meat was tasty too, but her stomach craved something soft and easy. The flavorful potatoes were perfect, and Amy was right. Though Lettie hadn't realized it, she was hungry. Very hungry. She scooped a couple more spoonfuls.

"Well, thank you for humoring me. If your favorite meal didn't do the trick, I was going to get Cass to come over and we were gonna force-feed ya. She suggested a slingshot method, but I liked the hold-her-and-stuff-her plan myself."

"God help you both," Lettie mumbled, but she couldn't control her smile. It was good to have a caring sister, and a great friend, at times like this. Times like this being when she'd personally lost the best man she'd ever hoped to find by waiting too long to tell him the truth.

"Are you ready to talk?" Amy asked.

"About what?" Lettie knew the topic of choice, and in all fairness, she didn't know if she could talk about him yet. Lord knows if she could, she'd have talked to Amy, or Erika, before now. The two seemed to spend the majority of their days calling Lettie. Judging from the determination in Erika's voice whenever she called, Amy suspected she was probably also talking to Bill. As if that would change his mind.

"Damn it, Lettie. Why didn't you tell me?"

When would she stop hearing those words? Or the pain in every syllable?

Amy dipped a piece of steak in the well of brown gravy nestled in her potatoes, then plopped it in her mouth, rolled her eyes heavenward and chewed. "All right, it's been two weeks. Cass, Erika and I have been overly patient, and it took a mountain of convincing to keep them from coming over here tonight and forcing it out of you. But it's time for you to talk."

"Okay," Lettie said, surrendering, while Amy put another dollop of fluffy white potatoes on her plate. "Pick a subject."

Smirking, Amy moved the remaining pieces of steak around her plate with her fork. Probably trying to decide what topic she wanted to tackle first. Thankfully, she started with the easiest, which only informed Lettie that the subject matter would progressively get harder to handle.

"Tell me about the new job," Amy said. "You haven't let us know where it is, what you're doing or anything."

Lettie took another bite, but her appetite was slowing, so she rested her spoon on the side of the plate until her stomach got its second wind. "I haven't got the job yet."

"Then tell me about the job you're trying to get."

Leave it to Amy to ask the one thing Lettie wanted to talk about. For the past week, since she'd spotted the ad in the *AJC* classifieds and called Charlene Frank, the owner of faire l'amour, she'd worked nonstop on her sketches. Turning all her attention to the drawings on the page, to the goal in her head, instead of what went wrong with Bill.

"It isn't the dream job, yet," Lettie informed.

"Well, I didn't figure you'd start out owning a shop, but you are making headway, aren't you?"

Lettie still planned to own a boutique, carry her designs exclusively, someday. Unfortunately, she hadn't made enough money to cover the start-up costs when she left My Alibi, so she'd have to begin her career working for someone else.

She didn't care, though. No amount of money was worth what lying cost her with Bill.

"If the shop owner likes these, I'm definitely moving in the right direction. We're meeting this afternoon to go over them." Lettie timidly reached for the sketchpad, half expecting Amy to smack her hand, since she hadn't finished her dinner. But her sister merely scooted her chair around the table for a better view.

Seeing Amy on the maternal side of their relationship,

since that had been Lettie's role for the majority of their lives, felt odd. Odd . . . and nice. In fact, Lettie knew now more than ever that she'd done a good job raising Amy. Her little sister had turned into a well-rounded, productive woman, who was no longer afraid of love.

Lettie's throat closed in as Amy pulled at the pad.

"Let me see." She flipped the cover and slowly turned the pages, then oohed and ahhed, providing Lettie with the boost of confidence she'd been lacking since things ended with Bill. A confidence she'd direly need when she met with Charlene. "You really like them?"

"They're elegance and sexiness combined. What's not to like?"

Pride spiraled outward from Lettie's chest. "I hope she agrees. When I told her the concept, I wasn't sure whether she'd be interested."

"The concept?"

Lettie's cheeks burned. "Yeah." Bill had been the main instigator in her current theme, but now what she'd originally envisioned for her own destiny would never happen.

"Care to fill me in?"

"Each gown has a honeymoon-night theme, sweet and sexy and seductive combined," Lettie explained. Her finger ran down the sketch of her favorite, the actual wedding gown made for bed, with beaded bodice, rich satin and a train. "She said she needed a slogan for the line."

"Did you come up with one?"

Lettie nodded.

"And?"

"For the woman who makes the night of her life last

a lifetime," Lettie said, her heart pounding. That'd *so* been what she planned to do with Bill. Make the friendship of her life last a lifetime. Make the love of her life last a lifetime. Make everything with Bill Brannon last a lifetime.

"No wonder she's wanting to see your stuff," Amy said. "What time is your meeting?"

"Eight. She had dinner plans, but we're meeting afterward to discuss the potential for my designs."

"And to let her make the offer."

"Lord, I hope so. I sure don't want to end up mooching off my sister."

"Now that would be a switch," Amy said.

"You never mooched."

"Funny, I remember you taking me in and covering food, rent and bills for the two years it took me to find a job. In my book, that's mooching."

"I wanted you here," Lettie said simply. "I wouldn't have had it any other way."

Amy laughed, breaking the sentimental moment, then moved her chair back in place and returned to her steak. "You realize you have two hours to get ready," she informed.

"Is it six? Already?"

"Time flies when you're out of work," Amy said, fighting a smile, but unable to keep it from sparkling in her eyes.

"You're a riot." Lettie picked up her plate. "And I've gotta get ready for my meeting."

"Anything I can do to help?"

"No thanks. It's up to me and the sketches in that book now."

"She'll be lucky to have you, sis."

Desperately needing to feel positive about something, Lettie stopped midway between the kitchen and her bedroom. "You think so?"

"I know so."

Those tiny spots beneath both ears started burning. She really didn't want to cry. Not now. "Thanks."

Amy turned in her chair, propped an arm over the wooden back. "You know what would help you loosen up and get relaxed for this thing, don't you?"

"No idea."

"A nice, long shower."

Lettie's laugh trickled up her throat, then burst free. Although Amy probably thought she was laughing at her sister's perception, Lettie was actually laughing at the irony of Amy's inference. That showerhead wouldn't be getting any orgasmic action today, at least not from her.

She could tell her sister she hadn't had an orgasm in fifteen agonizing days, since that morning Bill controlled her body completely with the aid of a long-stemmed rose. But she wouldn't.

How would Amy understand?

There was no way she could climax without remembering Bill's tender touch, his coaxing words or the way she felt when they were totally connected—his hard length deep inside.

And she wasn't ready to remember that clearly. Not yet. It hurt too much.

"She made a promise to Amy," Erika said, flipping through a *People* magazine while Bill studied the notes for his newest ad proposal.

"So you've said." Bill didn't want to discuss this again. His niece had been pleading Lettie's case for the past two weeks and he'd heard quite enough from her. He'd heard nothing, on the other hand, from the woman in question. He'd been so certain she would want to work this out, for the sake of their friendship, if nothing more. But she hadn't made any effort to contact him. *That* hurt, particularly when coupled with the fact that she'd lied to him about Erika, her job and her residence. . . .

"She did plan to tell you."

"That's what she said," Bill confirmed.

"Well? She was going to tell you the truth. Isn't that enough?" Erika asked, accusation in every word, as if *he* were in the wrong.

He cleared his throat. Hell, you'd think two weeks of solid explanations would suffice. "Erika, she lied about her residence. She lied about her job. And she lied about your whereabouts, which, whether you agree or not, put you in danger. How am I supposed to believe that she'd ever decided to tell the truth?"

"Yeah, but—"

"You don't understand. She ruined the thing I loved most about her, her honesty. That was the one thing I could count on from Lettie. It was something we always guaranteed each other. I trusted her to tell me the truth. And you too, for that matter."

"I made a mistake, and you *said* you'd forgiven me."

"I have," he clarified. "And I totally believe you've learned from your mistake. But it's different with Lettie."

"Why? Why does she have to be perfect?" she asked,

dropping the magazine on the coffee table. "Well?" Erika goaded, obviously believing she'd found her winning strategy.

She hadn't.

"She doesn't have to be perfect," Bill corrected, his words slow and steady, to coincide with his harnessed emotions.

"Then what's the problem? Can't you forgive her too? You've been miserable for the past two weeks, and when you're miserable, I'm miserable."

"I'm going to pretend you didn't complain about my disposition over the past couple of weeks, particularly since your hiring of an alibi company started this whole mess."

Her mouth twitched as she fought one of those teenage smiles Bill loved, but he refused to reward her by grinning back. So he clenched his jaw and attempted to look even more stern.

"You know if I hadn't hired My Alibi, you'd never have hooked up with Lettie. And evidently, you always had a thing for her; you can't deny it."

"I'm not denying anything," he said.

"So, why can't you go for what you want? She made a mistake. Everyone does. Why can't you forgive her and the two of you be together?"

"I don't know," he said honestly. "And for the record, she hasn't asked."

Erika picked up another magazine and flipped it open with a bit more zeal than necessary, so the crisp swoosh of turning paper penetrated the living room. "I thought you loved her."

"I believed I did. Unfortunately, I was mistaken."

"I don't think so," she mumbled, knowing he would hear.

"What's that?"

"Nothing." She snapped a few more pages, then dropped the magazine on the sofa. "It's because of me, isn't it?"

After two weeks of beating around the bush, Erika had decided to lay everything on the table. He'd been waiting for it, trying to provide the patience any parent would need when a child disobeyed, particularly a child who, according to the government, now qualified as an adult. It damn near killed him to find her at that hospital, crying for the man who'd defended her when that idiot biker jerk had attempted to assault his niece.

His niece. Moreover, Ginny's daughter.

Evan Carter had done what Bill would've done, if he'd been told she needed help. Which he hadn't, since Erika had deliberately lied to him . . . with Lettie's help.

Problem was, Erika had gone there of her own accord. She had only decided she didn't want to be there when Butch had moved on to his next biker babe and then retaliated when Erika moved on as well.

Erika, a biker babe. Had *that* been what she was going for? He cringed. Ginny wouldn't be pleased.

"What's because of you?" he asked, knowing exactly what she meant, but wanting to hear her say it. God, he really was a parent.

"The reason you won't give her another chance. You may have forgiven me, or so you said, but you're still mad at me for lying to you about where I went."

"You did more than lie, Erika; you hired a professional company to help you in the deceit."

She drew her legs underneath her on the couch and leaned back, as though his accusation didn't faze her in the least. "You gotta admit, that took a lot of nerve to hire them, don't you think?"

Bill shook his head. If she only knew how much she sounded like Ginny, defending her wild streak. "Erika, you surely wouldn't do it again."

"No," she said, grinning. "But I'm just saying that most people my age wouldn't have done it. Wouldn't have even thought about hiring an alibi agency."

Ginny would have, but Bill chose to keep that thought to himself. "I'd say that's a given." He didn't hold back his chuckle. She was *so* Ginny.

Erika laughed too, and he was glad to hear it. He loved the kid and was immensely grateful she'd been okay when he arrived at Savannah. He hadn't wanted elaboration on what exactly had happened between his niece and Butch, the biker guy, and she hadn't provided any. She'd simply stated the guy she cared about had been hurt defending her. The *new* guy she cared about, Evan Carter, whom she now wanted to be with at the University of Georgia.

God help him.

Besides, he knew enough about his niece to know she was destined to follow her instincts with a bit too much impulsiveness, something Ginny had been known for too. Hell, Erika had believed she was in love when she decided to spend a week with Butch. Then when he found someone else, she'd been shocked beyond measure.

And hurt. Definitely hurt. Which pierced Bill's heart. Mainly because he knew Erika's young heart had been bruised. Thank goodness she already seemed on the fast track to a complete recovery in disposition. Her laughter verified the fact.

And she hadn't given up on love. That was obvious by the way she was trying to get him back with Lettie. And by the way she was trying to convince him to let her go to the University of Georgia.

God, he was glad she'd gotten away from Butch. *Butch*. The name fit right along with the tattoos on his biceps, chest and throat. Then again, those were the only areas Bill could see, since the ponytailed, skull-earring-wearing, wild-and-woolly Butch hadn't worn a shirt. Just a black leather studded vest.

And a nipple ring.

Bill tried to remember if he'd seen the back of that vest in the hospital, where the nurses had stitched up the guy's split mouth. Good for Evan, getting in a decent punch and having a heavy enough high-school ring to leave the guy a permanent reminder of the encounter.

He thought about the big lug in the emergency room. Nope, he hadn't seen the back of that vest. But he'd bet his next paycheck there was a big, blazing Hell's Angels emblem embroidered in the center.

"You know, Lettie couldn't help it. Her job had her helping me lie to you," Erika said.

"Yeah, she could," he argued. "When she found out who I was, she could have told me the truth. She knew that I was responsible for you, and she should've known that you could've been hurt."

"For the record," Erika said, and Bill knew what was coming. Braced for it.

"Yeah?"

"I'm eighteen now. I could've simply told you I was heading to the beach with Butch, and there wouldn't have been a thing you could've done about it. I didn't tell you because I knew how you'd react. I knew you'd be upset."

"If you're waiting for me to thank you, we're going to be here awhile."

She laughed. Laughed! "I'm not. And she's not either. I didn't tell you the truth about where I was going because I couldn't stand the thought of hurting you. Evidently, she didn't tell you the truth because of the same thing. And because she had promised Amy to let me talk to you first. She takes care of Amy; she always has. Amy has never made it any secret about how much Lettie has done for her through the years." Erika blew out an exasperated breath. "I'm sure she didn't want to hurt you, but she also had to think about not hurting Amy."

His chest tightened; thoughts traveled to those lengthy discussions with Lettie in high school. When she vowed to make sure Amy would be okay, would have a "normal" life, in spite of their mother's distance. They basically raised themselves.

But *they* didn't. Lettie raised herself *and* Amy. She'd been distraught her senior year over leaving Amy behind while she paved the way for both of them to have a better life. But she did leave, and she did take Amy in after she graduated.

Looking back, Bill knew there was more to her rejection back then. She couldn't start a relationship with him at that time, and it didn't totally have to do with ruining the friendship. Lettie had to leave to make a better life for herself, and for Amy.

Was Lettie still feeling guilty for leaving her sister behind while she tried to earn them a better life? Had she taken the job at My Alibi for that reason? To make things better for both of them?

He turned and looked at the phone. Hell, who was he kidding? He'd been waiting for the past two weeks for Lettie to call. Or stop by. E-mail would be better than nothing at all. But that's what he'd received from her—nothing at all.

And damn if that didn't bite.

Should he tell Erika the truth? That he'd secretly hoped he meant enough to Lettie Campbell for her to venture past her comfort zone, seek him out and demand that he take her back?

Sure, he'd been madder than hell that night, but he'd had good reason. She'd lied to him. The one trait about her that had hooked him from the beginning—her ability to be honest to a fault—had shattered into a million pieces. And yeah, he didn't want to talk to her then. Didn't want to see her again, or so he'd said.

But that time had passed. Now he wanted to see her, hold her, touch her. Take her in his arms and never let her go. Show her she didn't need to fear hurting him. She could tell him the truth. Always. The same way he'd tell her the truth. Always.

Hell, what was he doing? He'd lied to her too, hadn't he? Tried to pull off that bad-boy act, and in doing so, he made her think he only wanted her body. Why hadn't both of them simply told the truth?

"Well?" Erika asked.

"You're right. I should've forgiven her."

She smiled smugly. "You're miserable without her."

"Don't get so shook up over it."

"By the way, I'm right about lots of things," she said, fiddling with the remote. The TV clicked to life, and she pressed the "mute" button.

He shouldn't ask, but curiosity got the better of him. "Such as?"

"Such as whether I need to move into my own place. At the University of Georgia. I've got the orientation information, as well as dorm expenses, meal plans and class schedules in my room. I'll go get them."

"I thought we covered this last week," Bill said, really not wanting to go there again. "You can live here and commute to Georgia Tech."

"Okay, so I made a mistake when I told you I was living with friends, instead of telling you I was planning to share an apartment with Butch. And I made a mistake hiring My Alibi. And I made a mistake sneaking away to Tybee Island, when you thought I was in Tampa. But dang, I'm wanting to go to college here, and I'm wanting to spend some time with a nice guy." She held her palms up defensively, but didn't look apologetic.

"Didn't you think I'd notice the biker paraphernalia when I came to visit?" he asked, focusing on the one portion of the conversation he hadn't hashed out completely over the past two weeks.

She shrugged. "I figured Butch would grow on you."

"Right, like a tumor."

She snorted. "Anyway, I still want my own place. I'm sorry, but living at home, with my uncle, and trying to blend in college isn't going to cut it."

"You should've thought of that before your trip to Tybee Island."

"I didn't want to go to the University of Georgia before I went to Tybee Island," she said. "And, like I said, I made a mistake. Everybody does. Don't tell me you haven't made your share." She cocked a brow, and he knew better than to try to snow her on this one.

"Your point?" he asked, knowing she'd make it with fervor.

"You turned out okay, didn't you?" she asked.

Did he? Best he could tell, the answer to that question would remain unanswered until he talked to Lettie. In person. This was definitely not something he wanted to cover over the phone. If he hadn't screwed things up completely, then yeah, he'd turned out okay. If he had, well, that was another story.

"I don't suppose I have to remind you that I'm—" She stopped when he held up a finger.

"Let me guess," he interrupted. "You're eighteen and legally an adult."

"How'd you know?" she said, her dark eyes twinkling with mischief.

Damn, she looked so much like Ginny that sometimes merely looking at her broke his heart. He missed Ginny's smile. Her laugh. Her hugs. But he still had those things, all of them, through Erika.

As if reading his thoughts, she withdrew Ginny's letter from her pocket and held it to her chest as she spoke. "Tell you what. I'll make you a deal."

Bill decided not to point out she had no room to bargain. Besides, sitting on that sofa, looking like her mom, and holding Ginny's final letter—gave Erika all the bargaining power she needed. "Go ahead."

"If I find a decent roommate, someone you approve of, then you'll let me have my own place."

"I must have missed something," he said. "I didn't hear your part of the deal."

She grinned. "Shoot, I've got the hardest part. I have to find someone you approve of."

He shouldn't agree to this, but he really didn't want to clip her wings totally over one mistake. Even if it was a colossal one. With the name of Butch.

Besides, he didn't want to encourage a total rebellion, where she'd have to turn her back on him completely to get her way. And something about the gleam in Erika's eye—that new spark that had appeared magically the moment she technically had achieved adulthood—told him she would get her way.

"All right."

"Cool!" she squealed, leaping from the couch and wrapping both arms around him. "Well, I've gotta go now."

Had she merely been waiting for the right answer before continuing merrily with her life?

"Where are you going?"

"Going to the late movie with Lindsay. You can call her folks if you want to check up on me."

"No," he said, and grinned. "I don't want to check up on you. I want to trust you."

"Fancy that, that's what I want too." Another hug; then she grabbed her purse and bounded toward the door. "And don't waste any time working things out with Lettie."

"I won't," he affirmed, "but—"

She halted. "But?"

"But I'm going to do this right."

She cocked her head, giving him a sweet smile.

"What's that for?" he asked.

"Mama would've loved this."

He swallowed hard. "Loved what?"

"You, finding the one who makes you complete."

CHAPTER 22

Lettie stepped off the elevator with a smile overpowering her face and more pep in her step than she'd had in weeks. Two weeks, to be exact.

Charlene Frank had practically drooled over Lettie's designs.

According to Charlene, Lettie's lingerie would be the next must-have attire for the boudoir. And sold exclusively at faire l'amour.

Best of all, she wanted Lettie to head the production process, handpick the fabrics, oversee the details. Everything. Her career dream was sure enough coming true, her dreams for Amy were coming true, and Lettie couldn't imagine how her life could be any better.

Her step faltered. Yeah, she could.

Gathering her composure, she inhaled deeply, then blew it out in a thick *whoosh*. Tonight was not the night to dwell on her loss.

Au contraire, she thought, deciding to use a bit of Charlene's French. Tonight, she'd focus on her future. A future that would've undoubtedly been better with Bill

Brannon in the picture, but a future that wasn't near as dismal as it'd seemed a few hours ago.

Her designs. "Lettie Campbell Originals," Charlene had called them. Grinning, she fished her key from her purse and prepared to tell Amy the news. She totally expected her sister to be waiting on the other side of the door with a celebration cake. Chocolate, with butter cream icing. Lettie's favorite.

Ever since they were little, Amy had always relished a reason to celebrate, had loved giving and receiving surprises. And since Amy had spent the past two weeks trying to cheer Lettie up, she wouldn't miss an opportunity like this.

Lettie pushed the door open and, sure enough, inhaled the sweet scent of butter cream.

Amy would never let her down.

"She loved them!" Lettie exclaimed, sailing into the room on a cloud of pure bliss. "Charlene Frank loved my designs!"

Then she stopped cold and gawked at the three women perched at the kitchen table, apparently playing some sort of board game.

"Amy? Cass?"

All three heads turned. Lettie didn't address the black-haired stranger on the other side, since she didn't have a clue who she was.

Amy beamed. "Well, of course, she loved them. Why else would I have baked a cake? Congratulations, sis." She stood, crossed the room and hugged her sister. "I knew you could do it. I'm so proud of you."

"Thanks," she said, bewildered. Stepping toward the other two, Lettie paused to run her forefinger across a swirl of icing at the bottom of the cake. Then she stuck it in her mouth and let the sugary concoction tease her taste buds. "What's up?"

"I want you to meet someone," Amy said, indicating the newcomer to the group. She wore a snug red tank and her silky black mane fell like an ebony waterfall around her shoulders. Big dark eyes examined Lettie with interest.

Lettie extended a hand and embraced the girl's tiny palm. She looked familiar. "Hello, I'm Lettie."

"Erika Collins," she said.

Lettie recognized the voice instantly, since Bill's niece had called her religiously during the past two weeks.

"I'm glad to finally meet you in person," Erika added.

Lettie blinked. Now she knew why the girl looked so familiar. Erika favored her mother, from what Lettie remembered of Bill's older sister. And she also favored Bill. "Nice to meet you too." She looked to Amy and Cassie for guidance. "Is everything okay?"

"More than okay," Erika answered. "Uncle Bill has finally seen the light."

"Seen the light?" Lettie asked.

Dare she hope?

"Realized he made a mistake letting you go."

Dizziness swept through Lettie, and she grabbed the edge of the kitchen counter to keep her head from plopping straight down in the center of her cake. "*Letting* me go?" she managed.

"Probably not the best choice of words," Erika said, "but he realized he wants you in his life and that he messed up."

"You okay, Lettie?" Amy asked.

Was she? Why did this monumental morsel of information blurted from Bill's niece make her feel so nervous? So . . . scared?

"God help me," she mumbled, easing into a chair at the table.

"He probably will," Cassie said, then placed her half-eaten piece of cake in front of Lettie. "But eat this, anyway. Cake never hurts. Besides, I'm not all that hungry."

"*You're* not hungry?" Amy asked.

"Nope," Cassie said, grinning, then added, "I'll tell you all about him later."

Unable to argue with the hunk of sugar in front of her, Lettie picked up the fork and chomped a big bite. Oddly enough, it did help. "Erika?" she questioned between chews.

"Yeah?"

"He hasn't called—hasn't tried to see me—in two weeks. Why now? And why are you telling me, instead of Bill?"

"He didn't want to talk to you over the phone, and since Amy, Cass and I have been meeting every night to try to figure out how we could help things along, we thought we should help you handle this the right way. I mean, since he's willing to go out on a limb for you, you should do the same."

Lettie took another big bite of cake and decided to start at the beginning of Erika's information dump. "You three have been meeting every night? About me . . . and Bill?"

"At Cowboys," Amy said.

"Don't you just love Cowboys?" Cassie asked, cutting another slice of cake, then licking the icing from her fingers. "Slay is taking me there again tonight. I swear, I didn't realize line dancing could be so much fun."

Amy's mouth fell open. "Slay? As in Slay Silverstone? You're seeing him now?"

"Oh, he and the girlfriend were just together for sex," Cass informed. "And don't worry, he can still test your products. Matter of fact, I think we're scheduled to come in for a visit to your lab on Tuesday. By the way, I've found out all the juicy details about his O-time factor. Lord help me, that man's amazing."

"Cassie!" Lettie exclaimed.

Cass merely shrugged. And grinned. "Damn, Lettie, he melts vibrators. How's a girl supposed to resist that?"

"Wow," Erika whispered on a breathy sigh.

"Uh-uh. I got dibs," Cassie said, pointing an icing-coated finger at the younger girl.

"He melts them?" Erika asked again, her big dark eyes even wider.

Lettie dropped her head in her hands. "I can't believe we're talking about this."

"You're right," Amy said. "We were talking about you and Bill. And the fact that the two people we care about most"—she pointed to Erika—"want each other. And he's finally ready to do something about it."

"But we think it'll mean plenty to him, tell him how committed you are as well, if you do something first," Erika said.

"What do you mean he's ready to do something?" Lettie asked.

"Talk to you, tell you how he feels," Erika said matter-of-factly.

"Then why hasn't he called?"

"I told you, he didn't want to talk over the phone," Erika said, as though Lettie obviously hadn't been paying attention.

"But he did call, to see when you'd be home," Amy said. "I told him you weren't here and wouldn't be back until tomorrow morning, that you needed to get away for a while."

"You *lied* to him?" Lettie couldn't believe what she was hearing. "Tell me you didn't."

"Not really. I wasn't *positive* you were coming home. And you did get away, for your interview."

"I fibbed to him too, a little," Erika said, giving Amy a crooked smile. "I told him I was going out with Lindsay."

"You did what?" Lettie asked, shocked.

Erika merely shrugged. "I am going out with her later, so it wasn't a total lie. I just didn't tell him where I was going first."

Lettie frowned, and felt sick.

"We wanted you to get a chance to do something first, to show him how much you care," Amy said, repeating Erika's earlier comment.

"What do you mean—do something?"

Amy took a bite of Lettie's cake. "Erika said he thought you would call or come see him to try to straighten things out," she informed. "He's been waiting for you to make a move for the past two weeks."

Lettie shook her head. "He told me not to."

"He thought he meant enough to you that you would anyway," Erika enlightened.

"I was trying to give him what he wants."

"Exactly. But what he wants—" Erika began, but Cassie held up a hand and blinked through a man-size bite of cake.

Cass swallowed hard. "What he wants is you, Lettie."

"And we've got the perfect way for you to give him exactly what he wants," Amy added.

Lettie laughed. She couldn't help it. What had they done? And what were they planning for her to do?

"God help me."

"I already told you," Cassie said, catching a dab of icing from the corner of her mouth with her tongue, "He will. And we will too."

"Okay. I'm game. What do you have in mind?"

Before they could answer Lettie's question, a four-legged, caramel-colored and pointy-eared creature bounded in the room, yapping loud enough to wake the entire building.

"What in the world is that?" Lettie asked, her eyes bulging almost as much as the dog's.

"Uhm, today's surprise from Landon?" Amy lifted the teeny dog and let it lick her cheek. "It's a Chihuahua."

"I could see that much. And it's yours? As in, for good? To live here? With us?" Lettie asked.

"Pretty much."

Cassie laughed loudly, shaking her head and eagerly watching Lettie for her reaction to her new roommate.

"He's adorable!" Erika exclaimed, reaching for him, then pulling her hands back when he growled like a Doberman.

"Wheelie, calm down," Amy commanded.

"Wheelie?" Lettie asked.

"It's a sentimental thing. You wouldn't understand."

"Obviously," Cassie answered.

"Say he's housebroken," Lettie said, eyeing the little dog suspiciously.

"He is," Amy said, smiling with pride. "Aren't ya, Wheelie?"

And at that moment, the dog decided to prove beyond a shadow of a doubt that Amy wasn't so great at lying.

"Oh my!" she yelled, holding him away from the big wet spot on her shirt. "Well, he's just getting used to the place, and to me. That's all. He really is house-trained, Lettie."

"Sure, he is."

"I'm keeping him," Amy informed. She brought Wheelie back to her chest, then giggled when he started a thorough licking of her neck.

"As if I could talk you out of it," Lettie said while her sister went to the bedroom to change her shirt.

"Okay," Cass said when Amy returned. "You need to show Bill you're everything he's looking for. That you want to be honest with him from now on."

Lettie nodded.

"You do love him, right?" Erika queried.

Despite feeling odd revealing that privileged information to a girl she'd just met, Lettie answered. "More than life."

"Perfect," Erika said. "Then this should work."

"What should work?"

"Our plan." Amy wrapped an arm around her sister as Wheelie growled at the items on the table.

"Yeah," Erika agreed. "We're calling it 'Operation Seduce My Uncle.'"

"I never agreed to that name," Cass grumbled, taking Wheelie as Amy switched to infomercial mode, describing the unique props. And while Lettie set her sights on winning Bill Brannon's heart.

*C*HAPTER 23

Bill hadn't stopped thinking about Lettie since his conversation with Erika last night. His niece had been right. He should have let go of his pride and made the first move. And Amy's enlightenment that Lettie had "needed to get away for awhile" didn't help. Where had she gone? And why had he waited so long before trying to get in touch with her?

Had he waited too long?

He picked up his office phone, then promptly dropped it back on the cradle. He would not call again. She'd obviously received his messages, and she hadn't responded. That gave him his answer, didn't it?

But damn it, it wasn't the answer he wanted.

He logged off his computer, picked up his briefcase and decided to call it a day. He'd put in three extra hours and hadn't even noticed, with his attention focused on Lettie instead of his new campaign.

All day, he'd left variations of the same message, apologizing. Saying he should have let her explain, that he really did want to get to know her better and that he was sorry for being an ass. That pretty much summed it up, didn't it? But she hadn't returned his calls.

Not one.

Driving home, he replayed the events of the last two weeks, then backtracked over the past nearly two decades, since the first day he'd seen the blond beauty when she'd marched into fifth grade.

Bill had spent most of his life wanting Lettie Campbell, not merely physically, but emotionally as well. Then, when she'd given him her body and expressed the desire to give him more, he'd thrown it all away over one mistake.

He jerked the wheel to enter his driveway. Erika's car was MIA, as usual. Probably out with her friends, and she probably told him where she was going, but he couldn't recall.

Wasn't that befitting? He'd botched the one relationship he wanted, might as well fail at his parental skills too.

With his head pounding and his body itching for a strong drink and a hot shower, he entered his house. And inhaled the distinct scent of flowers.

Candles flickered around the room, reminding him of the Landmarks Lounge. Yet the intimate lighting within his home provided an even more vivid semblance of romance. Even more because he suspected, hoped, he knew who had decorated.

Please.

It took a moment for his eyes to adjust, but they did, and what he saw took his breath away. Roses. Everywhere. More than he could count. Roses in vases, roses on the countertops, and petals on every piece of furniture, making the room resemble an elegant mosaic composed of solid . . . pink.

"Lettie?"

"Hi." She stepped from the bedroom, the candlelight shimmering behind her forming a curvy silhouette that made his mouth go dry. "I got your messages."

Swallow. Salivate. Speak.

"You did?"

"Yeah. And one of them caught me off-guard."

Bill struggled to remember each apology he'd left on her machine. He'd wanted to talk to her so urgently he'd rambled.

What the hell had he said?

"You confessed," she supplied, stepping closer. "Said you lied too."

"I did."

"Did confess? Or did lie?" Another step forward, and her shiny gloss caught the light, made her lips even fuller. More tempting.

"Both."

She laughed, a seductive, sexy sound. "You said you really aren't the wild and wicked guy I met this past week. That you were really more the friend I trusted more than anyone else way back when."

He didn't speak, merely watched her hand fiddle with the highest button of her blouse. She wore the same sleeveless white top she'd had on the last time she'd come to his home, the same fitted black pants and heels.

Was she trying to remind him of when he'd messed up? Because he really didn't need any reminders. All he had to do was look at her and he knew. He'd messed up. And he wanted another chance.

Was she giving him one?

"I kind of liked that wild guy."

Well, hell.

"And I'm not convinced that he isn't part of you. Maybe not something you show to everyone. Maybe . . . he's just for me?"

Bingo. "Definitely."

"Good." She stood in front of him, still teasing him with her fingertips on that button. "Because I'm not always a wild girl either."

"No?"

"No. And maybe, the wild girl is reserved for one person." She took her finger from the button and placed it on his cheek, tenderly tracing it down his jaw. "Maybe she's just for you."

"I should've let you explain," Bill said. "You were trying to tell me you were sorry, but I didn't listen. That won't happen again."

It was the truth, if only she'd believe it.

She tilted her head. "I brought something to help us figure all this out."

"Figure what out?"

"Us. You. And me."

"Okay."

Her hips swayed as she crossed the room. She paused and looked over her shoulder at Bill, giving him a soft smile. Then she ran her palm over an item on the dining table, and a blanket of pink petals fell to the floor. "Come here."

Bill followed her command; he'd follow any command from Lettie Campbell.

"Sit down."

He sat without regard to the flower petals on the chair.

"We're going to play a game." She moved two additional candles to the sides of the table, then pointed to the name on the outside of the box.

"Truth or Bare?" Bill asked, his heart rate quickening at the possibilities.

"It's Amy's latest creation, and it'll serve our needs."

"Amy's latest creation?"

"I never told you what she designs, did I?"

"No, you didn't."

"Sex toys."

He didn't respond, simply grinned. Were the Campbell girls always filled with surprises?

Lettie smiled, and it washed over his body like warm rain, covering him completely.

The gold flecks of her eyes caught the light of the candles, and he saw much more than mere color in their depths. He saw desire, and unless he was sadly mistaken, he saw more.

"When you gave me those pink roses in high school, then again at my apartment, you said you wanted to get to know me better, right?"

"Right."

"You meant it?" she asked.

"You know I did."

"Well, tonight, I gave you pink roses."

He swallowed. "You want to get to know me better, Lettie?"

"Yes." Her voice was deliciously sexy. Excited. Anxious.

"And this game will help?" he asked.

"That's the idea."

"Then what are we waiting for?"

Sliding her hand from his, Lettie opened the box and withdrew two pieces of white paper and two red pens. She handed one set to Bill, then kept the other. "Can you see the questions, or do you need more light?"

Bill scanned the sheet, clearly visible in the candle-light. "I can see them."

"Answer the questions."

"That's it?"

"For now." Her lips curved into a sneaky smile. "Answer honestly."

"Of course." He looked at the questions, read them all, then peered at Lettie, writing her answers.

"Some of these are rather interesting."

"Yes, they are," she agreed, fighting a smile and looking even more seductive.

She tucked her blond curls behind her ears. Bill eyed the tender lobes, remembered sucking them, whispering erotic words against the shell as she came.

"Bill?"

Evidently, Lettie had noticed he hadn't written the first thing on his page.

"What's the object of the game?" he asked.

"Simple. To get to know each other better."

"All right." There weren't that many questions on the paper, so he answered them fairly quickly, though a few of them required more thought.

"You ready?" she asked.

"Yeah."

"Hand me your pen."

He placed it in her hand, rolling the smooth cylinder in her palm before letting go.

She hissed in a breath, straightened in the chair, then placed the pens back in the box. "Okay. Now the rules."

"I'm listening."

Lettie recited the short set of rules listed inside the box lid. " 'Number one. Both players answer a corresponding list of questions. The number of questions varies, depending on whether you've selected an easy, normal, or advanced game.' "

"What did we select?" Bill asked.

"Easy."

"Didn't think I could handle advanced?"

She smiled. "Didn't think I could."

Bill liked the sound of that.

" 'Number two. In this game, ladies always go first.' "

He nodded. "Agreed."

"Here's the nitty-gritty. 'Play commences when the female reads the first question and identifies what she believes the male answered.' "

"You're going to try to guess what I wrote?"

"Exactly."

He scanned his list. This should be fun. "Then what?"

She continued reading, " 'If she guesses correctly, the male removes one item of his clothing. If she guesses incorrectly, she must remove one clothing item. Then the male follows this pattern, with a correct answer requiring the opponent to remove clothing, and an incorrect answer requiring the player to remove clothing.' "

"Damn fine game," he said. "How do you know who wins?"

She continued reading: " 'You both win, because you learn more about your compatibility; however, at the end of the game, the player with the most articles of clothing still in place, technically, wins.' "

"What if no articles of clothing are in place?"

"Seems to me, you still win," she said, laying the lid aside.

"Works for me."

She leaned toward the box, a motion that pushed her breasts together and gave him a glimpse of cleavage.

"Nice view."

She gave him a coy smile. "It could be better, if you answer right."

"Or if you answer wrong."

"That too."

"Trust me, Lettie, one way or another, those clothes are coming off. And when they do, whatever I haven't learned about you, I will learn. Eventually."

Her slender neck pulsed as she swallowed. "That sounds like a promise."

"It is."

She handed him a long board with sliding pink tabs. "Put your answers in this."

Bill slid his paper in the slot. The tabs covered each of his answers. "Clever game."

"Amy's a clever girl."

"So is her sister."

Her eyes brightened. "I've got some news." She couldn't contain the excitement in each word, and Bill realized her announcement had nothing to do with the game. It did, however, have everything to do with Lettie's happiness. He saw that much in her facial features, glowing and bursting to tell him.

"Looks like good news." His mind fast-forwarded.

What would her face look like if she ever told him she had some news, then finished the sentence with "I'm pregnant"? He knew that wasn't what tonight's "news" was about, but one day, hopefully. . . .

"You know how I was always doodling in high school? Couldn't hardly pay attention in class if I had a sketchpad in hand."

"Doodling—no. Designing—yes. Of course, I remember. You wanted to be a fashion designer." He lifted one shoulder, gave her a crooked smile. "I confiscated your drawings one day and took a look, remember?"

She blinked, and he knew she recalled that day in tenth-grade English.

"I went to turn in my homework, and you snatched my sketchpad." Another blink. "You said my designs were really good."

"They were."

Her head shook slightly as she spoke. "I thought you were just being nice."

"I was telling the truth."

"Yeah, you were." She straightened in her chair. "I took a new job this week, designing a new lingerie line for Charlene Frank. She's—"

"*The* Charlene Frank?"

Her pride surged forth, and he was thrilled to see it. A truly confident Lettie Campbell was a very pretty thing. "You know her?" she asked.

"Everyone in advertising knows her. She single-handedly turned the media's eyes toward Atlanta as the newest city for up-and-coming fashion."

"This afternoon, she hired a new designer for her lingerie line."

"Then Ms. Frank is as intelligent as they say."

Lettie beamed. "You think so?"

"I know so."

"Bill?"

"Yeah."

"Let's play."

$\mathcal{C}$HAPTER 24

He loved her. He loved her and he believed in her and he wanted her.

Lettie had gained all the information she needed to know from the look in his eyes, from the pride in his voice, the sensitivity in his touch.

Bill Brannon wanted her, not only her body, but her heart as well. The friend *and* the lover. He'd understood her dream, and he'd understood how much it meant to her. Even more, he'd believed in her as far back as tenth grade.

But she hadn't believed in him. Had thought he was merely being nice. The irony didn't go unnoticed.

"You go first," Bill reminded.

"Right." She extended her answer card. He met her halfway with his, but they didn't swap them quickly. The moment their fingers touched, their eyes met.

"We don't need the game, do we?" she whispered.

"No, we don't. I will get to know you, Lettie."

"You already do."

"So, do you still want to play?" he asked.

"We probably should." At his cocked brow, she added, "Amy hasn't put this out for distribution yet."

Bill laughed out loud. "In other words, she's using us as test subjects? You were letting me play guinea pig on a date that could change our lives?"

She grinned. "Funny, we never thought of it that way."

"We? How many people were in on this?"

"Me, Amy, Cassie." She paused, then shrugged. "Erika."

"My Erika?"

"She wanted to help. By the way, she's spending the night at my apartment tonight with Amy. She said it'd be okay with you."

Another rumbling Bill Brannon laugh trickled down her spine and warmed her already-moistened core. "You're incredible, Lettie."

"How incredible?"

"Why don't we play, and then we'll find out."

She took his card and read the first question out loud. "List your favorite animal." She looked at him, remembered the little Benji-looking creature that always followed him to school. "Dog," she said, then flipped the pink tab and read his scrawled answer. "I'm right."

"That you are." He removed a shoe.

Lettie frowned.

"What?" he asked.

"A shoe?"

"Isn't that the way this game works? Much like strip poker, I assume. You save your ace for last." His confident smile sent liquid pooling to her thighs.

How would she make it through every question?

"My turn," he said. "Favorite animal. Dog." He flipped the tab; then those chocolate eyes widened. "Monkey? You've gotta be kidding."

She laughed.

"Really?"

"That was my answer, wasn't it?" she teased. "Now, another article of clothing, please."

He removed another shoe.

"Spoilsport."

"I'm learning something new about you already, Ms. Campbell."

"What's that?"

"A lack of patience."

"Only where you're concerned," she said. "Okay. Next question. Favorite color. Black." She flipped the tab. "Ha! Right again."

He lifted one leg and removed a sock, holding up his bare foot for her perusal before placing it back on the rose-petaled floor.

Had she always had a foot fetish? Funny, she hadn't realized it before, but the sight of Bill Brannon's foot was definitely doing *something*. Then again, as hot as she was right now, and as long as she'd been without an orgasm, seeing anything associated with Bill Brannon would do *something*.

"My turn," he said. "Favorite color. Pink." Turning the tab, he read, " 'Purple'?"

"Purple," she agreed. "Now, do your thing."

Another sock hit the floor.

Yep, she definitely had a foot fetish.

"Next question. Career goal. Advertising executive." She looked behind the tab. "Bingo. Pay up."

He removed his watch.

"You're going to regret that," Lettie said, glaring at the leather band.

"I'm counting on it," he answered. "Career goal. Fashion designer." He viewed her answer and grinned. "Take it off, Lettie."

With every one of her seduction skills in place, she slowly unbuttoned the first button of her blouse. Then another. And another. Then she pushed her chest out as she slid the garment down her arms and dropped it to the floor.

"You didn't wear a bra." His voice was forced.

"I decided to follow your rules."

She watched his mouth open slightly, obviously remembering the other part of his bad-boy rule.

"That was for the car," he reminded, though the words were clipped, with his jaw so tense.

"I assumed it applied to your house as well." She shrugged, then cheered inwardly when his eyes watched her breasts move with the action.

"And if you didn't wear a bra . . ."

"I, of course, didn't wear panties either."

His eyes grew pretornado dark, and she was anxious to set the storm free.

"Lettie."

"Yeah. Oh right. My turn. Number of children. Two." She peeled back the tab. "Four?"

His brows lifted. "That okay with you?"

She grinned. More than okay. "Perfect." Then she lifted one leg, removed her heel and tossed it to the floor, following his example by wiggling her toes. "Your turn."

"Number of children. Four."

"You tricked me," she said as he turned the board toward Lettie so she could read her own answer.

"Yeah, I did," he admitted.

Sighing, and smiling, she removed the second shoe.

She lifted his card. "The day that changed your life more than any other."

He scooted forward in his chair, steepled his fingers beneath his chin.

"This is a tough one," she said.

"Wasn't for me."

"No?"

"No."

"I'll say." She pondered, *What did he write?* She desperately wanted to get this correct, and not simply because a wrong answer would remove her only other stitch of clothing. Clearing her throat, she answered, "The day Erika came to live with you."

She didn't turn the tab. Instead, she looked at him for her answer.

"That day did change my life, but not in the same way as my answer. Go on, Lettie. Look and see."

Taking a deep breath, she lifted the bright pink rectangle. Her throat closed in. Chest tightened. And the tiny spots beneath both ears tingled before her tears burst free.

"Say it, Lettie."

" 'The day a beautiful blonde showed up for fifth grade, ready to take Sheldon by storm, and more than ready, and able, to claim my heart.' " She swallowed and looked at him with tear-filled eyes.

"I love you, Lettie."

"God, I love you too." She circled the table and

climbed on his lap, wasting no time at all sealing their proclamation of love with a hot, heated kiss. Lifting her lips from his, she stared into his eyes. "I make mistakes."

"I do too."

"I'm not always good," she said.

"And I'm not always bad." He lowered his head and took a nipple in his mouth, sucked it hard, then released it. "But right now, I'd say I am."

"Works for me," she said, then laughed through her tears.

"Did you really follow my rule? Completely?" he asked.

"Of course."

"Then you definitely owe me a pair of pants."

"I guess I do, don't I? But first, tell me. What would you have said?"

"Said?"

"For my final answer. The day that changed my life forever. What did you think I'd say?"

"Today," he answered, then lifted her card and pulled the tab aside, revealing that very word. "I'm right."

"Yeah, you are."

"Looks like you're going to owe me another item of clothing."

"I'm only wearing one more," she said, shimmying off his lap and unbuttoning her pants.

His jaw flexed as she slid the zipper down, then pushed her pants to the floor. "You did follow the rules," he said, his eyes drinking in her nudity.

"I did."

"I don't expect you to be good all the time." He

reached out and ran his hand down her side; her entire body quaked with need.

"And I don't expect you to be bad all the time," she said. "But if you're going to be bad some of the time . . ."

"Yeah?"

"Right now would be . . ." She sucked in a breath as he pulled her body close, kissing her belly, then moving in a direct path to . . . "Oh!"

"A very good time," he whispered, his words feathering against her pulsing need. "A. Very. Good. Time."

*E*PILOGUE

Four years later

She here yet?" Evan asked, nudging his way into the shoulder-to-shoulder group peering through the glass window.

Cassie laughed. "Oh, she's here, all right." She held her camera near the glass and snapped another shot. "And she's making certain the world knows it."

"Of course, she is," Amy said, tears streaming down her cheeks as she watched the wailing infant get her first bath. "Can you blame her? She's going to be beautiful, she's going to have a real family, and she's going to find love." More tears flowed steadily.

"Lordy, Amy, you've got her grown already. Give her time. And this *is* a happy time here, right?" Cassie asked.

Landon laughed and dug a handkerchief out of his Wranglers. "Hormones are getting the best of her. Isn't that right, baby?"

Amy smiled, rubbing her enlarged belly. "Two more

months, and Bo Brooks will be on the other side of this window." She shed another batch of tears, then sniffed so loudly she snorted.

"That's my girl. Such a lady," Landon said as his wife elbowed him.

"Look," Erika said, "there's Uncle Bill."

Bill entered the nursery, where his daughter was getting her first bath and was none too pleased about it. He grinned. She was going to be a feisty one, or so the doctor had said when the wiggling, squealing baby entered the world merely minutes ago. And wouldn't it be surprising if she weren't?

He stepped closer and watched the nurses place the tiny diaper in place, swaddle his little angel in a pale pink blanket, then extend her to her daddy.

Her daddy.

While his heart pounded thickly, Bill brought the baby toward his chest. He grinned at the wide eyes, still shiny from tears, the sweet rosy mouth and the curls of downy hair, so blond it was nearly white, peeking from beneath the top of the blanket.

He turned her toward her admirers, their noses all pressed against the nursery window, then grinned while they took photos of Daddy and his little girl.

"You've got a beautiful little lady there," a nurse said from behind him. "You can take her to your wife now."

Bill breathed in deeply and exhaled. His wife. And his daughter. Life didn't get any better.

He turned toward the group at the window and indicated he was taking the baby to Lettie. With Erika and Amy leading the way, they turned and headed down the hall and into Lettie's room.

"Oh my, she's absolutely gorgeous!" Erika exclaimed as he entered.

"Did you expect anything but gorgeous from these two?" Cassie asked, her camera clicking madly.

"Nothing less at all," Amy said, her tears still dropping heavily down her cheeks.

Bill maneuvered through the crowd to view the woman in the bed. Her hair was tousled, cheeks flushed, mouth red from biting her lip during those final pushes.

He moved to the bed and sat on the edge, then tenderly handed the squirming little girl to Lettie.

"She's amazing, isn't she?" Lettie asked, touching a finger to their baby's perfect nose.

"As amazing as her mama."

Then Lettie Campbell Brannon kissed the top of their daughter's head. "And as lucky as her mama," she said. "Aren't you, Ginny?"

Bill's chest tightened. How he wished his sister could be here to see her beautiful, perfect namesake. "As lucky?" he managed, while their baby's tiny face turned instinctively toward Lettie's breast.

"Because she has a daddy," Lettie said, lifting her eyes to Bill's, "who makes dreams come true."

About the Author

Kelley St. John's previous experience as a senior writer at NASA fueled her interest in writing action-packed suspense, although she also enjoys penning steamy romances and quirky women's fiction. She is a member of Romance Writers of America (RWA) and a 2005 double finalist in RWA's prestigious Golden Heart Contest.

Writing has always been St. John's first love. She thrives on creating new worlds and bringing readers along for the ride. St. John follows the philosophy that in order to write about life, you have to live. Therefore, she makes it her business to enjoy life to the fullest. Traveling is one of her favorite pastimes and one she doesn't indulge in nearly enough for her tastes, especially since some of her best ideas have been sparked by weekend getaways. She loves extended car trips that involve marathon plotting sessions and swears that she can plot an entire novel in the time it takes to drive from Atlanta to Orlando.

And if you can't get enough of Bill and Lettie's story, read the prologue and deleted scenes, only available via the author's Web site www.kelleystjohn.com.

See below for a preview of
Kelley St. John's
steamy new novel.

Real Women Don't Wear Size 2

◈

Available in mass market
September 2006.

Clarise Robinson slid the last button through its hole and let her blouse fall open. Stripping in the employee lounge wasn't the way she spent her usual Thursday lunch hour, but then again, this wasn't a usual week. Typically, she'd already have her weekend activities mapped out, courtesy of TV Guide and her Dining for One cookbook.

But not this weekend. This weekend, she'd bare her soul, and everything else, in Tampa. And if she was going to put all of—she glanced down and flinched—this out there, she sure wanted to get it right.

Encouraged by the chants and cheers of the partying crowd on the video, she quickly released the front closure of her bra before she had a chance to change her mind.

The Robinson Treasures, as Grandma Gertrude called them, sprang free.

Personally, Clarise had never seen the heavy things as more than a nuisance. Certainly not jewels. As a matter of fact, she'd been under the distinct impression that one woman's treasure was another woman's junk. Particularly when Granny Gert's endowments included more than boisterous bazookas. Clarise had also been blessed with the Robinson Rump.

She turned her attention back to the Gasparilla Pirate Fest video, where a tall, drop-dead-gorgeous Adonis stood in the center of the crowd with one hand cradling his drink and the other pressed to his heart.

Clarise's pulse skittered, and she prayed Jesilyn and Rachel, her coworkers at Eubanks Elegant Apparel, had kept their word about leaving for lunch. If they were standing outside the door listening—and wondering if she was actually accomplishing this bizarre task—she'd never forgive them. True, if she followed through with her promise to attend the store's trip to Tampa this year, she'd be semi-stripping beside both of them tomorrow. But for now, she needed privacy. And a whole lot of what Granny Gert called "gumption."

A puff of cool air entered the room when the heating unit whirred to life. The Robinson Treasures tingled as the breeze quickly converted from frigid to toasty.

She swallowed. January in Birmingham, Alabama didn't lend itself to the necessary warmth for baring your body at a downtown parade. However, her coworkers had promised that Tampa would provide plenty of heat . . . from the climate as well as the partying crowd.

"Come on, darling. You're killin' us," Adonis drawled, his Southern accent even stronger than his alcohol.

Clarise examined the hand against his chest. Wide palms. Long fingers. She ran her top teeth over her lower lip and wondered if it were true what they said about men with big hands. Ethan Eubanks, the owner of Eubanks Elegant Apparel, and coincidentally, the object of her every fantasy, had big hands. Nice. Big. Hands.

Clarise had noticed. A few times.

When Ethan displayed clothing samples from new product lines at the weekly staff meetings, Clarise forced herself to concentrate on the exquisite quality of the garments, rather than those captivating hands. How was she supposed to watch those long fingers reverently touch a Hermès scarf without wondering what it would feel like to have them caressing her skin? And as head of the Women's Department, Clarise really needed to pay attention to the details. Which she did, as long as she kept her mind off those hands.

"Aren't ya gonna show us something?" that sexy Southern accent continued. He flashed a megawatt smile and made her belly flutter.

That was her cue. Clarise knew he'd ask, and she was ready. Sucking in her breath, she waited for his next instruction. It would come in exactly forty-eight seconds.

She'd timed it.

One thousand one . . . one thousand two . . .

Exhaling thickly, she focused on his baby blue eyes. She loved blue eyes, always had. Probably because her own were so dang dark she couldn't tell where the iris began and the pupil ended. Not an ounce of color, nothing attention-grabbing at all. Just as well, since she spent most of her time trying to hide the remainder of her abundant body.

But not anymore.

After thirty years of perfecting her wallflower image, she had a chance to set herself free. Let all her insecurities and inhibitions disappear and show the world, or at least most of Tampa, the real Clarise Robinson. The one she dreamed of each night, a girl who would drink and dance and party and have fun. Bare her body and be proud of its bounty.

And have monkey sex before the Pirate Fest ended.

She licked her lips. Swallowed hard. Monkey sex typically required two people.

While the blond Adonis called his friends over, Clarise pretended this was the real deal. Her ready-for-anything sister, Babette, would have no trouble baring her body to the masses at Gasparilla. She'd done it last year, in fact, when Clarise had chickened out of the trip and asked her sister to take her place. But then again, Babette's body was worthy of a Pirate Fest showing. Clarise's, on the other hand, was more conducive for a Fat Fest showing.

She frowned, a little, then remembered Granny Gert's motto: "Curves are where it's at, Clarise."

Taking a deep breath, she boosted her confidence once more. She did have curves, lots of them, and tomorrow she would flaunt her surplus and get what she wanted. One way or another, she wouldn't let opportunity pass her by. When the last parade ended, she'd have wild, frantic sex with . . . someone.

But who?

Jesilyn and Rachel had suggested Clarise cozy up to one of the gorgeous guys from work during the trip. All of the department heads were going, since Ethan footed the bill for each of them to attend the annual "corporate bonding" excursion. No doubt, each was planning to get hot and heated with someone at Gasparilla.

Would any of them think twice about having a bit of no-commitments, no-holds-barred, wild and frantic sex with "best buddy" Clarise?

She blew brown bangs out of her eyes while her shoulders dropped a notch. Who was she kidding? Wild, frantic sex? Shoot, she'd settle for mild, lukewarm. Or any activity that involved a male pressed against her. As long as it'd been, that'd be all she needed to work into a lather.

No, she silently commanded, straightening her back and lifting her chest. She refused to settle for tepid. She wanted hot, boiling, exhilarating sex, and that's what she'd get. Toe-curling, eye-glazing, heart-stopping sex.

Better than she'd ever had.

Clarise winced. Better than she'd ever had wasn't saying much. Sex with the lights on would extend her current bedroom repertoire. She needed a better goal, or several better goals.

She glanced at her blue notebook, perched on the coffee table in the center of the lounge. For the past few days, she'd studied the Pirate Fest travel brochures, the parade schedules and practically all of the Internet sites advertising the event. And while she'd outlined the must-see parades, she hadn't acknowledged the activities she most wanted to accomplish during her trip. Not on paper, anyway.

Flipping past the pages of parade routes, Clarise grabbed a pen. She'd always been a list person. Loved setting goals and feeling that major sense of accomplishment when she checked them off one-by-one. Why should her "Naked in Tampa" adventure be any different? After all, she knew what she wanted.

Sex with the lights on, for starters.

She wrote it down, smiled. Finally, a real goal. But that wasn't nearly enough, and if she was going to do this, she wasn't going halfway.

Grinning, she scribbled sex outside.

Sex. Outside. Her nipples puckered at the mere thought. But she didn't want just outside.

With her pulse racing, she amended her list to include different kinds of outside. In the grass, for sure. And on a beach. Those beach scenes in romance novels sounded hot. Water sloshing around her legs while she and her lover tore into each other like animals in heat. Yep, she'd try that.

Tampa definately had plenty of beach to offer.

She bit her lip. There was one more kind of outside sex she wanted more than the others. Before she lost her nerve, she wrote it down.

Under-the-bleachers sex.

Clarise had listened to those locker room conversations throughout her teen years. When they talked about bleacher sex, that had been the most intriguing thing she had ever heard. She definitely wanted bleacher sex.

Yeah, all of those for outside sex. That'd work. And lots of inside sex too. Standing up looked rather nice in the movies. And shower sex. How could she forget her shower sex fantasy? She'd want to get in a bit of shower action this weekend.

Hot water. Hot bodies. Well, his body would be hot. Maybe, if he'd had enough of those hurricane drinks everyone was holding in the video, he'd believe hers was, too.

She added the last two to her list.

Clarise giggled, then moved her hands to her chest when the action made her unbound treasures bounce.

Sure, Tampa offered a multitude of opportunities for sex, but she hadn't seen a single beach or football stadium in the travel brochures.

No problem. Even if she couldn't get her bleacher fix, she'd still have kinky sex with . . . someone. Oh, how she wished she could fill in the great big hole in that image.

One Pirate Fest partier to spend five delicious nights with. And what if he ended up being Mr. Right? It could happen.

She imagined Jake Riley, the Men's Department hottie, offering her one of those big, tall drinks. Or Miles Watkins, Formal Wear connoisseur, the guy Rachel called "sweet eye candy."

Or Ethan Eubanks, her friend, her boss . . . and her ultimate fantasy. Ethan Eubanks, whispering in her ear, telling Clarise he wanted her more than anything in the world. Ethan, having fanatical sex with her for five sizzling days, then professing his undying love.

Granny Gert always said if you're gonna dream, you might as well dream big. Then again, everything about Granny factored as abundantly proportioned, dreams, bosom, and behind included.

Besides, Ethan was the only hottie from work who wasn't making the trip. Probably just as well. Clarise had wisely decided not to risk their friendship, or her job, by confessing her crazy obsession. No need to jeopardize either for a weekend romp with the boss.

The blond hunk stared at her via the television screen as though willing her to grant his next request.

Go on, Blue Eyes, ask.

And, since forty-eight seconds had passed, he did.

"Shimmy for them, darlin'," he said, removing a strand of gold beads from his neck and dangling the glittering loop from one of those beautifully long fingers. "Come on. Give us a little shake."

Clarise flashed a siren smile, trying her best to imitate the one the woman tossed him on the video. Then she leaned forward and flitted her shoulders back and forth, sending Granny Gert's heritage swinging like heavy water balloons in front of the screen.

The knock on the door caught her mid-shimmy, and she abruptly stopped moving. Well, most of her did. Boom One and Boom Two still had a whole lotta shakin' going on.

She slapped at the TV/VCR combo to stop the tape. However, in her haste to get rid of the evidence, she hit the volume button instead. Within half a second, blonde and friends screamed their approval at the hooters on display.

"Yeah, baby, show us what you got!" one yelled.

"Have mercy!" blue eyes added.

"Bon dieu, sweet mother," the third decreed.

"Ohmigod," Clarise whimpered, grabbing a fistful of bra and shirt with one hand, while the other frantically punched the POWER button on the television.

"Clarise, is that you? Miles said you were in the lounge," Ethan called from the other side of the door. "Are you okay in there?"

Great. Just great. While she was playing exhibitionist with the blond hunk on the screen, the real deal was perched outside. The most gorgeous sandy-haired, turquoise-eyed male she'd ever seen, who happened to be her boss and one of her closest friends, was merely feet away. Listening.

Or was he? God, what had Ethan heard?

She immediately regretted her decision to have Jesilyn and Rachel vacate the premises for lunch. She should have had them on watch duty. Or rather, on Ethan Eubanks watch duty. And she should have told Miles Watkins to keep his big mouth shut about her whereabouts. Good Lord, she hoped he didn't tell Ethan what she was doing, too! The eye candy factor took an abrupt turn from sweet to sour.

She attempted to control her pulse. Miles only knew she needed privacy; she hadn't mentioned why. Thank God.

"Clarise?" Ethan repeated.

Didn't he say his lunch meeting would last two hours? And did he realize how he had surprised her by coming back early? Or how big a surprise it was? As in, a surprise heart attack for Clarise?

She was usually pretty good at hiding things from Ethan. They'd grown close, but she still kept her secrets guarded. Not many secrets, mind you. Only two. One, her real career goal. And two, the fact that he made her head swim and her heart tremble.

Heat crept up her body, starting with her bulging boobs, then worked its way up her throat to settle in her cheeks. "I'm—fine."

"I need to speak with you about this weekend," he said, that sexy, raspy voice making her nipples salute.

Would it be too much to ask for her weekend lover to sound like Ethan? Look like him? Act like him? Since none of her coworkers met any of the preceding criteria, she'd bet it was definitely too much to ask.

"Sure." She yanked the mega-cups of her bra together and fastened the closure without taking time to situate the two mounds in their holsters. As a result, righty had a hefty portion plumped over the top and lefty had some side action happening, with a paunch of flesh poking her armpit.

The doorknob jiggled, and her pulse skyrocketed.

"Do you need me to come back?" he asked, with more than a hint of curiosity in his tone.

"No," she gasped. Lord, did stripping in the employee lounge qualify for a pink slip? Probably, although she'd bet Ethan would chalk it up to progress. He'd been trying to get her to come out of her shell for the past three years. If he only knew, she'd do more than that. By tomorrow, she'd be coming out of her top. Then, if she did it right, she'd be coming period. With the lights on. Or outside. Or on the grass. Or all of the above.

Clarise fumbled her way with the buttons then jabbed the ends of her blouse into the top of her skirt, all the while thanking God and heaven above for elastic waistbands. Then she snatched her red scarf off the couch and quickly tied it at her waist as elegantly as possible, given her shaky fingers.

Making certain the television was off, she took a deep breath, unlocked the door and opened it.

Dang if his eyes weren't bluer than she remembered. Double-dang if he didn't look even better than last night's dream.

Clarise swallowed. She would not think about that now. Wouldn't picture the way she'd envisioned him tearing her clothes from her body in a frantic effort to touch her, hold her, get inside of her.

She focused on those waves of sandy hair, thick brows, strong jaw, totally kissable mouth, broad shoulders . . .

Heavens, what was she doing?

Blushing. That's what. And from the brilliant grin on that gorgeous face, he'd noticed. If he ever found out how he made her pulse pump, she didn't know what she'd do.

"You wanted to talk about this weekend?"

"Yes, I do." He indicated the television and the neon green glow from the VCR portion. "Watching a movie?"

Great. The tape was still rolling, even though the screen was off. And he could see that blinking arrow, dadgummit.

"Yeah," she said, stretching a finger toward the machine and punching the STOP button. A surge of relief flooded her when that tattletale arrow disappeared.

"Sounded like a Gasparilla parade. Trying to get an idea of what's in store for the weekend?" He crossed the lounge, opened the refrigerator and withdrew a Coke. "Hey, I didn't mean to make you nervous yesterday, but I thought I should warn you about some of the—activities—down there." His mouth crooked to the side. Then he took a long drink from the bottle, as if he had to do something with those enticing lips to keep from outright laughing at her attempt to blend with the wild women of Tampa.

Clarise wanted to spout some smart remark about how she could be sexy if she wanted, but she couldn't concentrate on anything beyond watching his neck pulse with each swallow.

Ethan lowered the bottle and grinned. "Not that I think you should pass on the trip. I'm glad you're going, but you've never been around anything quite like Tampa during Gasparilla. I just want you to be prepared."

"I'm ready," she said, and couldn't keep her smile from bursting free.

He laughed, and the luxurious sound rippled down her skin like hot shower water, touching her everywhere.

"I have no doubt you're ready, but is Tampa ready for you? Clarise Robinson, letting her hair down? I thought you said you'd never be caught dead at one of those parades."

"That was last year, and I had a case of cold feet. This year is—different."

"Different how?" he asked.

Clarise had a hard time hiding things from this man. Truthfully, the big 3-0 had been a major factor in the decision to bare the Robinson Treasures at Gasparilla. She sure wasn't getting any younger, and she sure wasn't finding her way into Ethan Eubanks's bed. So she might as well find her way into someone else's, right?

She turned away from him and prayed he wouldn't realize that the combination of her birthday and his apparent lack of romantic interest had convinced her to go through with the trip. Their friendship had developed so steadily over the past three years that typically Ethan could look at Clarise and know her every thought, dream, and desire. Matter of fact, it amazed her that he hadn't instinctively recognized her obvious attraction.

But he hadn't. And she thanked heaven above for that small miracle.

"You told me repeatedly I should take this trip, and now that I've decided to go, you're trying to talk me out of it." She pivoted, crossed her arms beneath her chest and glared at him. "I'm old enough to have some fun, and I'm going to," she added, her frustration at having been caught mid-strip wedging its way into the words. Then again, was she frustrated that Ethan had caught her, or that he'd never realized the one she really wanted to strip for . . . was him?

He took another drink and stepped closer. "I'm glad you decided to go, Clarise." The corner of his mouth dipped down, and he shrugged. "I just hate it I'm going to miss the show."

"The show?" she asked, trying to keep her attention on his eyes, rather than his mouth.

"Yes, the show. Clarise Robinson, unplugged. I've got to tell you, I'm jealous."

"Jealous?" she asked, her vocabulary taking a momentary nosedive while he stepped even closer.

"Of all the guys in Tampa. I've been waiting to see you let that airtight guard down for years. Now you decide to set the wild side free, and I'm stuck in Birmingham with a major meeting. Hell, yeah, I'm jealous." He grinned, and her frustration dissipated.

"Stop it, Ethan." She playfully shoved his arm. Problem was, the rock solid bicep stopped the momentum of her palm. And started the momentum of her uterus. Clarise chuckled through the sexual tension that existed only on her side of this fence. Yeah, he flirted with her on a daily basis, but it was merely a sociable banter. He didn't mean anything by it, and Clarise was smart enough to realize that. Why would a guy she'd classify as "God's gift to females" even think twice about an abundantly proportioned best friend with plain hair and a semi-cute face? A great personality and business smarts could only go so far in the world, and evidently neither went far enough to gain Ethan's attention beyond friendship.

"All right, I'll confess. Miles told me you were in the lounge practicing your flashing technique, and I was curious. One, I can't believe you're actually going on the trip, though I do think it'll be good for you. And two, I am envious of the men who get to be on the receiving end of your shimmy." He grinned. "By the way, I heard the guy's command from the video. Did you give him what he wanted?"

Her blush came fast and furious, making her cheeks burn. She wasn't about to answer his question. Instead, she focused on the guy who ratted her out. "Miles told you?" Then she shook her head. "He didn't know."

"Rachel told him."

"Is anything private here?" She moved toward the television and pushed the EJECT button on the VCR.

Ethan shrugged. "Obviously, not much. So, come on. Let me see what you've got."

Another trickle of heat burned her chest. Heck, she'd love the opportunity to show him aplenty, probably more than he wanted to see. Twenty or thirty pounds more, she suspected. She grabbed the video and looked up.

His expression had altered from teasing buddy to compassionate friend. Had he realized how embarrassing this was for her?

"Clarise. I'm not serious." He placed his Coke on the table and moved toward her again.

Clarise gripped the video like a lifeline, while she waited to see just how close he'd come.

Ethan stopped merely a foot away, leaned casually against the wooden cabinet enclosing the television unit. "I wouldn't do you that way. You can save your secret shimmy for the guys in Tampa. It was a joke."

She blinked. Nodded. "Right, I knew that."

"But I am pleased that you've decided to have some fun. And…"

"And?" she whispered.

"And I really do wish I could go down there and see you at your first Pirate Fest. You deserve to have a good time."

His sincerity touched her heart. He really did care about her and wanted the best for her. Delight radiated from her center. Unfortunately, it was followed by the sudden urge to fling her body against his, wrap her legs around his waist and kiss the living daylights out of him.

Thank goodness for self-control. She shifted from one foot to the other and backed away from the too-close-for-comfort situation.

"Why don't you head out early and finish up your packing. That way you won't forget anything you need."

Forget anything she needed? She'd already packed the only real necessity, an industrial-sized box of condoms.

"Sound good to you?" he prompted, reminding Clarise she'd yet to respond.

She looked at the round clock on the wall. Two P.M. "I have three hours before I get off."

"I'm giving them to you. You work too damn hard anyway. Besides, Abby is working in the Women's Department today. She'll be running the place while you're gone; might as well let her go ahead and get started. Take the afternoon and prepare to have fun." His face sobered. "Do you plan to take someone along?"

She blinked. "Take someone along?" How would she have a weekend of wild sex if she took someone along? And who would she take? Babette was currently visiting their folks in Florida and was leaving tomorrow on a cruise that would celebrate, yet again, her December graduation from college. Clarise wondered if her sister would ever stop celebrating and start working. Probably not.

Then there was Grandma Gert, who would come to Tampa in a heartbeat and strip down to her enormous brassiere and equally enormous panties, regardless of whether gold beads were involved, if someone like Blue Eyes tossed her a come-hither smile.

"Tampa tends to be an interesting place for couples to visit," Ethan continued.

Oh. Well. She should've figured that one out, but leave it to Clarise to hear "bring someone along" and immediately think of her whacked-out family. "I'm not bringing anyone along," she said, "but I do plan to have fun."

"Obviously," he said, nodding toward the television. "I'm betting you'll have the best shimmy there."

That itch to fling against him pulsed through her again, and this time, she didn't completely resist. "Thanks!" She wrapped her arms around him, and the video and notebook slapped against his broad back with a loud smack.

Clarise barely noticed. She was too lost in her close proximity to Ethan to care.

He smelled like sea salt and soap, and she inhaled it thoroughly. But then reality teased her senses, and she realized he'd tensed against her attack. So she backed up. Quick.

Sure, they were friends, but she'd never been a hugger. Maybe if she'd started out hugging him as boss or friend, this could have been a regular occurrence.

Heck, she should've hugged him after her first interview.

"You're welcome," he said, his voice thick and awkward.

What had she done?

Clarise forced a snigger. "Sorry. Carried away, I guess."

"No problem." He ran a hand, with long fingers, she noticed, through his hair. The short blond and brown waves rippled with the touch and made her wonder how those locks would feel running between her fingers.

Then he smiled.

Her thighs clenched, a typical response to an Ethan Eubanks smile. Man, she had to get over this thing for her friend.

Friend.

"Clarise?"

She looked directly into those blue-green eyes and instantly remembered all of those afternoon coffees, the two of them laughing and chatting and learning more and more about each other. As friends. "Yeah?" she asked.

"Be careful while you're gone," he said, depicting genuine concern and reminding her that he was truly a friend first and a boss second. He inhaled, as though he was going to say more, then he slowly exhaled.

Hoping to hear the rest, Clarise waited a heartbeat before responding.

"Have fun, Clarise." He gave her an easy smile, then left.

She sighed. Maybe it was the preparations for stripping in Tampa that had caused her to cross over that invisible boundary that existed between friends. The line that says friendship is here; more than friends is there. She'd never even attempted to venture to the other side before, but she sure had today. And Ethan, being a true gentleman, graciously ignored her momentary lapse in good judgment and even told her to have a good time.

If she accomplished the items on her list, "having fun" wouldn't be a problem. "Don't worry, Ethan," she whispered. "I will."

THE EDITOR'S DIARY

Dear Reader,

All's fair in love and war . . . even a few white lies, a little bloodshed, and a dash of attempted burglary. And that's just in love. Check out our two Warner Forever titles this December to see why.

Romantic Times BOOKclub Magazine raves **Shari Anton's** previous book is a "charming delightful romance" that "sparkles with originality." Well, prepare to be enchanted by her latest, **MIDNIGHT MAGIC**. Though she is betrothed to another, Gwendolyn of Leon finds the King has given her hand in marriage and her land to a knight with her family's blood on his hands. His arrogance astounds her, his steady gaze and teasing smile intrigue her. But on this knight's hand rests the ring Gwendolyn needs to activate an ancient magical legacy . . . and she will do anything necessary to wrest it away—even seduce him. With the seal of the dragon slipped on his finger, Alberic of Chester has gone from landless knight to titled baron. Marrying Gwendolyn would secure his position and Alberic is intent on taking what is rightfully his by king's decree. But winning the heart of his sensuous and fiery wife-to-be may prove his most daunting fight yet.

Good girls never lie . . . unless it's their job. Lettie Campbell from **Kelley St. John's GOOD GIRLS DON'T** knows that all too well. As a well-paid cheating consultant for *My Alibi*, the cover stories come easily to Lettie . . . until she discovers the man on the receiving end of one of her whoppers is none other than Bill Bannon—her best friend in high school. How can she lie to him now? But even more shockingly, when did the boy next door have the power to make her heart flutter and her toes curl? As the lies pile up and Lettie and Bill start to burn up the sheets, Lettie knows she has to come clean. Will she 'fess up before Bill discovers he's been conned? Grab a copy of this sassy and sensual debut from brand new Warner Forever author Kelley St. John today.

To find out more about Warner Forever, these titles, and the authors, visit us at www.warnerforever.com.

With warmest wishes,

Karen Kosztolnyik, Senior Editor

P.S. Believe in love and the afterlife vampire-style in these two irresistible novels: **Susan Crandall** delivers the poignant story of a woman who lost her husband and unborn child in a fire and the man who gives her a reason to believe in love again in **ON BLUE FALLS POND**; **Michelle Rowen** tells a death-defyingly funny debut about a girl who goes on a blind date and comes home a vampire in **BITTEN & SMITTEN**.